# Asda Tickled Pink

*45p from the sale of this book will be donated to Tickled Pink.*

*Asda Tickled Pink wants to ensure all breast cancer is diagnosed early and help improve people's many different experiences of the disease. Working with our charity partners, Breast Cancer Now and CoppaFeel!, we're on a mission to make checking your boobs, pecs and chests, whoever you are, as normal as your Asda shop. And with your help, we're raising funds for new treatments, vital education and life-changing support, for anyone who needs it. Together, we're putting breast cancer awareness on everyone's list.*

*Since the partnership began in 1996, Asda Tickled Pink has raised over £82 million for its charity partners. Through the campaign, Asda has been committed to raising funds and breast-check awareness via in-store fundraising, disruptive awareness campaigns, and products turning pink to support the campaign. The funds have been vital for Breast Cancer Now's world-class research and life-changing support services, such as their Helpline, there for anyone affected by breast cancer to cope with the emotional impact of the disease. Asda Tickled Pink's educational and outreach work with CoppaFeel! aims to empower 1 million 18 - 24 year olds to adopt a regular boob-checking behaviour by 2025. Together we will continue to make a tangible difference to breast cancer in the UK.*

*Asda Tickled Pink and the Penguin Random House have teamed up to bring you Tickled Pink Books. By buying this book and supporting the partnership, you ensure that 45p goes directly to the Breast Cancer Now and CoppaFeel!.*

*Breast Cancer is the most common cancer in women in the UK, with one in seven women facing it in their lifetime.*

*Around 55,000 women and 370 men are diagnosed with breast cancer every year in the UK and nearly 1,000 people still lose their life to the disease each month. This is one person every 45 minutes and this is why your support and the support from Asda Tickled Pink is so important.*

*A new Tickled Pink Book will go on sale in Asda stores every two weeks – we aim to bring you the best stories of friendship, love, heartbreak and laughter.*

*To find out more about the Tickled Pink partnership visit www.asda.com/tickled-pink*

Penguin
Random House
UK

ASDA
Tickled
pink

## STAY BREAST AWARE AND CHECK YOURSELF REGULARLY

One in seven women in the UK will be diagnosed with breast cancer in their lifetime

## 'TOUCH, LOOK, KNOW YOUR NORMAL, REPEAT REGULARLY'

Make sure you stay breast aware
- Get to know what's normal for you
- Look and feel to notice any unusual changes early
- The earlier breast cancer is diagnosed, the better the chance of successful treatment
- Check your boobs regularly and see a GP if you notice a change

Jo Thomas worked for many years as a reporter and producer, including time at Radio 4's *Woman's Hour* and Radio 2's Steve Wright show.

Jo's debut novel, *The Oyster Catcher*, was a runaway bestseller and won both the RNA Joan Hessayon Award and the Festival of Romance Best EBook Award. Her book *Escape to the French Farmhouse* was a No. 1 bestselling ebook. Jo loves to explore new countries and discover the food produced there, both of which she thoroughly enjoys researching. Jo lives in Pembrokeshire with her husband and three children, where cooking and gathering around the kitchen table are a hugely important and fun part of their family life.

Visit Jo's website: jothomasauthor.com
or follow her on:

 Jo_Thomas01
 JoThomasAuthor
 JoThomasAuthor

www.penguin.co.uk

## Also by Jo Thomas

THE OYSTER CATCHER
THE OLIVE BRANCH
LATE SUMMER IN THE VINEYARD
THE HONEY FARM ON THE HILL
SUNSET OVER THE CHERRY ORCHARD
A WINTER BENEATH THE STARS
MY LEMON GROVE SUMMER
COMING HOME TO WINTER ISLAND
ESCAPE TO THE FRENCH FARMHOUSE
FINDING LOVE AT THE CHRISTMAS MARKET
CHASING THE ITALIAN DREAM
CELEBRATIONS AT THE CHÂTEAU
RETREAT TO THE SPANISH SUN
KEEPING A CHRISTMAS PROMISE
SUMMER AT THE ICE CREAM CAFÉ

*Ebook short stories:*
THE CHESTNUT TREE
THE RED SKY AT NIGHT
NOTES FROM THE NORTHERN LIGHTS

# Countdown to Christmas

## Jo Thomas

PENGUIN BOOKS

TRANSWORLD PUBLISHERS
Penguin Random House, One Embassy Gardens,
8 Viaduct Gardens, London SW11 7BW
www.penguin.co.uk

Transworld is part of the Penguin Random House group of companies
whose addresses can be found at global.penguinrandomhouse.com

First published in Great Britain in 2023 by Bantam
an imprint of Transworld Publishers
Penguin paperback edition published 2023

Lyrics on p. 10 from 'Merry Xmas Everybody',
written by Noddy Holder and Jim Lea.

A CIP catalogue record for this book
is available from the British Library.

ISBN
9780552178693

Typeset in 11/14pt ITC Giovanni Std by Jouve (UK), Milton Keynes.
Printed and bound in Great Britain by Clays Ltd, Elcograf S.p.A.

The authorized representative in the EEA is Penguin Random House
Ireland, Morrison Chambers, 32 Nassau Street, Dublin D02 YH68.

Penguin Random House is committed to a sustainable
future for our business, our readers and our planet. This book is
made from Forest Stewardship Council® certified paper.

To Ffion and Josh, sending you love on the
next chapter in your journey together.
I am so proud of you both. x

# 1

*1 December: 24 days until Christmas*

*Do not screw this up!* I repeat to myself, over and over again. My nails dig into my palms as my knuckles clench and my eyes squeeze so tightly shut that my nose wrinkles like a bulldog's. *Do not be embarrassing!* I hear my voice in my head, stern and firm.

I breathe in the familiar smell, savouring it and saving some for later. I'd know it anywhere. It's home. Not the house, or the furnishings, just a place where I feel I belong. And I'm wondering how I'll cope without it. Like a boat set adrift from its mooring, I expect. Without that smell, that feeling, a house is not a home.

'Mum.' There's a tap on my forearm, gentle at first, like a paw from a pup wanting attention. Then it becomes more urgent, like a wrestler tapping his opponent to time out. My eyes ping open.

'I can't breathe!' Ruben looks up at me, but only just. He's grown again. Any time now he'll be taller than me. Not that that's hard, I'm only five foot three, but it seems weird that my child will be the same height as me and that I shall soon be looking up at him. But it happens. Time flies. I want to stop the clocks. Stay as we are. Keep things just like this. But I can't.

'Sorry, sorry.' I loosen my grip on my son's neck. I seem to have him and his big parka in a tight head lock – I splashed out on his coat as an early Christmas present, even though I was worrying about where the money would come from. It's always the same at this time of year. Work is on hold for the next couple of months: the campsite café is closed. That's how it is. You take the money when the tourists are in town and hope it'll keep you going when they've departed. I just have to be careful. It's not only me who relies on my small pot of savings.

I look at Ruben. I mustn't embarrass him! Mums are known for it. The one thing I definitely mustn't do is cry.

I feel his arms slide around my waist, hugging me back. A smile pulls at the corners of my mouth and I breathe in deeply, trying to hold back the tears behind my screwed-up eyes. Breathe, Chloë! I'm reminded all over again of the day he was born, the rush of love and the fear of never being good enough. 'Breathe!' the midwife told me, and I did. I do now, closing my eyes and trying to remember each note I can smell. The freshly washed hair. The detergent I've always used. Sweet chewing gum and something else, something that makes him Ruben. My little boy. I'm imprinting this moment into my brain and onto my heart so that I can remember it when I need it.

He lets go of the hug and I release him and his teddy bear, Joe. He's had it since he was a baby, bought for him by my dad, a proud grandfather, and named after my great-grandfather Joseph, Dad's grandfather. Dad said if I wasn't going to call the baby Joseph, the bear would be Joe. Ruben has never slept without him, and after Dad died, Joe seemed even more important. I grabbed him as we left the house to stuff into Ruben's case. Along with a jar of Marmite. He has it on toast every morning, always has.

I take another huge breath and smile widely.

Ruben looks at me quizzically. 'You going to be okay, Mum?'

'Of course! And you are going to have the best Christmas ever! With your dad . . .' I hear the crack in my voice and push on through it '. . . and meeting your new sister – in New York, for heaven's sake! Who wouldn't want to go to New York for Christmas?'

'I just wish you were coming too. I hate the thought of you being here on your own at Christmas.'

I'm hugging Joe and the jar of Marmite to my chest. 'Don't worry about me! I've got so much planned. And I want to hear about everything you'll be doing. Go and have the best time.' I straighten the hood on his coat by way of a distraction. 'Have you got all the numbers stored on your phone?'

He rolls his eyes. 'Yes, Mum. And I've got my emergency money, separate from my wallet. And I won't speak to strangers. Or get into cars if I'm offered sweets.'

'I'm serious, Ruben.' The panic I've been trying to harness since this was first arranged rushes up inside me, like a wave gathering speed and size.

He smiles, and the wave of panic falls back. I pull him in for one last hug. 'Don't forget the work school has set you and the Zooms you need to join. They've been really good letting you have this time off to see your dad. Make sure you finish all the stuff they've given you to do. It's an important time for your studies now you're in secondary school.'

'We'll be fine, Chloë.' I hear his voice and my head shoots up. The familiar figure is standing behind Ruben at a thoughtful distance. I'd almost forgotten he was there. And it seems weird to see Lucas in person. It's been so long. 'We'll make sure he does it. And I promise to look after him and bring him back in one piece.' He smiles.

'I know you will.' I try really hard to smile back, but my cheeks hurt as the muscles are so tense. 'You're his dad!' The word catches in my throat and I cough to clear it. 'And we put presents for you, Lizzie and the baby in his case. And there's some Marmite – just in case you can't get it over there. I know it's your favourite too!' I wave the jar from the security of my chest. 'I forgot to put it in his case!' I say, feeling very distracted.

He laughs. 'Thank you! But he'll have plenty of new things to try when we get there. Lizzie is a great cook.'

I swallow. I used to cook, come up with new ideas for the summer season in the café. But this year I've had neither the ideas nor the inclination. Summer at the café next year will be much like last year.

There's a moment's awkward silence. I can tell Lucas doesn't want to rush me or make this difficult for Ruben, but I also know they have to go.

'Come on, move along there,' says a member of the airport staff, as we stand at the entrance to Departures, people having to navigate around us. 'You're blocking the way,' he says impatiently.

Ruben turns to look at his dad, then back at me, anxious now, knowing they have to go. 'We'd better go through before Mr Grumpy tells us off again,' he says, trying to inject a little light-heartedness into the situation.

'Yes, of course. Go!' I wave my hands around, hoping the wafts of air will keep the tears at bay, which are still threatening to put in an unwelcome appearance. 'Go and have fun with your dad and new baby sister,' I say, as Ruben backs towards Lucas.

'Wait till you see the Christmas tree in the apartment,' Lucas adds. 'Lizzie's waiting for you to decorate it.'

Lucas gives me another look and a nod of reassurance. With a huge effort, I smile as Ruben stands beside Lucas, who puts an arm around his shoulders. It's like the small spaceship has made it to its docking station. I have passed responsibility for my child to his other parent for a whole month.

'Thank you for this, Chloë,' Lucas says. 'He'll be fine. And he'll FaceTime lots.'

Ruben is finally looking excited.

'Thank you,' I say, and mean it. It's such a great opportunity for Ruben – a month in New York at Christmas with a new half-sister.

'Go!' I say, and they move towards security. As I wave and smile, Ruben drops his scarf. I go to run forward but Lucas stops to pick it up and wrap it around his son's neck again. He gives me a thumbs-up and a familiar smile. He might have filled out, got a few lines round his eyes, lost a bit of hair, but the smile is still the same. He's got this, I tell myself. They'll be fine. It might have been a couple of years, what with Covid, since they've spent time together in person, but they've FaceTimed every Saturday.

I just wish this wasn't so hard, as if I'm letting my

child go off with a stranger. Lucas and I were together for a bit. We tried to make it work. You might have called us friends with benefits, until we were caught out. We tried to make a go of it as a couple, but we weren't in love, and didn't make each other happy. Not as a couple. We made the decision before Ruben was born: we'd be there for him but we couldn't be together.

He takes Ruben's small rucksack, which is sliding down his shoulders, and puts it over his own as they hurry towards security, laughing. They're making the most of their time together already. I'm lucky Ruben has a dad who loves his son as much as I do.

Around me, the airport is full of sparkling Christmas trees, baubles hanging from the ceiling, tinsel garlands. Families and others are heading away for the Christmas holidays, even though it's only 1 December. There is a choir singing, wearing Christmas hats and light-up jumpers, shaking charity collection boxes. The air is full of love. I feel like I'm watching a happy Christmas film from inside a snow globe, unable to be part of it.

Ruben stops and turns, and I can barely hold back the tears now. Don't embarrass him, I repeat to myself, with a huge ball in my throat. He raises his hand and waves. I raise a hand too – and realize I'm clutching Joe the Bear by the neck.

'Ruben! You forgot him!' I brandish him in the air.

But he's turned away and Lucas is saying something, making him laugh, and then they're gone.

Despite the blur of tears filling my eyes, I stumble out of the airport to the car park, where I fiddle with the keys to unlock the car, get in, slam the door and collapse over the steering wheel, holding Joe to my eyes. I sob my heart out, regardless of the huge fee I'll have to pay for outstaying my drop-off time, or the people around me staring as they get out of their cars with big cases. It's just me, for a whole month, on my own at Christmas. I have no idea how I'll get through it with nothing but Netflix and a tub of Celebrations for company. And Joe the Bear.

I catch a glimpse of myself in my rear-view mirror, slide off my bobble hat and put it on the seat next to me. I rub my hand over my shoulder-length dark hair and wonder where the years have gone. It seems only yesterday that I was a twenty-six-year-old with a new-born baby, terrified that I wasn't going to be a good enough mum, and now I'm putting my twelve-year-old son on a plane with his dad, wondering what I'm going to do without him. I rub my red nose with the back of my glove, and hear a ping from my phone.

*Through security!* Ruben sends me a picture from a café, with a milkshake and a giant Toblerone from Duty Free.

*You forgot Joe the Bear! And the Marmite!*

*You look after him for me. And they wouldn't have let me take the Marmite through security! Save it for when I'm back. I'm planning to try out some new breakfasts in New York. Dad says they have everything there!*

I nod and send him a kiss. I should have put the Marmite in his case, I think crossly to myself.

*Don't forget your present!* he texts. *I made it for you. It's under the cheese plant in the lounge. Open it when you get home.*

Thank you, Ruben, my lovely son, making me forget I was cross and making me smile. I hold the phone to my lips for a second or two. I need to take this one day at a time, I tell myself, and turn on the ignition. I just have to count down the days until Christmas is over and Ruben is home.

# 2

'So here it is, Merry Christmas,' the radio blares out as the car throatily fires up. I hit the off button with more force than I'd intended and the knob flies into my lap as the radio falls silent. I stare at the rain on the windscreen. We'd had the radio on and Christmas tunes playing all the way to the airport. Now that it's 1 December, the Christmas songs have been released from their seasonal stabling and are running amok over all the channels. I push the button back on and try a few other stations, but they're all the same and I turn off the radio again, gentler this time. Our road trip to the airport had been fun, singing along at the tops of our voices. Now the songs seem to taunt me, reminding me of everything I'm missing already.

With the engine running, I hold the steering wheel. I just have to get through December and Christmas.

On New Year's Eve he'll be home again. It's only a month. Christmas is cancelled this year. I put the car into gear as my phone rings. I snatch it up without looking at the name or number, in case it's Ruben and the flight's been cancelled or something.

'Hello, is that Chloë Namid Jones?'

'Who's that?' I snap, my nerves jangling, not sure whether I'm relieved or disappointed that it's not Ruben.

'Ms Jones, I'm calling from Berry and—'

'I'm sorry, whatever it is you're selling, I'm not interested. Sorry,' I say again, apologizing for my rudeness, but I'm really not in the mood for a cold call. I close the phone and give my nose a big blow.

My phone pings with another picture of Ruben, pointing at the departures board and giving me a thumbs-up.

'Happy Christmas, Ruben,' I whisper, and find myself smiling. He'll have the best time, I know it. I put the car into reverse as my phone rings again inside my handbag. This time I let it go straight to voicemail. I know it's not Ruben, who's happy with his dad. He'll soon be on that plane and on his way to New York.

I join the busy lanes of traffic heading out of Heathrow and on to the motorway, taking me back towards the Prince of Wales Bridge and home to Wales, to Cardiff.

As I drive home, I try not to let every lit tree and decorated shop window make my heart break a little more, knowing that this Christmas will be my first without my boy in twelve years. It starts to rain harder. The wipers swish forward and back, the lights from the streets melting into each other as they slide off the windscreen.

After a few hours, I pull into our street, a walk away from town, sometimes used as a cut-through by cars to get to the cheap supermarket at one end. But it's quiet and friendly enough. I look for a parking space. The one I left this morning has been taken and I'll have to go further up the road.

I park, get out of the car and walk slowly past the row of houses, already decorated, to ours, a little two-bedroom that we've rented for years, ever since Lucas and I broke up. I brought Ruben home to it, and it's been fine for the two of us, but Ruben would love a dog and we can't have one here. When we own our home, we'll have a dog.

I spot my neighbour, Mae, putting more Christmas lights into her front garden and run my hands over my eyes to get rid of any last trace of tears. She's tinkering with her inflatable snowman, and has strung more lights around the neck of the inflatable Santa at the other side of the front door. The energy crisis seems not to have dampened her usual enthusiasm for her outside lights.

'He's gone, then?' she calls, as I make a dash for my front gate.

I can't really speak. My throat is too tight.

'You changed your mind about coming to us on Christmas Day? You know you're more than welcome to spend as much of Christmas with us as you like. Always a houseful here.' She smiles as her inflatable snowman pulls himself up to his full height, waving and smiling at me. 'Looks like he had a slow puncture. That's sorted him. Always keep a few corn plasters in the cupboard for that sort of thing,' she says.

I scrabble for my front-door key in my bag, where my phone is lighting up again.

'Can't imagine how you must be feeling. It's always just been you and Ruben,' Mae says kindly, her words threatening to start another sobbing session.

'I . . .' My throat tightens even more, making it impossible to speak. I don't want to be rude but the last thing I want right now is to talk about how much I'll miss Ruben. I find myself inadvertently accepting an invitation to Christmas lunch, which makes me feel like another of Mae's waifs and strays, animals and people. There's Wilf who works at the corner shop, who lost his wife a few years ago, two sisters she plays bingo with and the Tesco delivery man, who spends all month delivering Christmas but goes home to eat alone. Now he's at Mae's, with her daughter and her partner, and the three grandchildren.

It always sounds like glorious, happy chaos through the walls. It's not something I've had since my parents died. I miss them. Before Dad went, we were a small but tight little family, but afterwards it was just me and Ruben. It's all different from when he was still alive – everything has changed. We used to know people in the street but nowadays it's full of students moving in and out with the new term. There's only Mae left. Christmas is quiet as the students go home for the holidays. These days, we usually have breakfast, presents and lunch together, then go next door to join Mae and her crowd. So I suppose I *am* another of Mae's waifs and strays. I'd love to be part of a bustling family Christmas, and I know Ruben would too, where we'd all join in cooking, sharing presents and stories. But Mae's small front room, with a collection of strangers, most of them dozing when we arrive, is the best I can do right now. If it wasn't for Ruben, I probably wouldn't go. I'm not sure either of us really enjoys it, but I'm grateful that Mae always includes us. Just sometimes, I wish it was different.

My phone is still lighting up and ringing. 'Unknown number'. I grab it and my keys and wave the phone at Mae. Tucking Joe under my arm, I find the right key, fit it into the lock and push open the front door with my shoulder, shutting it firmly behind me. I lean against it, the phone in my hand.

'Hello?'

I've missed the call. Now my brain has flipped into overdrive. What if something's happened to Ruben or the flight? You hear of hostage situations. I check my text messages. And my WhatsApp. Nothing. I check the flight tracker, and Ruben's flight is where it should be. I hold the phone to my lips for a moment, shut my eyes and think of my boy. He's taken off. He's on his way. Slowly I open my eyes. He's there and I'm here. And none of this feels quite right.

I look around the little living room. There's no sign of Christmas, other than the few baubles Ruben has hung on the Swiss cheese plant and the gift he told me about. I stare at it and my heart could explode.

*Open it when you get home!* I blink a few times. It's one month. I just need to get to the end of December and he'll be home. Everything will go back to how it was.

I walk towards the present, pick it up slowly. Everything about it makes me feel as if Ruben is right here with me. The wonky Sellotape, the rocket wrapping paper I saved from his last birthday, or maybe the one before that. I like to reuse as much as I can. And the familiar handwriting on a handmade label from another piece of wrapping paper, with balloons on it: 'Happy Christmas, Mum, love you always.'

If I let emotion overwhelm me this could get too messy. I rip open the parcel, letting the paper fall to the floor. Inside I find his advent calendar. I made it years ago from an old pillowcase, putting pockets all over the front and a Christmas tree I drew with Sharpie pens. It comes out every 1 December. I usually fill it with a small gift for each day in the run-up to Christmas. A sweet or a small present. Just little stuff I collect through the year. We add to the decoration on it each time it comes out, baubles, tinsel and cut-out pictures. I'm a dab hand with a glue gun, a Sharpie and recycling. He must have gone to the cupboard under the stairs to find it. It's kept in the box with the other decorations, which I won't be bringing out this Christmas.

I run my hand over the pockets. They crackle and crunch, each one puffed out, filled with expectation. It's mostly paper, I think, probably messages or jokes. Another fat tear plops onto the calendar. Damn it! I take a deep breath and tell myself to pull up my big-girl pants. Ruben would!

I sit on the sagging sofa and reach into the pocket with 1 on it. There's a note. I put down the calendar beside me and unfold the piece of paper, which has been torn from a school exercise book. It's got a little drawing of a snowman in one corner.

'1 December: Pour a glass of wine and drink it! A big one! And eat the crisps too!' There's another drawing of a glass with red wine in it and a bowl next to it, then a smiley face with a bubble coming out of its mouth, saying, 'Hic!'

I laugh and sob at the same time. He did this to

make me happy. Well, I'd better do as I'm told. He wanted to picture me here, in front of the telly, with a drink and crisps. Like we do on Saturday nights. He has a bottle of orangeade and I have wine. We put the crisps into a bowl. It's always a Saturday night, a birthday or another special occasion if the crisps go into a bowl.

I hold the piece of paper in my hand, head for the kitchen and the fridge, then look at the open bottle of wine in the door. Why not? I pour a glass and grab the bag of chicken and thyme crisps that Ruben threw into the basket last time we were at the shop – because he knows they're my favourite – put some into a bowl and head back to the sofa. There's a miaowing at the back door. It's Whiskey, one of Mae's cats. I open it and he squeezes in. Whiskey is not a small cat. In fact, he's fat, but maybe that's because Ruben feeds him bits of meat from his plate. When he goes home to Mae's she feeds him again. He's not our cat but I know Whiskey will miss Ruben. He jumps onto the sofa and I sit down with the wine, the crisps and Whiskey next to me.

'Looks like it's you and me,' I say to Whiskey, and stroke his damp fur. 'And Joe the Bear.' I place him on the sofa, too, where Ruben would be. Then I put an empty glass in his paw and a small bowl of crisps next to him, hold up my phone and take a snap of him. I create a message for Ruben: *Hic! Did you mean me or Joe the Bear?*

Smiling, I press send. It'll be there for when he lands and turns on his phone. I'm feeling brighter already.

Christmas is out there. In here, I can avoid it as much as I like.

I turn on the television. *Santa Claus: The Movie* blares back at me. I change the channel. It's *The Muppet Christmas Carol*. Definitely not. Ruben and I watch it every year together. Traditions have gone out of the window this year. Just give me anything that isn't Christmas! Hallmark, no . . . Netflix, no . . . Last year's *Great British Bake Off Christmas Special*, no!

My phone rings again. I click the TV off and look at the screen. Unknown number again! I pick it up.

'Ms Chloë Namid Jones?' comes the same voice as before. 'I'm ringing about an exciting opportunity that—'

'Look, I'm sorry, I've told you that whatever you're selling I'm not interested,' I repeat to the salesman.

'Ms Jones, I'm in your area at the moment and would be happy to come and speak to you in person.'

'No!' I say, ruder than I meant to.

'If you could just—'

'No! Please, don't ring this number again.'

'I left you a voice message earlier,' he says. 'Just listen to it. I'm not trying to sell you anything. If you're interested, ring me back. Any time. I just want to explain.'

And this time he hangs up, leaving me puzzled. Whiskey has curled up and gone to sleep. I turn the TV on and immediately off again when more Christmas music plays at me. I look at my phone. Not trying to sell me anything? Wants to explain? What is he on about?

I look around the silent living room. I'm not going to listen to his message. I have no idea how he got my number. I don't know who he is. I sip the wine and follow it with a crisp. I check my phone, then Ruben's flight tracker. Not too long to go now. I run my thumb over my Instagram account. I check my voice messages. There's just one. Wants to explain? Curiosity is tugging at my thumb as it hovers over the message. I could just listen. See what it is, probably an elaborate prank, and then delete it. It must be some kind of scam. With nothing else to distract me, and Whiskey snoring beside me, I press the play button and cautiously listen to the voice-mail, and let it play to the end.

# 3

*2 December: 23 days until Christmas*

This is a wind-up, right? It has to be, I keep telling myself. But where's the catch? I just couldn't see it. Instead, I called the number back and listened to what he had to say.

'Is that Chloë Namid Jones?'

How would he know my name, including my middle name, which I hardly ever use, without some kind of proof? He'd need to have proof, which he said he has.

Now here I am in a busy steamed-up café, Christmas music playing and shiny lightweight paper lanterns hanging from the ceiling. Christmas seems to start earlier these days, I muse, with a hint of Scrooge. As soon as the kids go back to school in September, the shops are gearing up for the festive season. Once Halloween and Bonfire Night are done, it's full-on Christmas decorations, music and adverts of happy families sitting around a groaning table. Don't they realize it's not like that for everyone?

There are parents with shopping bags weighing down buggies, and overtired and overexcited children hyped to their eyeballs about Christmas, which is still a whole twenty-three days away. It's busy, but that's good. I'm not stupid. I'm not meeting this man, who is apparently 'in my area', in some car park or inviting him to my home. And how does he know where 'my area' is? I have lots of questions.

I think about Ruben and this morning's advent-calendar gift. A teabag! For tea in bed. And a note: 'Say yes! You might have fun!' He's talking about Mae, I bet. He wants me to spend Christmas Day with her, but it'll be a reminder of all the things I'd usually do with him, I thought, as I drank my tea in bed. That was when I finally rang Nigel Berry back and arranged to meet him here, in Bella's Big Bakes. Bella knows me and waves.

She's lucky to keep going through the winter period. I wish we could in the café on the campsite. But no one wants to be in a tent over December and January. Bella is known for her generous portions, huge bacon butties and slabs of syrup sponge. Different from the cakes I bake at the café, but just as popular – the place is packed, people getting out of the rain.

21

I think about Ruben. He FaceTimed late last night from the apartment in New York, his dad with him, waving and smiling too. They're so alike, both dark, with dark eyes, and happy to be in each other's company. It was good to see him smiling. Ruben's happiness is all that counts. I told him about the wine and crisps. This morning I messaged him, although I knew he wouldn't be awake, and told him about the tea in bed. I didn't mention the phone calls or the man I've agreed to meet this morning. I told him in my message that I'd said yes and was off for coffee with a friend. I'll just have the coffee, listen to what Nigel Berry has to say, then go home with the bundle of DVDs I bought from the hospice charity shop next door, which have nothing to do with Christmas, and another bag of chicken and thyme crisps from the Co-op over the road.

I wish I was working, I'm sure that would help. Actually, baking. But with only me in the house it seems pointless. Usually the break over December and January works perfectly for me. Ruben and I spend lots of time together, even if money is a bit tighter. But even the thought of cooking in the café doesn't cheer me up. Not like it usually does. Maybe I'll go over and give it a deep clean. I usually do that the week before we open, but there's no harm in keeping on top of things. Perhaps I'll get some ideas for next season's bakes if I'm actually there. Then I remember that Suzie the owner has the keys, and the floorboards are up, to sort out a slow leak from the Ladies.

'It's not a joke or a scam,' says the man now sitting in front of me, wet from the rain but smart enough in a shirt and festive red tie. 'I know how this must look. But I really am from Berry and Brandy, Heir Hunters.' I roll my eyes inwardly. Even the company's name sounds like a Christmas cake from a Marks & Spencer's television advert. 'I presume you Googled us?'

'Yes,' I say. I did. They have a website and seem a legitimate company but you can never be too sure. I've heard of heir hunters, but only through a television programme.

'I'll get straight to the point. You had a distant relative who sadly died recently and, as it stands, you're the only surviving heir we can find to inherit his estate.'

'Right.' I laugh. 'Really, you've got the wrong person. I'd know if I had any relatives, and I don't. It's just me and my son.' I stop myself wittering on, avoiding giving him any more details about Ruben.

'I know. Your mother died when you were four. Your father brought you up with his parents until their deaths. He died seven years ago. You have one son by your ex-husband. You're divorced.'

I stare at him. He pushes a piece of paper towards me, showing a family tree. I frown. This seems very personal information. He's right: Lucas and I did marry. We'd thought it was the right thing to do. But we very quickly realized it wasn't and were divorced soon after Ruben was born. And Ruben was five when Dad died. Since then, it really has been just me and my boy. Before that, this area still felt like home. Now it's just somewhere I went to school. It's familiar. I kept Ruben here so that he could go to the same school. Besides, where else would I go?

'I don't have any other family,' I say firmly. This is surreal, like I've stepped through a sliding door into a parallel universe, one where the boiler isn't leaking, there isn't damp in the corners of the bedrooms and I'm preparing for a big old family Christmas.

'That's as may be, with regard to your immediate family. But on your father's side, you had a remaining distant relative. A cousin.'

'A cousin? I'd know if I had a cousin.'

'This is not a first cousin. You can see here.' He gestures to the family tree. I look at where he's pointing and my name.

'So is that a second cousin or a cousin twice removed?' I say, not really understanding, but I'm fascinated.

'You are the only blood relative we can trace at the moment to Harold Jones, so his legacy is legally yours, if you choose to claim it.'

I stare back at him. I feel as if I'm in some kind of

film. Perhaps he'll turn out to be a modern-day fairy godmother.

'If I choose to claim it?' I give a little laugh that sounds as if it doesn't belong to me at all.

'That's right.' He nods with a small smile, letting me take in the information.

I can't help it, I laugh again.

'So now you're going to tell me I'm on some kind of reality TV show – *You've Been Framed!* Remember that?' I'm wittering again. 'Or *Beadle's About*. Now you're going to tell me I've inherited a huge house and a million pounds, then watch my reaction when you tell me it's all a joke!' I can't even believe I came to meet this man, as nice as he seems. I shouldn't have said, 'Yes'! I pick up my scarf and start to wind it round my neck, ready to leave. My huge scone is untouched.

He shakes his head as I push back my chair. 'Sorry, no house or a million pounds in the bank.' He pulls out a file of papers.

'I didn't think so. Look, thank you, it was good of you to tell me about my . . .' I swallow '. . . distant relative.' I didn't know anything about him, and that's sad, I think. Would we have got on? Would I look like him? There's no point in wondering. Just like there's no point in wondering about me and Lucas. What if we hadn't split up? Sometimes at night I do wonder where it all went wrong, but maybe it was just wrong from the start. We liked each other, a lot. We were friends. We got on. We enjoyed each other's company. But we made the right decision. And it was better in the end that we went our separate ways before we started arguing in a way that could impact on Ruben.

I remember the night when I realized that trying to make our marriage work because of the baby was doing neither of us any good. We needed to be allowed to leave the relationship. It was over a supermarket ready-meal. We were about to be new parents, but we weren't a proper couple. He felt guilty. And so did I. Him for thinking about leaving, me for him staying. We had limped on, trying to make it work, but slowly, looking at baby equipment and attending antenatal classes while our lives separated. He'd been offered a job in New York as a journalist. What did I think? Should we go? A new start. I stared into the orange chicken tikka masala I'd craved earlier, which was now the very last thing I wanted to eat. I took a deep breath. 'You should take it,' I told him.

'But what about you? I mean, a fresh start could be just what we need.' But we knew that wasn't true. We were never going to make each other happy.

I shook my head and he gave a sigh of relief.

'You sure?' he said gently.

I nodded again. Large plops of tears joined the soggy mess on my plate.

'I'll always be there for you, both of you.'

'We'll make it work,' I croaked, but I had no idea how. I wanted to focus on bringing up Ruben. I didn't want Lucas to feel guilty. He would be a good dad, a great dad. I didn't want to hold him back, and we knew the New York job was the get-out we needed. But every now and again I still wonder what life would be like if we'd stayed married. What if I had moved to New York with him? Would it have been a fresh start? But I wanted to keep things as they were, for Ruben's sake, and I had Dad to help me.

Now, I just need to think about Ruben. This is his home. I didn't know this relative, and I certainly don't feel entitled to his money or whatever he's left behind. There must be someone far more deserving, someone who knew him at least.

It all sounded too good to be true.

I stand to leave, swinging my bag over my shoulder, just as a buggy, without a child in it but with bags of Christmas shopping hooked over the handles, tips back and catches me on the back of the ankle, making me wince in pain. Suddenly I'm very hot and short of breath. This is all too much to understand in the cacophony of mother-and-toddler coffee meet-ups. I can't wait to get out of here, away from all this noise, which is reminding me of everything I'm missing.

'Look, let's go somewhere quieter where I can explain,' says Nigel-from-Berry-and-Brandy.

I look at him through narrowed eyes, wondering

again about the relative I'd supposedly had. How come I never knew? There are questions I'd like to ask, but getting out of the hot, noisy, crowded café would be good.

I end up sitting in the bus shelter, with the number 44 driving away.

'So you see,' Nigel continues, 'you're in line to inherit a large parcel of land that could be worth a lot of money.'

'A parcel of land?'

'Yes, and from what we gather, it's an important one.'

'Right,' I say, trying to process it as the rain tips down. 'Where is it?' I ask. I'm not sure that really matters, but I can't think what else to ask.

'Canada. Québec. It's where Harold Jones lived. The land has passed through the family for some generations. But he never married or had children and died with no direct heirs. So the line comes to you.'

I chew my bottom lip. *Canada?* I don't have relatives in Canada! My mind is whirring, trying to spot all the pitfalls and possible scams here.

'All you have to do is agree to us going forward with the claim. This is how it works. We take a percentage for getting all the ducks in a row. Once the land is sold, we take our fee from the proceeds and you have the rest.'

I still stare at him. 'How did you get my phone number?' I suddenly ask.

'You're on the website for the café at the campsite

where you work. This phone number is on it. A contact for holiday staff.'

Oh, yes! How could I have been so stupid? I must take it down. 'And you're an heir hunter,' I say.

'Yes.' He nods. 'Just like on the television. We research people who have died without leaving a will and find their relatives. Of course we knew it was you we needed because of your middle name. Very few people have it and it's been in your family for generations.'

'My father's. I don't know why. And I don't have anyone to ask.' I swallow, feeling very alone, despite everything around me being familiar.

'I can email you a copy of the family tree, as we have it so far,' he says kindly, holding his file under his arm. 'Lots of the younger staff carry iPads for this kind of thing, but I'm too old for all that. I like to see things in black and white.' A big wet raindrop splashes onto the middle of his red cardboard file as another drip falls from the joins in the shelter roof.

I hand over my email address. It's better than him phoning me.

'I need to think about this,' I tell him, trying hard to find the holes in the story where the scam reveals itself.

'Okay, take your time. Well, not too long. If no one claims it, the land will be sold and the money will go to the Canadian Treasury.'

'Really?'

'It's a sizeable amount, Chloë. It would be a shame

for it to go into the Treasury coffers. You could do a lot with a legacy like this one.'

'How much?' Curiosity is creeping in. 'I mean, presuming this is real, how much are we talking?'

He shrugs. 'Enough for it to be worth our while. Maybe a top-of-the-range car, a pension pot—'

'Enough for a house – or at least a deposit?' I cut across him, my mind working overtime – *what if, what if, what if?*

'I would say almost certainly.' He smiles kindly. 'It's not a scam, Chloë. It's all up front. We get a good commission from finding you, then getting the legacy sold and the money to you. There's nothing hidden. Look, to be honest, you're my last client. I'm retiring, so I'm keen to get this job wrapped up. If it'll help,' he gives an impish grin, 'let's push the boat out. I'll even organize for you to visit the land if you like, pay for your flights and accommodation. I'll need your signature. You just have to say yes.' And once again I think about Ruben's piece of paper from this morning's calendar.

Surely I can't say yes to this. That would be absurd! Or is it more absurd that I turn this down? A house of our own, for Ruben's sake . . .

We say our goodbyes at the bus shelter and I let him know I'll be in touch. He tells me again to be quick. I assure him I won't take long.

As I drive home, I rack my brains for any Canadian relatives on my father's side. Back in my street, I go to

Mae's. She may know. There used to be a tight little community here. People knew each other and everyone's business. Now we smile and raise a hand to anyone coming and going, but familiar faces are few and far between.

'Mae, do you know anything about a relative of my dad's in Canada?' I say, clasping a jolly Santa mug of tea.

'A relative of your dad's?' She frowns, putting a plate of mince pies on the table. 'I'm not sure. There was a story about your great-grandfather going to Canada with his brother. But he came back. Took over the corner shop, as you know. Not sure what happened to the brother, mind. Why?'

'He's died.'

'I expect he did. It was years ago!'

'I mean, the last of the line, a man called Harold.'

'Oh, that's sad,' she says. I can hear *Countdown* in the background on the television in her living room. It doesn't matter whether I'm in her house or on the other side of the wall in mine. It's always *Countdown* at this time of day.

'How do you know?' She pushes the mince pies towards me.

I take one and eat it. 'Because I'm in line to inherit from him.'

'What? How?'

'An heir hunter came to find me.'

'Oh, I've seen that on the telly! They find people

31

who are legally entitled to inherit and they get money they were never expecting.'

'Yes. Apparently, it could be quite a bit.' I swig my tea to wash down the mince pie.

'Really? How much?'

'I'm not entirely sure. It's land, apparently.'

'So, you're saying you've inherited some land, but you're not sure how much it's worth?' She dunks her mince pie in her tea and catches it in her mouth as it disintegrates.

Now she says it, I'm doubtful again. But Nigel answered all my questions. He didn't avoid them.

'Where is this land?'

'Québec. Like I said, he lived in Canada.'

'Well, that's a turn-up. A man you don't even know and now you're going to inherit the money from his land. I wonder who he was exactly. Fancy dying with no one.'

Suddenly I have an overwhelming urge to find out more. I feel I owe it to the man whose land I'm told I've inherited. Mae's words run around my head: *Fancy dying with no one*. And I feel so sad for him. I don't know who he is or why I've inherited from him, but something is making me want to find out, to pay my respects, not just take the money. I think about Ruben and the piece of paper.

*Say yes!*

# 4

'So you'll come here after Christmas dinner as usual for charades and mince pies?' says Mae, the next morning, as I'm stepping outside my house. 'But you're welcome for lunch as well, you know that.'

I shake my head. 'Sorry, Mae, and thanks, but this year there's been a change of plan. I'm going to Canada!' There. I've said it. As mad as it sounds. 'I rang Nigel Berry yesterday after I left you and said yes, I'll sign with his company, visit Harold's land and find out more.' I have butterflies in my stomach.

'And they've booked a flight for you?'

'Yes.'

'When?'

33

'Today.'

'*Today?*'

'Yes.'

'That's a bit quick, isn't it?'

'Well, if I leave it a week, I'll probably get cold feet. I just said yes, that I'd like to go as soon as possible. So I'm going.'

'When?'

'Now!'

'*Now?*'

'Yes,' I say. It sounds as surreal as it feels.

'But – but you can't just go to Canada! It's Christmas!' She puffs out her cheeks. 'You always come here.'

That is exactly why I *can* go to Canada.

'This year is different. I did what Ruben told me to do. I said yes!' I'm trying to convince myself that this isn't totally mad. It *is* mad. But exciting too.

'But it was only suggested yesterday!'

'And that's why I'm doing it now. If I think about it for too long, I won't do it. I'm just saying yes and seeing what happens. I'm going to look at the place and try to find out who this relative was. I just feel I should.'

'And what will you tell Ruben?' She frowns, her hands on her hips now.

'That I'm going to meet an old friend.' I've spent the night thinking about this.

She throws her hands into the air. 'But anything could happen!'

It has to be better than sitting at home on my own and missing Ruben.

'I'll be fine. I'll text you the flight details, and the place I'm staying, and I'll message you when I'm there. The heir hunter has helped set it all up – even paid the air fare.'

'This land must be worth a sizeable amount if they're prepared to do that,' she says.

'Yes,' I say, guilt scratching at me like a rough blanket for taking money from a man I never even knew existed.

I look down at Ruben's advent calendar. Today, 3 December, he'd given me a train timetable and a toffee. 'Take a trip!' he said, in a note. 'Go somewhere different.'

I'm certainly doing that . . .

I'm mentally checking I've turned everything off when I see Whiskey safely back with Mae, sitting in the window behind the flashing fairy-lights curtain. I slide the advent calendar into my case and zip it up, then shut the door behind me. I move towards Mae, on the other side of the garden wall, trying to dodge the waving arm of the inflatable snowman.

'You're really going to do it, then?' Mae is walking towards me in her slippers.

'Yes, I am.'

'We'll miss you at Christmas,' she says, looking tearful.

'It's just this once, while Ruben's away,' I say. 'I've got

to find out if any of this is true, if I really did have family I never knew about, so I can tell Ruben how we came by the money – if I decide to take it,' I add.

'You could end up with a home of your own from it.'

I can't think about that now. But she's right. This might be the lucky break we need.

'Now, give me a hug.'

I feel my bravery slipping and need to hurry. Ron the taxi pulls up outside to take me to the station. I'm not sure this was the train journey Ruben had in mind, but I said yes. I'm not just sitting inside, counting the days until Christmas is over and wondering what to do with my time. At least I'll have something interesting to tell Ruben.

Mae reaches over the wall and I hug her as best I can with the wall between us and the snowman batting at us.

Ron the taxi beeps his horn.

Mae gives me a final squeeze. 'Off you go. And, remember, you can always come home if you don't like it.'

If only it felt like home, but it doesn't now. Not without Ruben. I blow Mae a kiss, jump into the waiting taxi and shut the door behind me. I can still hardly believe I'm doing this, but I am. And at least I'm going to be on the same continent as Ruben. Somehow that helps. I look at Mae waving and Whiskey in the window, then at her inflatable snowman and Santa.

Everything I usually love at this time of year means nothing without Ruben.

'Off on your hols, are you, love?' says Ron. 'Can't say I blame you. Could do with some sunshine myself!'

'Not sure it's sunshine I'll be getting, Ron.'

I think back to the conversation with Nigel Berry.

'If you need convincing this isn't a scam, go and see it for yourself,' the heir hunter had said.

And that's what I intend to do. I need to see it's for real.

'Where are you off to?'

'The station, please.'

'And what about your holiday?'

'Heathrow . . . and Canada,' I tell him.

'Didn't one of your relatives go out there? What happened to them?' he says, to my surprise, in the rear-view mirror.

'I'm not sure, Ron,' I say, as we drive past the old corner shop that my grandparents once owned, my great-grandfather before them. 'That's what I need to find out.'

I text Ruben from the train to tell him I'm going to stay with an old family friend in Canada. He's delighted for me. I promise to let him know about all the exciting things I'll see and to keep up with my advent calendar. And he promises me that he's keeping up with his schoolwork.

'Where are you off to?' says the inspector, checking the ticket I pull out of my pocket with the train time-table and some toffee.

'Québec, Canada,' I say casually, while inside I'm as giddy as a newborn foal trying to find its feet.

He frowns. 'I meant your station. Reading, is it? Change there for Heathrow Express.'

I blush.

'Sorry,' I say, holding out my ticket. 'Heathrow.'

Now he smiles. 'But Canada sounds great. You'll have a perfect Christmas!'

But Christmas is the last thing on my mind. Leaving it behind is the best thing I can do.

# 5

'*Où?* Where to?' The taxi driver, wearing a red Santa hat, asks me to repeat the name of the town as I bend over and speak through the window, but my teeth are chattering so much I'm not sure if he's understood me. It's snowing heavily. And it's so cold. I pull my scarf around me as my nose freezes and turns red.

'Forêt des Esprits,' I repeat, but my accent is terrible, not helped by my teeth still chattering uncontrollably.

'I thought that's what you said. Get in. You look freezing!' he says, in English with a French-Canadian accent, and I grab the taxi door handle. I push my case onto the passenger seat, then squeeze in beside it. I slam the door, glad to be in the warmth of the car. I don't even mind that the radio here is playing Christmas tunes too.

'Okay, and you're sure it's Forêt des Esprits?' he asks.

I peer at Nigel's email. 'It is,' I say.

'Okay,' he says, and we set off, crunching along the snowy road from the airport.

I gaze out of the window as we leave Montréal. I'm wishing I had the chance to take in its beautiful French-style buildings with wrought-iron balconies and railings, soft pastel colours and shutters, as we head out into . . . well, a winter wonderland. The trees at either side of the road are covered with snow and remind me of Christmas cards. Snow like I've never seen before. I mean, I've seen snow and it has closed Ruben's school a couple of times. Once, early in the morning, we waited on the council's website as schools posted closed-for-the-day notices. We waited with bated breath until the name of Ruben's popped up. Closed for the day! A snow day! We cheered, and got ready for a day of snowman-building and sledging. But this is a different level of snow. It hangs from branches and is banked up beside the road, leaving a clear path down the middle. The driver hurtles along, too fast for my liking.

'You're not from round here,' he observes.

'No.' I shake my head, mesmerized by the houses, their terraces lit with multicoloured lights, as we pass other cars, mostly pick-up trucks, far too close.

He catches my eye in his rear-view mirror. 'Not used to Canadian winters, I see,' he says.

I'm thinking I've underestimated the cold. I'm ridiculously underdressed for this weather.

I wonder what on earth I'm doing here. What made me think this was a good idea? It's like I've stepped into a different universe! I know I wanted to get away from Christmas, but right now, my front room with Whiskey, posh chicken-and-thyme crisps and *Strictly Come Dancing* on the telly seems a very safe, warm place to be. I don't even speak French! What am I trying to prove? That I can take a break while Ruben is with Lucas, his new wife and their baby. That I have a life of my own, that I'm happy being single, grabbing opportunity with both hands. I'm adventurous . . .

Or am I just scared to be without Ruben for the Christmas holidays? Scared of wallowing in my misery, wondering what it would have been like if Lucas and I had tried to stay together all those years ago. I'm trying to find out if I had family I didn't know about, if this story about inheriting money that will buy Ruben and me our own home is true. It's not that I don't believe Nigel Berry, but after Lucas left and it was just me and a small baby, I couldn't trust or let anyone into our lives easily. Lucas moved on quicker than I'd expected, although it took him a few years to start dating seriously, to settle and remarry Lizzie. And I know it's taken a lot longer for them to have the baby they wanted. In some ways that hurt all over again. They were trying for a baby, and there were clinics, appointments, IVF, hope and disappointment. For a while it felt Lucas was more focused on the baby he didn't have rather than the boy he had already. And I wonder how Lizzie must have felt, wanting the one thing I had and she didn't.

'You have friends out here in Forêt des Esprits?' the taxi driver asks cheerfully, breaking my thoughts.

I shake my head.

'Seems like an unusual place to spend the holidays,' he says. He seems as intrigued as I'm unsure about what I'm doing here.

We head further and further into the forest, and the houses thin out until there are none, just trees. And snow.

Finally, after about an hour, we come to a small town. 'Forêt des Esprits.' He points to a snowed-over wooden sign.

'So, you here on business?' he asks.

'I . . . just wanted to get away from Christmas – I mean for Christmas,' I reply, taking in the little town as we pull up in front of a hardware store opposite a square and a bandstand. I see driveways, almost small streets, with postboxes at the ends. Some turnings seem to lead to houses set deeper in the forest and cabins nestled in the shadows of the trees. I look back at the hardware store. Its veranda has been cleared of snow, like the steps, but all around is deep snow and more is falling in tiny flakes, like glitter. I'm dreading stepping out of the car.

'You might want to get some warmer clothes,' the driver says, nodding towards the hardware store.

'Oh, I'm not staying long,' I say. If I wear nearly all my clothes at once I might just be warm enough.

'Well, if it's getting away from Christmas you wanted, you've come to the right place.' He glances around at the cheerless store, the diner next door and a small grocery on the other side. This place may be exactly what I need. There's no sign of Christmas anywhere.

'Here, take my number for when you need to get back to the city,' the taxi driver says, handing me the card machine and his business card. I take it. Just in case. And put the taxi fare, which makes my eyes water, on my credit card to deal with when the café at the campsite is open again.

Slowly I step out of the taxi into the snow, clinging to the door. I pull my case from the seat beside me. I shut the door and the hairs up my nose freeze and tingle. I've barely stepped away from the cab when he sets off. I watch him leave at speed, as if he can't wait to get out of the place. The little glow of the light on the top of his cab, and the artificial tree on the parcel shelf at the back, disappear into the white distance.

Part of me wants to run after him, shouting, 'Come back!'

But he's too fast for me. In no time, he's gone. It's just me. I look around the small town square. There's a bench next to the bandstand but not much else.

Mostly it's just trees, with cabins tucked between them off the small tracks and driveways leading from the square, and no one's around. It's silent.

I lift my phone and take a photograph, ready to send to Ruben. Then I hear a rustle. I look round. It's coming from the trees opposite.

'Hello? I mean, *bonjour*?' I look into the snowy shadows.

'Hey, hey!' says a voice, in a forced whisper.

I spin round but can't see anyone.

'Psst!' I hear, not from the direction of the trees.

I look at my phone. I was told to meet someone here to pick up the key to my accommodation. I look back in the direction of the 'psst'. A man is standing in the doorway of the store, frowning at me.

Let's hope it's not him, I think.

I look back in the direction of the rustle in the forest.

'Moose!' he says.

'Excuse me?'

'Moose!'

'Hello? I'm looking for . . .' I say loudly and clearly.

But I've barely got the words out when suddenly I'm knocked off balance, bundled backwards, and hijacked behind a pick-up truck, my head pushed down. Well, that's how it feels. 'Hey . . .' I try to say but the words won't come out.

I'm in shock. I stand and glare at the tall man, the size of a bear, my hijacker. 'Well, really!'

'Get down!' He motions.

Instinct tells me to do as he says.

'I have no idea what's going on, but I demand you let me go!' I say, as he peers over the back of the truck.

He doesn't say a word.

I just have to phone my taxi driver and leave. He was right: this is not somewhere you come to spend Christmas.

The man's still staring out.

'Excuse me!' I say indignantly, but inwardly terrified.

He turns to me. 'That's what's going on around here,' he whispers, pointing, and I look out over the pick-up. A large moose with antlers the size of television aerials is moving out of the woods, and behind her is a baby. She's looking this way and that. My heart is thundering, not at the thought of being kidnapped, but at the size of the animal, so close to me, here in the wild.

'It's huge!' I whisper.

He nods.

I can smell him next to me. A mix of woodsmoke and the outdoors.

'And with young. You don't want to get in the path of a moose on the move with her young,' he murmurs, and I can feel his warm breath on my cheek. Suddenly in each other's personal space, yet complete strangers.

The moose stands tall, lifts her head, high and majestic, looks around again, then slowly moves off.

I feel the man next to me breathe a sigh of relief.

'She's close to town today. Hopefully she'll move on now.' He stands and heads towards the steps of the wooden veranda underneath a sign saying 'Store'.

'At least she's on her way,' he says to no one in particular.

I'm gathering my thoughts. 'So,' I clear my throat, 'that's what that was about.'

He looks back at me from the foot of the steps, somewhat surprised. 'Yes. Like I say, you don't want to get in the way of a moose with young. You were right in her path.'

I straighten and dust myself down.

'You're welcome!' he says, and takes the steps.

'You could have explained.' I'm still ruffled. 'I thought I was being kidnapped!'

I hear him laugh, which infuriates me.

'Oh, yes, stupid of me! I could have explained while you got trampled!' He comes back down the steps. 'Instead I did what needed to be done and got you to safety.'

I'm starting to blush, and I look around nervously.

'Hey, the coast's clear. She's gone. But tell everyone to keep an eye out.' He's on the phone. 'Nancy!' he calls. 'She's gone!'

A woman at the store looks out of the window and gives a thumbs-up.

'You here to see Bea?' he asks, picking up some boxes by the door and pushing it open. 'Bea, next door in the diner?'

46

'Um, I'm not sure.'

'Right,' he says, and carries the boxes inside. The door slams and suddenly I'm terrified of the moose coming back. I look at my phone. My heart sinks. Yes, the instructions tell me to go to the store to collect my key. I hope this isn't where I'm staying.

I head up the steps. I open the door. The bell rings loudly. I shiver, expecting to be hit by a wall of warmth and a bit of Christmas cheer. But there's nothing. Other than a big black fur rug on the floor. The man's nowhere to be seen.

'Hello? Um . . . *bonjour*?' I call.

The rug moves and lifts its head, taking me aback. It's a dog and it's huge. It looks at me, drops its head down and continues its snooze. It's not too bothered about me being here.

I am in a large wooden cabin, with a big worn counter and an old-fashioned till on it in the middle of the room. There's an eclectic mix of shovels, rolls of wire, higgledy-piggledy boxes of boots, racks of checked jackets and waterproofs, head collars for horses and lead ropes.

'*Bonjour*?' I call again.

The dog lifts its head again but doesn't move and gives a deep 'Woof!'

'*J'arrive*!' comes the voice.

A flight of wooden stairs leads to a mezzanine with more coats and hats, by the look of it. In fact, this is

47

the sort of place you could find anything you wanted, if only you knew where to start your search.

I stamp my feet and wrap my arms around myself. It's cold in here and I'm chilled to the bone. I hear footsteps coming down the wooden staircase and turn to see the man again: tall and broad-shouldered, in a thick checked jacket, work jeans over solid thighs that I try to look away from and heavy-soled boots, pulling off yellow work gloves and frowning.

The dog gives another bark.

'Okay, Hagrid,' he says, to the dog.

'Hagrid? As in Harry Potter Hagrid?' I can see the resemblance: big black beard and mane of hair. Ruben would love him.

'Yes?' he says, gazing at me quizzically, as if it's perfectly normal to have a dog the size of a horse lying in the middle of the floor. 'So, what can I do for you? Lost? It happens, especially when the weather's like this. Or did you come to thank me?' His voice is a deep, rich mix of French-Canadian flippancy.

I blush again. 'About that, sorry. I didn't realize. I . . . didn't know.'

He stares at me, challenging me almost.

'And, yes, thank you,' I add.

He nods. 'You mean *merci*.'

'Pardon?'

'You're in Québec now. Not "thank you", *merci*.' He's not joking.

'*M-merci*,' I echo.

He clearly thinks I'm some stupid city type from out of town, and doesn't suffer fools gladly. But I need to find my accommodation.

'So, it's not always like this?' I gesture at the deep snow lying outside.

'No.' He looks straight at me with dark brown eyes, hair falling forward, which he brushes away, and a square jaw that makes something inside me illuminate with colour and light, as if it's brought its own set of lights to the Christmas party.

He raises an eyebrow. 'No, it's not always like this. Only in winter.' He laughs gently. And the lights inside me are extinguished. I'm annoyed all over again.

'Sorry, I didn't mean to appear rude. Just my humour. We don't get many visitors at this time of year. Not on their own. Like I say, you're either lost or here to see Bea next door in the diner.'

Despite his questionable humour and my irritation, my eyes are drawn back to him, taking in his broad shoulders, the wide jaw, close-cut beard and dark eyes. This hasn't happened in a very long time, which intrigues me. When was it? When I first met Lucas? Have I ever felt like that? Suddenly I realize I'm staring.

'So,' he claps his large hands together, snapping me back to the here and now, 'what can I get you? You're not dressed for the weather out here,' he says, indicating my boots and insubstantial coat.

It's an effort to pull away my gaze, and I have no idea why. He seems to be staring at me too. Why am I feeling like this? I put it down to tiredness from the flight. And the speed at which this has happened. I'm in the middle of nowhere, and I have no real idea where nowhere is. I had a knee-jerk reaction to Ruben going away and did the first mad thing that crossed my path. I take a deep breath. I have to find my accommodation and get some sleep.

'If it's not better clothing, what can I do for you? You need directions?'

'Something like that,' I hear myself say.

'Well, if you drive straight out of the town . . .' He points.

'No. Er, I was told to come here to pick up the key.' I try hard not to catch his eye again and look down at the details on my phone. I'm not making myself clear. 'I've got accommodation booked,' I say, starting again. 'Cabane de l'Étoile?' My eyes are drawn back to his.

'Star Cabin?' He's surprised. 'The forester's cabin?' He frowns.

'Hoping it's not actually in a forest!' I laugh nervously.

He isn't laughing. 'Everything here is in a forest.' He raises an eyebrow, gives me a querying look. 'This is maple country.'

'Yes, yes, of course.' I wave a hand over my face. 'Sorry. Long flight.'

'Come far?' he says, opening the till and taking out a chunky wooden key-ring.

'The UK,' I say, remembering my instructions to Ruben not to give out details to strangers.

'Here for the holidays?' he asks, as if bemused by my arrival in his store.

'To get away from them, actually.'

'Ah.' He tosses the key up and catches it. 'Then you came to the right place. Follow me. I'll take you to the cabin.'

# 6

'This place isn't often used until the sap rises,' he says, after a short but freezing walk through high trees along a cleared snowy path. My boots are now saturated and definitely not made for 'all weathers'. Each step is hurting: the cold is stinging my toes through sodden socks. I can hear my footsteps on the snow and every now and again a *boomp* that makes me jump.

'Is that the moose?'

He shakes his head. 'She's moved on. Neighbours texted me. Saw her go off back into the forest. It's just the snow, falling off the branches.' He turns and smiles at me, making me shiver with some sort of excitement. Something I haven't felt in . . . Well, haven't ever felt. It must be the cold, the tiredness, the shock of the moose. It must be to do with being in the middle of nowhere, surrounded by huge trees. And the silence. There's barely any noise.

'What did you say about sap?' I ask, following him as he carries my case on his shoulder, out of the snow.

'This place.' He points at a small wooden cabin in a clearing surrounded by more tall trees, and lots more snow. 'It's only really used in the spring.'

He steps onto a terrace and kicks a pile of snow away from the front door.

I take in the log cabin, made of large tree trunks, each with snow clinging to its rough edges.

'Cabane de l'Étoile!' He puts the key into the lock. It doesn't work straight away and he shakes the door, snow falling from the lintel overhead. My teeth start to chatter. 'As I say, it's not used much other than when the sap rises, at the end of winter, when the ground starts to wake and warm up. When the sap in the trees starts to run.' He waves at the trees all around us. 'That's when we tap them for their syrup.' It's as if he's happy to be back with old friends. And I feel that excitement in my stomach again, like a tangle of Christmas lights being plugged in.

'Did you say tap? Like a kitchen tap?' I give a little laugh.

'Yes,' he says directly, and then, 'You do know you're visiting a maple forest, right?'

'Of course!' I bluff. No idea about any of this, maple sap, taps and forests.

He puts his shoulder to the door and it gives, showering snow from the veranda roof, and I jump back. The snow lands right in front of and over me. He steps into the cabin with my case. Another lump of snow falls from a tree behind me.

'And it's just me here, is it?' I say, stumbling through the thick snow.

'And the trees.' He smiles.

'Of course, the trees. Erm . . .' I look around the dark, cold cabin. 'Is there a town anywhere near here?' Perhaps with a hotel, I think.

'Just the store, where you were dropped off. And the diner next door. Good pancakes. And then Nancy's grocery store. She'll order in anything you haven't got.'

'Great,' I say. 'Pancakes. I'll be sure to try them.'

'I'll get the porch cleared of snow. Like I say, it's been a while since anyone stayed out here. Usually it's just used for the harvest. The sugar shack is just over there.'

'The sugar shack?'

'Where we take the sap and boil it, make the syrup. The cooperative around the town takes it in turns and we work through the night to keep the fires lit and the syrup boiling when the sap is rising, for about six weeks. We use this place to be near the still.'

'The . . .?'

'The still. Where we boil the sap. We collect from the trees. Most of it trickles through tubes that connect to each other and feed into a collecting vat. Other trees that are harder to get to and some of the older ones we tap by hand. We make a small hole in the tree, push in a tap and collect the sap in a bucket. Then it goes into the still and is kept boiling, through the night, until we have syrup – the stuff you put on your pancakes,' he adds, with a grin.

He puts the key on a wooden table with two chairs. The cabin is what you'd describe as basic and freezing.

There's an awkward silence as I take in my lodgings. Then he takes pity on me. And his pity is something I really don't need on top of everything else. 'We'll soon have this warmed up,' he says, and opens the doors to a wood-burning stove. 'I'll make some kindling. If you need to make more, the axe is outside by the log pile.'

'An axe?'

Not for the first time in the last twenty-four hours I'm wondering what I'm doing here or, with talk of an axe, if I'm about to be murdered in my bed.

He goes outside and I watch as he places a log on a larger stump and swings the axe. The log splinters into shards. He carries them in. 'I'll bring in some bigger logs too,' he says, clearly realizing this is way out of my comfort zone. I'm used to pressing a button to turn on the heating at home. And I want to say, 'Don't bother, I'll do it,' but I'm dead on my feet, and colder than I've ever known. I let him get the logs, then light and feed the fire, kindling first, bigger logs on top.

He closes the doors on the stove and opens the vents at the front. Flames begin to appear, jump-started into life.

'There's plenty of bedding here,' he says, going to a big cupboard by a high wooden bed. 'Let's get the bed made.' He throws open the cupboard.

'I can do that,' I say, my voice high and urgent. I don't want him to do any more for me. I can manage. But the idea of bed when I'm in the company of this attractive man is making me feel light-headed.

'Okay, if you're sure.'

'I am, but thank you,' I say firmly.

He checks the fire again, putting on a bigger log, then turning on the lamps, which give a dim glow. 'They'll warm up,' he says.

'Like the fire,' I say, with another little laugh. It's higher pitched than I intended.

'So . . .' He stands in front of the now blazing fire. 'Let me know if you need anything. Perhaps we should start again. I'm Theo, owner of the hardware store.'

'I'm Chloë Jones,' I say. And, once again, I find I'm staring at him and drop my eyes from his face.

'Pleased to meet you, Chloë. Like I say, let me know if you need anything. There are supplies in the cupboards but in the fridge there may just be beer. Nancy and I can order in anything else you need . . . although the delivery truck is often late, due to the snow.'

I wonder if I should offer him tea or coffee, beer

even, but then he says, 'I need to get back. The deliveries won't take care of themselves.' And I'm relieved and disappointed all at the same time.

He reaches for the door, then turns back. 'What was it you said you were doing in these parts over the holidays?' he says.

'I didn't,' I say.

'No, of course, sorry. Small-town syndrome. We're not used to visitors, really. I mean, why would you come to a town like Forêt des Esprits at Christmas?'

I wonder whether to tell him but something tells me to take my time. Like he says, this is a small town and I don't want to make a fool of myself within the first hour of arriving. I should take things slowly, see what I can find out – if my inheritance is real. If it is, it could change everything for me and Ruben. This could be the only way I'll ever get the money to put down against a home of our own.

'Like I said, avoiding Christmas.' I'm glad there's been no attempt at Christmas decorations in the cabin. I just have to get through the next twenty-seven days before Ruben comes home. And this seems like as good as place as any to do it, maybe while I'm finding out why my father and his family were estranged and how my cousin came to live here. I think Dad would have liked to know more, so I'm doing this for him as much as myself. And for the man who's died alone, with no one. I feel I need to be here for him too.

'Well, you've come to the right place,' Theo says. 'Forêt des Esprits is certainly no Tinsel Town! Anyway, I'll leave you to settle in. Nice to meet you, Chloë Jones. I hope you manage to avoid Christmas spectacularly well here.'

'Thank you, Theo,' I say. I think I've made the right choice.

'Oh, if you're walking back to town, the store and the diner, keep an eye out for the moose. If you see her, stand still or get to cover. Let her pass. Don't alarm her.'

As he walks away, he waves.

'The moose,' I say, and look around at the snowy, wilderness. Tall trees, behind which any amount of moose could be hiding. 'What about wolves?' I call after him. 'Do you have any?'

'Sometimes. They're around,' he says, as he starts to walk again.

'Why's it called Cabane de . . .?' I'm wondering if it's haunted.

'Just look up,' he says, pointing. 'On a clear night.' He smiles and I watch him go.

I look around the clearing. It's just the trees . . . and me. I throw myself inside, shutting the door firmly. Me, in a forest, on my own, with moose and wolves. Then I take out my phone with shaking hands to text Ruben that I'm here, safe and sound, although that may be misleading.

No signal.

'Of course!' I sigh, sitting heavily on the bed, exhausted. Could this get any worse? I grab a huge patchwork quilt from the cupboard and wrap it around myself. I'm really tired and tearful. My stomach rumbles. I can't remember when I last ate or slept properly. I open my case and there is Ruben's advent calendar. And there is the toffee! Heaven! I rip open the shiny purple wrapping and put the sweet into my mouth, closing my eyes and letting the chocolate melt. 'Thank you, Ruben.'

I shut my eyes. Tomorrow, I tell myself, everything will look different.

# 7

*4 December: 21 days until Christmas*

'Whassat?'

I wake with a start to the sound of a bear roaring. Which surprises me – first, because there's a bear outside and, second, because I didn't think I'd slept at all. My heart is pounding as I sit bolt upright in bed, my back to the wooden headboard, pulling the covers right up under my chin and gripping the patchwork eiderdown. I haven't felt like this for a very long time, not since Ruben was a baby. It's fear, my heart pumping so fast I don't know whether to run or fight. I remind myself that I'm in a cabin, in the middle of a forest. Last night, as I lay in bed, waiting for sleep, I could hear the distant howl of a wolf. I'm in a cabin, in a maple forest, on my own in the dark . . . It's not helping.

And now this: a noise so loud it could almost be in the cabin.

I grab my phone and turn it on for light.

It's dark and cold. And, frankly, very scary.

Was I dreaming?

But there it is again, a roar and . . . it's coming from my stomach. I'm starving. I try to remember the last time I ate. Was it yesterday lunchtime? What, even, is the time? Am I really still here?

I hear another noise, from outside this time.

It's nothing, I tell myself.

Could be anything, my overactive imagination replies unhelpfully. Wolves, bears – did he say there were bears here? The moose! Dangerous if they've got young with them! I remember yesterday's close encounter.

Or maybe it's the wind in the trees and the snow falling from the branches. I remind myself of the *boomp*s I heard yesterday on the short walk here from the store.

I hear the sound again, like shifting snow. Different from yesterday. Could definitely be a moose with young. Or a bear.

My phone dies. Brilliant. I forgot to put it on charge when I fell into bed last night.

I grapple for the lamp beside the bed. Find it. Knock it over, then freeze in case it alerts whatever is outside. I'm shivering with cold or maybe fear. Bears can smash windows, can't they? And what about that moose, with its long antlers?

My shaking hands finally turn on the lamp. I peer at the window latches to make sure they're shut but can't tell for sure. I swing my legs out of bed, and drop onto the floor, dragging the quilt with me. I shuffle across the floor, the quilt wrapped round me, and double-check the window latches, just to be on the safe side, trying to see out of the windows without getting too close or pushing my nose against the cold panes. I stand back, listening hard.

There's a thump against the door. I muffle a shriek into the quilt and reel backwards, knocking over a chunky wooden coffee-table with a lamp on it. I stand with my back to the wall out of the way of the window. My heart is racing. Slowly, after what seems like for ever, I lean forward to peer out of the window again.

It must have been a lump of snow from the overhanging branches. Just like when I arrived here yesterday . . . or whenever it was. I pick up the lamp and the table I knocked over. The fire has gone out. I shuffle over to it.

I reach for the paper, kindling and matches next to the wood-burning stove. But I can't do it while I'm holding the quilt. I drop it, freezing and shivering, scrunch up some paper, then strike a match, once, twice, three times. I could cry with frustration. Finally, on the fifth attempt, broken matches all around me, the paper lights, flames licking upwards. I put on the kindling, careful not to smother the flames, and watch as the fire grows. Then I pick up the quilt and wrap it around me again, relishing its warmth.

I didn't end up making the bed last night, just wrapped the covers around me and lay on it. Now I shuffle back to it, wrapping the quilt around me, like a cocoon, to see if I can get a little more sleep.

I decide to leave the light on. With the covers tight around me, I remember how I used to lull Ruben when he couldn't sleep. Count sheep. Ridiculous idea. Never works. Instead I take myself off to a happy memory and, try as I might to avoid it, it's Christmas with Ruben and Lucas. Our first Christmas. We weren't together, but we spent that Christmas Day with the baby. I wish things had been different . . . I think back to before our paths went in different directions. Well, his did. Mine stayed where it always was. And I won't do anything to change that: I don't want anything else to upset Ruben's world. And definitely not another man in his life, as Mae keeps telling me I need. He has enough adjusting to do as it is, with one step-parent and a new sister.

I hear the *boomp* again and remind myself that it's just snow falling from the trees. This time I don't jump. And finally I must have fallen back into an exhausted sleep.

I sit bolt upright, wide awake again. Something is out there – I can hear scratching, right outside the door. I hold my breath. There it is again. Scratch, scratch, scrape, scrape.

I'm thinking about the moose with its young. On

the veranda. Or even the wolf I'm sure I heard howling in the night.

Now what? I can't phone anyone. No signal or battery.

I'll wait, like Theo told me, stay calm and still. Surely the moose will clear off soon when she realizes there's nothing to eat here. My stomach rumbles again.

I think about the advent calendar. Maybe there's another toffee in it.

Then I see a shadow cross under the door. Oh, my God!

I have to do something.

I crouch, then shuffle across to the fire. It's died again. I pick up the poker from beside it.

What am I going to do with it? Wave it, just in case something or someone tries to break down the door, I tell myself, and slip on my still soggy boots.

I stand behind the door, shaking.

The noise outside stops. I hold my breath. Maybe it's gone.

Then there's a knock.

I jump out of my skin. It hasn't gone.

Another knock.

I stare at the door handle and raise the poker.

'Chloë, *bonjour?*'

What the . . .?

I try to turn the knob. After a couple of attempts I un-stick it, yank open the door, and stare.

# 8

I've never been so relieved to see someone. I could hug him. 'Oh, thank God!'

Theo is staring at the poker. 'Just wanted to get this porch cleared before you got up. Hope I didn't wake you,' he says. 'Everything okay?' he adds warily, in his French-Canadian accent.

I take a deep breath. The air is cold, but it feels really good so I take a couple more breaths. It feels almost invigorating.

'It's just you,' I say, with relief, then realize how rude I must have sounded. 'What I meant was—'

'It's no problem,' he says, raising a gloved hand, with a small smile. Yesterday's strange swirling sensation in my stomach is back.

'You planning on doing something with that?' He points at the poker.

'Oh, sorry, I was . . . I didn't know what the noise was. Thought it was the moose back again,' I say quickly, feeling stupid.

He shakes his head. 'I told you, if the moose is around, stay still, keep calm, don't scare her. But we'd have heard if she was here. Neighbours call each other if they spot her or anything else round and about.'

He attempts to look past me into the cabin. 'You kept the fire going?'

'Yes, no problem,' I lie, teeth chattering as light snow falls onto the cleanly swept porch. 'Th–thank you,' I stutter. 'For doing this.'

He raises a teasing eyebrow.

'*Merci*,' I correct myself.

'*De rien*. No worries. I was doing the store's porch and the diner's so I thought I'd pop over.'

Now I can barely speak. My toes are cold, as are my nose and ears.

'Well, I'll leave you to it. You know where to find me if you need me.' He turns to go, then turns back. 'You need to keep feeding it,' he says, indicating the stove.

I turn to look at it. 'Bugger!'

He climbs up the two cleared steps in chunky boots and worn jeans.

'May I?' He raises an eyebrow and points at the stove. I nod, hoping he knows how grateful I am.

With the fire roaring once more, he straightens from his crouch. 'Keep it going now. Feed it. Don't let it die out.' He pulls on his gloves over his large hands. 'Once it's hot, after about twenty minutes, close this vent at the front. You control it by this one on the side. Open it if you want it hot, and close it if you want it to tick over, like at night.'

'Thank you. I'm not used to having one.'

'No fire at home?'

'Just radiators. Gas ones. I flick a button.'

'Ah. Well, this is a little different, but very effective.'

'Thanks.'

This time, he leaves. 'Don't forget, the diner does great pancakes and coffee. Not much else at the moment,' he shrugs, 'but it's something.'

I raise a hand from the top of the quilt and my stomach roars to let me know that that sounds like a very good idea.

I shut the door and turn into the cabin. It's not half as scary as it felt last night. In fact, I could see why some people might think it the perfect getaway, but not me. This was not what I had in mind when I agreed to come here. I was thinking more small and cosy hotel. Some shops, cafés and maybe a library where I could find out what I need to know about the relative who owned land. I didn't plan to be abandoned in the middle of that land without a clue about how to stay warm.

I plug in my phone to charge, then go to my case and pull on as many layers as I can, leggings then joggers, three pairs of socks, and the same for jumpers. I tie my scarf around my neck, then squeeze into my boots and jacket. I'm warmer, if a little restricted in movement.

I grab my bag, then remember my advent calendar. I pull out the little slip of paper from the pocket with number 4 on it.

'Go out for coffee! Smile at someone and ask how their day is going!'

He's read my mind – about the coffee, I mean. I'll take a picture and send it to him, if I can get signal.

I'll put another log on the fire, I think. Open the door at the front carefully, just as Theo has shown me. I get the swirling sensation again when I think about the smile he gave me, aware that I was lying about the fire. Damn it! I need that coffee and some pancakes – maybe they'll get rid of the strange sensation. The very last thing I want is this man to have some kind of effect on me when he's around. I haven't had a relationship with another man since Ruben was born, and I don't intend to. Who knows? One day in the future, when it's just me, I may want to meet someone. But definitely not now! That would be far too complicated. I don't want to do anything to upset what Ruben and I have.

I head for the door and take the key out. Then I shut the door, lock it and slide the key into my bag. It's still snowing, flakes gently falling, and there's already a layer over the porch where Theo swept it. I take another couple of deep breaths, hoping the fresh, dry air will pep me up. And it does.

Despite Theo's reassurance, I look left and right, just to be sure there's no sight or sound of the moose. I head for the cleared pathway towards the store where Theo walked with me yesterday, wondering how it's kept so free of snow. Is it a council thing? Like gritters back home? I try to get my phone from my bag to take pictures for Ruben. I can't. I pull off a glove with my teeth and find it, then need to take off the other glove to hold it and take pictures. My hands freeze, but I decide to take a video. I press the button and start to turn in a slow circle, pointing the camera upwards to take in the trees. There are lines running between them, like piping. Some kind of fencing to keep wild animals out? My thoughts turn to the moose again. I hear a rustle and stop. I hold my breath. My heart is racing. It was nothing, I tell myself. Then I hear it again. I lower the phone, turn in its direction and slowly start to back down the cleared path towards the town. Suddenly there's a louder rustle and something big jumps out of the snowy bush, flapping its wings at me. I don't know what it is, so I run.

# 9

I'm running as fast as I can but the big bird behind me is doing exactly the same.

I trip, stumble, and eventually throw myself at the bottom steps of the store porch and cling to the post there.

'Hey, Ike!' Theo is waving a hand at the huge bird. It has big red jowls. It stops and looks around. 'Wow! You can run!' he says to me.

I'm puffing for all I'm worth, dragging cold air in so hard that it's hurting my throat and lungs. I can't help but scowl. 'Didn't know . . .' I try to explain as plumes of condensation, hot breath meeting cold air, puff out of me. I'm still clinging to the post at the bottom of the steps.

'Ike! Behave!' Theo calls, as if it's some kind of pet.

'What . . . is . . . it?' I manage.

'Who, Ike? A turkey. Escaped Thanksgiving lunch one year and he's been part of the community ever since.'

'Ike?' I stand straight to look at him.

'He's harmless, just likes to think he's big and scary.'

'He *is* big and scary!' Ike is wandering about in front of the store, jowls wobbling.

I'm finally getting my breath back when I hear a ping. 'Signal!' I pull out my phone. My heart lifts. 'Ruben!'

'Ruben?'

I send him a picture of me, and tell him I'm off for breakfast.

I wave a hand at Theo, relieved and excited to hear from my boy, scrolling through the photos he's already sent. 'I'm going to get tea and ring him while I've got signal.'

He raises both eyebrows this time. I should probably explain that Ruben is my son but I've no reason to explain anything. It will only lead to more questions and the last thing I want is for anyone to ask me questions. I just need to listen and learn, I think, as I walk to the neighbouring porch, which belongs to Bea's Diner.

I open the door to a rush of warm air and the aroma of coffee. It's like a very welcome hug.

'Hi!' says an exhausted-looking woman sitting on a stool behind the counter, an apron barely covering her large bump. She's probably in her mid-thirties, maybe a little older. It's hard to tell. Her blonde hair is scraped back in a scrunchie off her pretty face.

The diner is warm. There's a fire in the wood-burning stove and two checked wingback chairs at either side of it. There are tables with red-checked tablecloths to match the curtains at the windows, which are steamed up with condensation and gathering snow outside. At each window a tea light flickers in a lantern and there are more on the tables.

'Take a seat.' Her smile betrays her weariness. I remember feeling like that when I was in the final trimester of my pregnancy with Ruben. 'What can I get you?'

'Tea, please?' I'm gasping for a cup.

She laughs. 'This isn't an English tea room! We've got coffee,' she holds her hand to the jug on the coffee machine, 'and pancakes. That's it.'

I've been put in my place. 'Coffee would be lovely, thank you,' I say. 'And your pancakes come highly recommended.'

'That'll be Theo, I'll bet! He eats enough of them to keep me in business – just!' she laughs, but I can still hear her weariness. 'It's about all I can manage to rustle up right now.' She slides off her stool. 'But some business is better than none at all.' I try not to feel bad that she's on her feet when she'd rather be sitting with them up by the fire.

what else to say and feel ridiculous at the idea that I might own a piece of the place.

'Well, enjoy your stay. I mean, there's not much to do at this time of year. There's usually the tree lighting, the Christmas fair and then the sap run on the twenty-sixth, but it's taking a bit longer to get sorted this year.'

I drizzle the amber syrup over the golden stack of pancakes on my plate, knowing I'll never be able to eat them all. 'What's the sap run?'

'It's a run through the forest, following the sap trail. The trees have hoses connected to them so that when the snow melts in the spring and the ground warms we harvest the sap. We put taps into the trees, and siphon it off.'

'So the tap thing isn't a joke?'

She shakes her head. 'We really hammer taps into trees. We drill a small hole, put in a tap. In most cases we attach pipes and the sap runs from tree to tree through the pipes to the vat. We collect it and take it to the sugar shack.' She seems to have slipped into her comfort zone, talking about the trees. 'Or in harder to reach trees, older ones, we sometimes just siphon it off into a bucket.'

I have a fuzzy memory of Theo telling me this as we went to the cabin yesterday. But I was really too tired to take it in. Or maybe it was jet lag. Or maybe just shock at finding myself in the middle of a maple forest!

'I . . .' I go to say that I had no idea. But like I say, I just don't think I was really taking it in. 'And, what happens at the sugar shack?'

She leans against the table. 'That's where we boil it. We get the fire good and hot and we boil the sap to turn it into syrup. The whole town comes to help and we take turns to keep the fire going and the sap boiling.'

I pick up the leaf-shaped bottle on the table. It practically glows in the light. 'Is it all the same? I mean the same flavour?'

'We have four different grades of syrup. From light to dark as the season starts and ends.'

'It sounds like this town is all about the syrup,' I observe.

'It's how we live here. It's our liquid gold. There's a reason we have the maple leaf as our national emblem. We're proud of it.' Her smile fades. 'If only everyone kept their sap as pure as we do.'

'Oh?' I ask, cutting into a pancake and breathing in the hot, sweet steam.

'We're just proud of our syrup. It's all natural and we're grateful to have it. We have the annual run through the forest the day after Christmas to celebrate what we've got, to thank our ancestors for the trees they planted, give thanks for the generations to come and for a good harvest, but . . .' she takes a big breath

'. . . a lot of things will be different this year. I'm not sure we'll be celebrating at all.'

I'm about to ask what she means when the door opens and two men come in, one leaning heavily on crutches, his foot in plaster.

'Morning, Bea,' they say, pulling off furry hats. One reveals grey hair, sticking out at wild angles, and the one on the crutches is rubbing a big bald patch. They bang the snow from their boots on the way in, the man with the crutches using one to knock snow from his good foot, and walk up to the wooden bar. They climb stiffly onto stools, one with the aid of a crutch, as Bea pours them coffee without being asked.

'How you feeling?' says the bald man.

'Like I could sleep for ever,' she says.

'I put some logs by your back door, save you doing it,' says the other. 'There's plenty more on the farm, so I'll just keep them coming.'

'And let me know if you need your supplies putting away. Just ask. We'll get the boys helping you out. You lads behaving? All ready for the game?' calls the man with the crutches to the group, who reply, '*Oui, monsieur*,' and 'Yes sir.' He nods and turns back to his coffee. 'Me and Eli can get the boys to come after our coaching sessions if you need anything doing. Just tell us if they get too boisterous.'

'They're fine,' she says. 'Shame the girls' team isn't

getting as much coaching from you two. If I wasn't like this . . .'

'You need to be taking it easy,' says the man with the crutches.

I watch them. They're in their sixties, I'd say, and are clearly concerned about her and the baby. She nods and says nothing more.

I think about Ruben's challenge. Ask someone how their day is going. I can't ask these two strangers. I really can't.

I return to my pancakes, breathe in their sweet scent and cut into them. It's like slicing through a cloud. I put a piece into my mouth.

Oh, heaven! Soft and fluffy, with salty butter and sweet maple syrup reaching into every corner of my mouth.

'All okay? Want any more?' says Bea, collecting my empty plate.

'No, thanks, but that was fantastic. I must make more pancakes when I get home. I should take some syrup back with me.' I haven't thought about cooking anything since Ruben left, but I'm absolutely going to make these for him. I experience a pang of homesickness.

'So, you here for the holidays?'

'I'm not sure, to be honest.' I'm gazing out of the window at the white landscape. I don't know what I expected to find here. A pot of gold?

'Let me top you up with coffee. We might not have

much in the way of Christmas cheer right now, but there's always coffee.' Her welcome is clearly genuine, and I feel a rush of gratitude towards her.

I accept the top-up, then scroll through the photos Ruben's sent me again. The joy of seeing him happy is mixed with sadness that Lucas is part of my past. There are pictures from days out in New York. The huge tree at the Rockefeller Center. Bloomingdales. With Father Christmas, many times. I think back to the days when he worried about Father Christmas coming into our house at night. A stranger in our home. He'd end up sleeping in my bed, leaving his stocking downstairs. He worried a lot as a youngster. Still does. And I often wondered if it had anything to do with Lucas not being there. But I'm so proud of him making this trip to see his dad. I try not to dwell on the pictures of Lucas and his wife in their new home, with the baby. I'm pleased for them, I am. I swallow. It's me who has to let go. I'm happy that they're happy. I just wish I could make things better for Ruben, with his dad and now his sister so far away.

I message him: *You free to chat?*

My phone immediately springs into life.

My heart leaps when I see his face. But he looks worried.

'Ruben? You okay?' I suddenly panic.

'Mum? Are you okay? You still in Canada? You need me? Whassup?' he says, panicking.

My heart twists. This caring boy, who does as much for me as I do for him, or so it feels.

'No, no! Everything's fine.' The lump in my throat puts in an appearance. 'I just wanted to say hello! Are you having fun?'

He breathes a sigh of relief. 'Yeah, great fun. And Jodie, the baby, she's really sweet. She's got my nose!' He lets himself smile.

My eyes well with happy tears. I would have loved to have another baby, but it was all I could do to bring up Ruben on my own, with Lucas gone. He always sent money, and rang, and when Ruben was old enough, he FaceTimed. But it hasn't always been easy for father and son to meet up.

'So tell me what you've been doing,' I say. And he can, now he's not worrying about me. I wish he didn't, and I wish, too, he didn't feel he was being disloyal by enjoying his time with his dad. I need to make this work for him. 'I want to know everything you've been up to and then I'll show you photos of my cabin in the woods.'

'Cool!' he says. And he tells me everything he's been doing and enjoying, with a grin. My heart is bursting with joy, and just a hint of sadness too.

'Tell me about the cabin!'

I talk about the cabin, the fire, the moose and Ike the turkey.

'Are you opening your advent calendar?'

'I am!' I raise my coffee cup at him. 'And I had the most amazing pancakes. With maple syrup, made from the trees around here. I'll bring some back.'

'Okay. And have you done it?' he asks.

'What?' I feign forgetfulness.

'Asked someone how their day is going.'

'Not yet.' I'm looking at the two men on the bar stools. 'I'm just, you know, being cautious. Stranger danger and all that!' It's a good opportunity to remind him to be careful.

'The next person you see!' he tells me firmly. 'As long as they're not a complete stranger!' he adds.

'Okay, okay!' I hold up a hand.

'It's good to meet people and make friends,' he says, and beams. 'Love you!'

'Love you too!' We hang up. I look out on the snow, bereft. It's just a few weeks, I tell myself. It's just Christmas. Suddenly this feels crazy. Maybe I should go home, not hide out in this one-horse town where I know nobody. I should just go to Mae's and join in. Ruben would like that. This has all been a mistake. I smile at my own stupidity. I don't know anyone here, not even slightly. Ruben is happy and that's all that matters. And in twenty-six days he'll be home. And that's where I should be too. Not hiding in a cabin in the woods, wondering if I'll be attacked by a moose or bears.

'Everything okay?' Bea says, maybe seeing the damp in my eyes.

'Delicious, thank you.' I'm feeling a little more human after the coffee and pancakes.

'You're a long way from home for the holidays,' she says, smiling kindly, and suddenly I feel another pang of homesickness. I'm not missing the house, just Ruben. But she's right. I am a long way from home. I should do what Ruben told me to do. Spend it with Mae and talk to him via FaceTime. As much as I like, he told me, so we feel as if we're together. That's what I'm going to do. I'm going home.

I open my mouth to ask her how her day has been, when the door opens. It's Theo.

My heart sinks. Please don't let it be him I have to ask.

She plants a kiss on both his cheeks. *'Café?'*

He nods, and looks at me. 'Hi,' he says. 'How were the pancakes?'

'Great,' I say, then take a deep breath and run at it. 'And how's your day going?'

He's taken aback. It sounded so forced. I've already seen him a couple of times this morning, too.

'Erm, fine. Thank you.'

'Good, good,' I say. There, I've done it. My cheeks are burning with embarrassment, but I can tell Ruben I did it. I asked the only person who wasn't a complete stranger around here how their day was going. I start to type a message, with lots of emojis.

'May I?'

I look up, surprised. He points to a chair opposite me.

I wasn't expecting this.

'Erm, yes. I was just leaving.'

'Leaving? Or leaving-leaving?' He does that smile from the corners of his mouth.

'Actually, something's come up and I'll be leaving as soon as I can get a flight. Going home.' The words catch in my throat.

'Ah, Ruben?' he asks, as Bea puts coffee down in front of him and tops me up without even asking. I'd feel rude turning it down.

'Ruben's fine.'

There's a moment's silence as the question hangs in the air, right in the middle of the table, over the candles, and the only sound is the crackling of the fire and the stillness from the snow in the woods outside.

'He's with his dad in New York.' It would be churlish not to explain.

'Oh.' He nods. 'Nice.'

'And his dad's wife and new baby,' I add slowly.

'Ah . . .'

He nods again, but says nothing. Then, 'So, somewhere without Christmas seemed like a good bet.'

'Yes. So Christmas really is cancelled around here?'

'Not cancelled. Bea does it all usually. And this year, well, it's different.'

I find myself frowning. Honestly, the poor woman,

heavily pregnant and still expected to organize the town's Christmas festivities. Looks like this place is stuck in the 1950s. The sooner I'm home the better. 'Well, if you'll excuse me,' I say, 'I have some calls to make.'

He stands and joins the men at the counter. They're talking and take occasional glances at me. My ears are burning and so are my cheeks. I didn't expect this. I'll just contact Nigel Berry and say he has my permission to sell. I don't need to know any more.

I look at my phone and my airline's flights. Pull out the taxi firm's number. I really don't belong here. I'm going home.

# 10

'No flights for another two days?' I repeat. 'Fully booked?'

'I'm sorry. It's a busy time of year,' says the woman at the other end of the line.

'Okay. I'll take the next available flight,' I tell her, and thank her, wincing as I give her my credit-card details, wondering if Nigel Berry is going to cover these costs too.

I close my phone. I have two more nights to get through. When I look up, Theo has gone.

I'm clearly not dressed as I should be for this kind of weather, I think, shivering as I walk along the decked terrace outside the diner, and make for the store next door to get some maple syrup to take home for Ruben. I shiver again. I'm only here for another forty-eight hours. I have to put up with the cold for just another two days. I need to keep busy.

'Hey again,' says Theo, as I open the door and the bell rings. 'How's things? You got everything you need?'

'Er, yes. Um, actually, no. As I say, I'm leaving. I've decided to go home. Maybe trying to avoid Christmas wasn't the best idea I've had.'

'Well, we've clearly made quite an impression on you! Mind you, Forêt des Esprits has a way of doing that to most people.' I see a flicker of tension on his face. 'When are you off?'

'Day after tomorrow. I'll drop in with the key before I go,' I say, by way of polite conversation.

He says nothing for a moment. Then, 'The cabin's been rented for the month.'

'Oh, that's fine. I don't expect a refund.'

He nods.

'In fact it wasn't me . . .' I stop myself saying it wasn't me who paid for it. 'It's fine.'

There's a moment's silence as I look around for maple syrup. Maybe now is the time to ask Theo more about the land, the old man who died and who he was.

'How were your pancakes?' he asks, not looking at me.

'Gorgeous!' I say, feeling the tiny spark ignite. 'Just really light, fluffy, golden on the outside, and with the maple syrup . . .' I feel the little rush of excitement I used to have when I was thinking of new flavours for cakes, then trying them out on Ruben. 'Actually,' I say, looking around, 'I came to get some maple syrup to take home with me. I'll make the pancakes for Ruben. When he's back. A homecoming celebration.'

'Well, if it's syrup you're after, you've come to the right place. We have plenty. But not here. Next door, in the food store. Nancy's place. I'll show you.' He holds out a large arm. He's wearing a checked flannel shirt, open over a tighter-fitting top. I follow his invitation to the door, where he grabs his thick coat, with hood, shrugs it on over his wide shoulders and pulls on his hat.

'Aren't you cold?' He frowns.

'I'm fine,' I lie, shoving my hands further into my pockets and looking at him with envy as he opens the door onto the snow and holds it for me. I head for the porch and pass him, feeling short in comparison, and he smiles, with his dark hazel eyes, from beneath the brow of his fake-fur hat. It frames his wide jaw, high cheekbones and the slightly crooked nose that adds character rather than detracting from his classic good looks. I step past him, smelling a mix of woodsmoke and pine. He pulls the door to behind him, Hagrid in tow.

'Okay, follow me,' he says, pulling his hat down further. 'Mind your step,' he adds, with a glance at my insubstantial boots. I wish I didn't feel so inadequately dressed.

'This is Nancy. Nancy, have you met our visitor?' He holds out a gloved hand to the woman behind the counter.

'Hi,' she says. 'You're staying in Cabane de l'Étoile, aren't you? Have you seen them yet?'

'Have I seen what?' I look at Theo.

'*Les étoiles!*' She beams. 'Beautiful from that spot!'

'The stars,' says Theo, quietly. 'I told you, just look up!' He smiles, and I feel a strange shiver of something like . . . anticipation.

'Oh, I will!' I swallow hard. 'But I need to leave sooner than I was expecting.'

'Don't tell me, you met the locals! Probably Eli and Philippe scaring people off. Honestly, those two. Like Statler and Waldorf in *The Muppets*!' She shakes her head. 'This town is getting greyer by the moment.'

'I'll show you the syrup,' Theo says, guiding me away from Nancy. He points towards a row of shelves. Rows and rows of bottles full of beautiful, gleaming syrup, varying in shades from dark brown to gold and right up to light amber. This must be what Bea was saying about the four grades. 'What's the difference in colour?' I ask.

'Well, the lighter syrup, the more delicate in flavour, comes as the sap first starts to run. The darker the colour, the stronger the flavour. We get the darker-grade syrup towards the end of the season. That's how we know the sugaring season is coming to a close.'

'And it's all made around here?' I ask, running my finger along them.

He walks over and picks up a bottle. 'The town works as a cooperative. We all harvest our syrup in the spring, pool it and sell it. No additives. Just syrup. Not like other companies and cooperatives around here.'

I raise an eyebrow.

'Not all syrup on the shelves is a hundred per cent syrup. Some add to it to make it go further. But here in Forêt des Esprits, we're all of the same belief. It has to be one hundred per cent pure. We've always worked together. Let's just hope . . .' He peters out.

'Hope what?'

'Oh, nothing.' He waves a hand. 'Just . . . something about part of our land, where your cabin is.'

'It's your land, is it?' I ask quickly.

'No. I've just been looking after it. Harold, a neighbour, was getting too unwell to manage it. So I've been helping.'

'Is it you who clears the footpaths?'

He nods. 'So we can do maintenance on the lines before the harvest in the spring. And look after the trees. You get to know trees. Each one is different.'

'Really?' I say, a little disbelieving.

'It's true. They're like family to us.' He smiles widely

and warmly and I'm wondering if he's teasing me again as the stirring in my stomach starts. 'Each year, in return for us looking after them, they give us syrup.' He puts his hand on the bottles and large cans on the shelf.

'Sounds like it works well!' I say, still wondering how seriously to take him.

'It has done. For three generations.' His smile slips. 'But no one knows what will happen now. But, hey, that's nothing to concern you.'

I have a feeling, deep down, that it might.

'How do you mean?' I say, trying to sound casual, like I'm asking Ruben how things are when I know he doesn't want to talk.

'Just . . . we lost that neighbour, Harold. Not long ago. And now no one knows what will happen to the land.'

'Around Cabane de l'Étoile?' I ask slowly.

He tidies the bottles on the shelf. 'It's at the heart of the cooperative. Where the sugar shack is. No one knows who owns it now, or what will happen to it. A lot of people are waiting to hear the plans for it. We just need to find out whom to ask.'

I'm frozen to the spot. Do I own this land? I gulp. Am I responsible for what will happen to the cooperative?

'Whoever it is, if they sell, they'll be damaging our community for ever,' says Nancy, with menace. 'I'd like to meet them and tell them so to their face.' Her expression darkens. 'Now, what can I get you?'

The sooner I leave the better.

My teeth are chattering again, and I'm not sure whether it's from cold or the fear of being found out.

'You could do with better clothing,' Theo says.

'You're right,' I say, wanting to change the subject. My brain is whirring and turning over the information. The land is at the heart of the community. What will happen if it's sold? Who will buy it? I want to ask but don't want to give myself away. I don't have the answers they and the rest of the town want to hear. I don't know what will happen when it's sold. I quickly choose four bottles of maple syrup, one of each grade, golden, amber, dark and very dark, and pay.

'A good jumper is what I need,' I say. 'Know where I can get one?' The least I can do is spend some money before I leave. Not that I have any. But the guilt in me is telling me to put it on my card and deal with it when the land is sold.

'Follow me!' says Theo, pulling open the store door. 'See you later, Nancy.' I wish I wasn't taking in his wide shoulders and tall frame as he leads the way.

'Nice to meet you, Chloë. It's good to see a new face around here. Shame you're not staying,' Nancy waves.

I wave back, but my cheeks burn. I certainly can't stay now. I follow Theo into the hardware store as the bell rings cheerily above the door.

I have no idea where to start looking for jumpers, or maybe a coat. I'm shivering. There are boxes everywhere that he still hasn't got round to unpacking and organizing.

'Here, let me help you.' He climbs through the boxes, rips open the tops of some and pulls out a checked flannel shirt. 'You could do with one of these. You need layers. Utility coats are what we wear around here. They have a fluorescent lining in case you're stuck in the snow. And a couple pairs of these gloves and a hat – everyone around here knows a good hat is important,' he says, putting some socks on top of the coat and handing them to me. 'That should keep you going until you leave.'

'Thanks,' I say, feeling the warmth from the clothes just being in my arms. I pull out my emergency credit card again, my eyes watering at the cost. But it's the least I can do. 'I'm not sure about the hat.'

'Believe me, you'll thank me. The hat is essential.'

I'm struck by the chaos of the boxes. 'Is it always like this?'

'Like what?' he says.

'Oh, I just meant no Christmas. No lights, music, nothing.'

'It wasn't always like this,' he says, picking up a box and moving it. 'But things have been a bit different this year, what with one thing and another. And Bea, well, as I said, she usually organizes Christmas around here.'

'Can't some of you help?' I say, unable to bite my tongue.

He stops what he's doing and studies me. 'You think we can't do it. We just let Bea get on with it and now she's pregnant we don't know what to do.'

'Well, you said yourself you rely on her.'

'We do. Maybe a little too much. But it's not that we can't do it. We're not from the fifties here!'

I blush.

'Bea's having a hard time. She won't let anyone else help, thinks she can do it on her own. Won't let anyone else do what she's always done. And it's not a good time for her to feel she can't cope.' He takes a breath. 'I have a feeling we won't be celebrating in Forêt des Esprits this year.' He puts down the box on top of another and leans against the pile. 'So, apart from changing your airline ticket and packing up, what do you plan for your last couple days here?'

'I'm sure I'll find something to do.'

I'm tempted to organize the boxes in this store, but I won't offer. I'll just keep my head down until it's time to go, pushing aside all thoughts of the parcel of land, answers to the questions I came with and Nancy's darkening face. I'm the last person these people want here. The sooner I go, the better.

93

'Well, how about I show you around today, show you the sights before you leave? I have some deliveries to make. See if I can apologize for this town letting you down so much you decided to leave already?'

'Oh, no, it's fine. It's me. I shouldn't have come. It was a ridiculous idea.'

'Well, sometimes it's the ridiculous ideas that turn out to be the best. Just not in this case?'

I shake my head.

He laughs. 'Now, get dressed. I'll give you locals' discount. Even throw in the hat! Call it a leaving gift.'

I laugh and blush. 'Isn't everyone around here a local?' I ask.

'Pretty much.'

'Then how are you going to make a profit?'

He tilts his head and my stomach flips. 'Sometimes it's about making sure people have what they need.'

Maybe he's not as bad as I first thought. Maybe he's just being kind. I feel warm already. He claps his gloved hands. 'Now, get yourself kitted out like a local, then let me see if I can show you the better side of our country. That's if you don't have anything else you'd rather be doing?'

'No.' I shake my head. 'I don't have anything better to do. And *merci*.' Maybe I might just get the answers I need before I leave and still be home in time for Christmas with Mae, where I belong.

'I'll get the sleigh sorted, plus the packages and parcels from Nancy.'

'A sleigh! You're joking, right?'

'Best way to get around out here. That and skis.'

He's joking, I think.

I go to the makeshift changing room and take a moment to look around the walls of the quiet store. There are photographs on the wall, black-and-white, of families among the trees, generations before Theo's. I pull on my checked shirt, warm socks and boots over them. Ah, the joy! I'm dry and warm. Finally the coat: I've put on a thermal blanket! It's glorious. And the hat Theo threw in as a leaving gift.

I pull back the curtain of the little changing area, surrounded by yet more boxes, when suddenly the bell goes over the door. 'Hey!' says a round-bellied man.

'Er, hey!' I'm fully dressed in my flannel shirt and coat with fluorescent lining, thermal gloves and a scarf. It's not like the ones I brought with me, which I'd bought in the local supermarket, but a thermal neck warmer, and it's bliss. I may never take it off.

I hope Theo's on his way back.

'He's just gone to load up the . . . deliveries,' I say, not feeling I can carry on the joke about the sleigh with a stranger. 'He'll be back in a moment.'

'Right. Well, perhaps you can help me.'

'Oh, I'm not—'

But he cuts me off and carries on: 'I hear Harold Jones's land is coming up for sale. Apparently they've found the relatives, who are ready to sell. Tell Theo – he owns this place, right? – tell him Thomas came by and I have the cash if he hears anything.'

I feel myself go from toasty warm to freezing cold. 'Okay, I'll pass it on.' My tongue seems to be tying itself in knots, making it hard to speak.

'Do I know you?' He narrows his eyes.

'A friend of Theo's,' I say, as confidently as I can manage.

'Really?' His eyebrows rise. 'Well, if you hear of anyone new in town . . . I heard someone was staying in the *cabane*, in the forest.'

'That'll be me. I've come to spend some time with my friend Theo.'

'Right.' He turns abruptly and leaves. The bell rings long after he's shut the door, like the atmosphere he's left behind . . . a chilly one. Finally I can breathe again. What if Theo had been here? What if they work out who I am? At least Jones is such a common surname that no one has guessed my connection to Harold.

'You ready to go?' Theo appears through the back door, clapping his gloved hands.

'Um, yes, of course. Er, there was a man here . . .' I tail off.

'Okay, that happens. We do get customers!' He's teasing me again.

'He didn't seem like a customer. He left a message. He said his name was Thomas and he'd heard some land was coming up for sale. I was to ask if you'd heard anything.'

Theo's face falls. 'That was Thomas Tremblay. What's he doing in town? Clearly there are rumours going around.'

'Who is he?'

Theo lets out a long, low breath. 'From a big company a few kilometres away. Tremblay Syrups. The biggest around. Always looking to pick up bits of land where he can.'

'And make maple syrup?'

'Yes, but not like we do. Round here we keep it real. I'm thinking he's been out to the farm sale. Come on, let's go. See what anyone else knows.'

I follow him out of the back door, open it and stop.

The snow is falling all around, heavier than before. The wind has dropped and there's stillness to the air. And there in front of me is a pair of beautiful ginger horses, tacked up, and behind them a large sleigh.

'You weren't joking!' I say, staring.

'Best way to get around, other than skis,' he repeats.

'I have to take a photograph for my son. He told me to take photographs to send to him.' I wave a hand, not really explaining, still surprised by the horses that are ready to go to work.

'Come and say hello.' He gestures. 'They're mother

and son. Always together, never apart, and always bickering.'

One gives the other a quick nip and they throw up their heads, then look in opposite directions.

'Climb on board,' he says.

I pull out my phone, get onto the sleigh and start to film. As Theo makes a click-click sound to the horses, they move off and I'm both terrified and thrilled, as the cold wind flies at our faces. I pull on my hat, knowing it makes sense.

Suddenly the forest isn't quite the scary place where I spent last night. In fact, as I look up at the tall maples, the fir trees and what I think may be silver birch, Ike the turkey trotting along behind us, I'm smiling for what feels like the first time in the long few days since Ruben left.

# 11

The cold bites my nose as we pass tall trees, snow-capped gateposts and mailboxes at the top of driveways to houses and cabins tucked away in the forest. Theo pulls up the sleigh in front of one such cabin. He takes in a box of supplies, stops to talk to the neighbour, then returns to the sleigh, click-clicks to the horses and we're off again through the magical snow scene. Yesterday I thought this was the end of the earth, but it may just be somewhere rather special.

'What's that?' I point at a group of trucks, pick-ups and Ski-Doos, on a snowy driveway to a rundown cabin on our way back to town. A sign at the top of the driveway, over the mailbox, reads 'Maple Lodge'. Several people, in big hats, coats and boots, are standing outside the open doors of a large barn next to the cabin, talking.

'Whoa,' Theo says, and the horses immediately slow down.

'It's a farm sale. The man who lived here just died. Harold Jones, the guy I told you about. He didn't have much. No relatives left that anyone knows of. No will, apparently. Well, none that can be found. We've looked all over the house. They're selling off his possessions to raise money for the new sugar-shack equipment. Figure whoever takes this place over isn't going to be keeping his second-hand slippers for sentimental reasons.'

'What did he die of?' I ask, trying not to give anything away, but I can't help being interested, curiosity clawing at me.

'A stroke. First he had a small one – that was when I stepped in to help with the trees. A few of us were looking after him. Bea did the most. Then he had a big one, which killed him. He was only sixty.'

I say nothing.

'He had a simple funeral. Folks are helping sort out the house and his belongings. No one wants to see everything just cleared out and dumped.'

I see neat rows of items laid out on the snowy porch and in the open barn.

'I should stop,' he says. 'Do you mind?'

'Not at all,' I say. This is why I'm here. I just hope no one else realizes it.

I get down from the sleigh into the deep snow,

crunching underfoot, but my feet stay warm and dry in my new boots. I pull down my hat and tug my scarf up around my chin.

There in front of me are, indeed, the contents of the tiny cabin. Despite its sad state, the porch looks pretty with the snow clinging to the balustrade around it.

'Hey, Theo!' says one of the men, who reaches forward to shake his hand.

'Anything?' ask Theo, and I'm guessing he's asking about the will. They shake their heads. 'He clearly didn't want it ending up in the wrong hands.' And they're all downcast. 'Silly fool!'

I shift from foot to foot nervously, feeling like an impostor. The tension in the air is unbearable. Maybe I should just admit who I am. Get it over and done with, then just hide in the cabin until I leave.

'This is our mayor, Philippe Martin. He's also the coach for the local ice-hockey team,' Theo says, introducing me, lightening the mood. I recognize him: he's the balding man from the diner, the one with the crutches.

'Not much of a coach, these days,' he says, pointing to his foot in the plaster cast, wrapped in layers of plastic. 'Could do with another pair of hands – or feet.'

'You're doing fine. Even one foot down.' Theo turns to me quickly. 'This is Chloë Jones. She's been spending time in Cabane de l'Étoile but is about to leave us.'

'Ah, Christmas in Forêt des Esprits a bit too low-key for you?'

I smile. 'I . . . just . . .' I have no idea what to say.

'She's decided running away from home isn't the answer.' Theo beams, chivalrously stepping in, and I'm grateful.

'Never is,' agree the mayor and the others.

'Despite my charms, she couldn't be persuaded to stay,' Theo adds.

'He didn't have a lot, poor man,' says Nancy, coming over to stand next to the mayor.

'Not financially maybe, but he found love in the end. Not everyone does,' says another woman next to her.

'True. If only they'd made it official, this would all be so different,' Nancy says.

'Bloody paperwork shufflers! Of course it should be different!' says the mayor, anger written all over his face.

'He'd have done better in life if he'd sold his land,' says the other man I recognize from the diner, joining the conversation.

'He couldn't do it, Eli. He was a good man. He wanted to keep the cooperative together,' Theo adds.

'But now what? Some stranger's gonna come in, sell up and the cooperative will be splintered,' Nancy interjects crossly.

'And where will the ice-hockey team train from now on?' says the mayor. 'That land includes the lake.'

Suddenly I want to put this right, make them less worried. Calm their fears, like I did Ruben's when he was starting at a new school or going to his first rugby training session, or visiting the dentist. I just want to make things easier for everyone.

'What will be wrong with selling the land? It might be a good thing,' I say, trying to make them feel better. They turn to me, eyes wide. 'It might bring in a new investor, wanting to put more into the area.'

There's silence. And then: 'It would be the worst thing for the community. The land has always been at the heart of the cooperative. We'll lose the syrup if another owner or cooperative sets up in the heart of the town,' Theo says evenly.

They all start to talk over each other.

'And the lake will go too. Nowhere for the ice-hockey team.'

'Just as our girls' team is starting up,' Nancy says.

'What if they block access through the forest?'

'Could be anyone coming in.'

'What if some idiot wants to take down the trees?'

There's a sharp intake of breath, and a dark cloud hanging over them. I should have kept my mouth shut like I planned to. I need to leave this place. Nigel Berry told me I was related to Harold Jones. I don't know how, and I'm not going to be here long enough to work it out. But I can see that anyone planning to sell that land could be run out of town.

'Sorry. I just want to go and . . . pay my respects.' Pay my respects?! It's the only thing I can think of saying.

I walk away from the group towards the small weatherworn cabin. It was clearly once red and white, but now the red is faded. There's a chimney on the snowy roof, four windows and the porch at the front. I wish I could know how Harold Jones came to be here, who he was and who he found love with 'in the end'. But I can't ask. That would give me away. And I don't want to play any part in ripping a community in two. I just want to get on the plane and fly away, I think, as I look at the worn books, pots and pans, boots, snowshoes and framed pictures . . . I stare at a black-and-white photograph in a wooden frame of a man in a coat and hat. He could almost be . . . Ruben. He's standing beside a First Nations man in a feathered headdress, and a woman with long black plaited hair is sitting next to them. This man has to be why I'm here. This has to be where the story begins. I look around. And this is how it's ended. What happened to the love Harold found? Did he fall in love with someone he wasn't supposed to? Someone married or gay? So many questions I'm dying to ask.

'Who's taking the cows?' I hear, as I walk back down the steps to rejoin the group.

'I'll give a hundred and fifty dollars for them,' says a younger man.

'It's for the new sugar shack. It's what was agreed. All proceeds to a new sugar shack with evaporator and sap-collection equipment. Theo's been working hard to keep the old stuff going but we need new.'

'Okay, okay, I'll give two hundred. But no more.'

'And I'll take this,' I say.

Theo looks at me, then the photograph in my hand. I swallow as our eyes seem to lock on to each other's. A load of unanswered questions bundle into my head, about Harold, of course, and then about why I feel like this every time I'm near Theo, stomach fizzing, head spinning. Why did it never happen with Ruben's father? Why do I know I probably won't feel like this again?

'For the sugar-shack fund,' I say, holding out some cash.

'That's very generous of you,' Theo says. We slip off our gloves and he takes the money. As our fingers touch, a bolt of electricity shoots through me, like a firework. I snatch my hand away.

'*Très gentille*,' says the mayor, with a huge smile in his voice. '*Merci!*'

I don't know what happened then with Theo. I've never felt that before. But I do know that the heir hunter might be right. I could be related to the man in the photograph and to Harold Jones. And, by the sound of it, Harold's death and the sale of the land will shred the community. I don't want to be any part of that.

We pull away from the yard on the sleigh. It's got darker and colder. Snow is falling heavily. I'm still holding the picture to my chest, the only memento I will ever have of how we had a connection with this land. This was my chance to give Ruben the security I've always wanted for him. Lucas is generous, but I wanted to provide something more, something for the future for when I'm not here. I look at the picture. A legacy. But how can I be part of selling this land when the people here don't want that to happen? Unless, of course, it's sold to someone who deserves it.

We whizz past the trees.

'Look.' Theo points, nudging me out of my thoughts. 'The moose, with her young.'

I peer through the trees to where he's pointing. A huge animal, her calf sheltering by her side. She stares at us as we pass, giving each other space. In that moment I feel we both belong.

Neither of us says a word as we travel back towards Cabane de l'Étoile. I can just hear the horses' hoofs on the settling snow and the whoosh of the sleigh. Every now and again I look sideways at Theo and find that he's doing the same. Snowflakes settle on his eyelashes and he blinks them away. What is he thinking? Does he know? What am I thinking? This is madness! I can't stop looking and neither can he. As we near the cabin, my mood darkens along with the sky. I bet the fire's gone out.

The horses slow as we reach the clearing in front of the cabin. I shiver, yet excitement is building inside me, urgency.

'Do you want me to come in and check the fire?' Theo says.

'No, no, I'll be fine!' I say, still holding the picture in front of me as if I can't trust myself around this man and the way he makes me feel. I wasn't expecting ever to feel like this. Certainly not now, with this stranger, someone I will never see again after tomorrow.

An owl hoots, startling me. The horses seem restless, pawing at the ground, steam rising from their warm bodies in the cold night air, keen to get back to their stable now the night is drawing in. I'm wondering what life would be like if I had the chance to get to know Theo and this place, to relish the feeling that I belong.

Theo turns to me. It's stopped snowing. We look up. The sky is dark but clear and stars are popping out, like a sparkling sea of diamonds.

'Wow!' I say. '*That*'s why they call it Cabane de l'Étoile.'

'Uh-huh,' he says. 'Like the best Christmas decorations you could imagine.'

107

We stare up at the glittering sky. Eventually I pull my gaze from the stars and am drawn back to his eyes.

He's searching my face, as if he's waiting for me to say something.

Suddenly, I have no idea why, I lean in, looking at his lips, wishing they were warm against mine. And for just a moment time stands still, as my eyes flick between his eyes and his lips, slowly drawing closer to him. Then one of the horses whickers and flings up its head. The sleigh shifts and we're thrown apart.

I put a hand to my face.

I didn't kiss him, thank God. But he must know that that was what I was hoping would happen. I suddenly felt attractive, and as if something was missing from my life.

'I'm so sorry! I have to go!' What on earth is wrong with me?

'*Bonsoir*,' he says, clearing his throat, looking forward and settling the horses.

'I shouldn't – I mean, I'm leaving the day after tomorrow.'

'Really, it's fine. Have a good trip back.'

We talk at once, the words tumbling out of us. I push the thick blanket off my knees, feeling the cold despite my warmer clothes. I slide and bump myself off the sleigh. 'Thank you. *Merci*. It was lovely, seeing the town and everything.'

He nods slowly, gazing straight ahead. 'There's plenty more to see in these parts if you go looking for it.'

We slip into an awkward silence.

'Well, thank you again, and goodbye.' I go as quickly as I can to the steps leading onto the porch where new snow has settled.

'*Au revoir*. Safe journey home,' I hear him say. Then he clicks his tongue, and the horses move on.

I pull off a glove and find the key in my pocket on the big key-ring.

I throw myself in through the cabin door, shut it, double-bolt it and lean against it. The fire has gone out.

'What on earth was I thinking?' I say aloud. I need to get out of here before anyone works out who I am. And before I try to kiss any more local men. Suddenly the hole inside me, where I'd felt something was missing, has grown into a crater. But I have everything I need at home with Ruben. I don't want anything more.

I try without luck to light the fire. I wrap myself in the big quilt, wearing all my clothes, and vow to book myself into a hotel near the airport tomorrow, somewhere warm, with room service, hang the expense. I drift off to sleep, but instead of dreaming about the hotel room, I'm dreaming of feeling Theo's lips on mine.

I should never have come.

## 12

5 December: 20 days until Christmas

The following morning, I bump my case up the steps to the diner, having dragged it from Cabane de l'Étoile through the snow. Ike jumped out at me, trying to give me a fright, but I wasn't in the mood. When I ignored him, he waddled along beside me, flapping his wings, almost cheerily.

The cold freezes the hairs in my nose making it itch, but there's nothing I can do with my big gloves on, holding the picture I bought at the farm sale under my arm. I only just remembered it before I left the cabin. I'll pack it safely away when I get into the diner, where I intend to hand in my key. I don't want to see Theo again if I can avoid it. I twitch my nose. I plan to leave the key with Bea rather than face the embarrassment of seeing Theo again, and letting him think I fancy him, which I don't. I mean, he's good-looking but I really don't fancy him. I don't know what happened but I nearly made a complete fool of myself. It's a good job the taxi's booked and will be on its way shortly. I'm going to check into a hotel in the city for my last night in Canada, rather than stay here any longer. However, I have time for coffee and pancakes before I'm picked up. A plate of pancakes and syrup, with a cup of Bea's strong coffee, to set me up for the day. I could get a taste for that coffee – I may even drink it at home.

I push open the door of the diner, expecting to be hit by the same warmth that welcomed me yesterday. But it's cold, really cold. The wood-burning stove on the far end wall, blazing last time, is out, cold.

Maybe the diner's shut. But, if so, why would the front door be open? I glance back at it, then walk towards the counter. There are no candles in the windows and no smell of coffee from the ever-hot pot.

'Hello? *Bonjour!*' I call towards the back room. There's no smell of sweet pancakes, like there was yesterday. In fact, if anything, there's a smell of . . . burning.

I slam the picture I'm carrying onto the counter with my big handbag and rush around it to see smoke rising from an empty pan, butter burning in the bottom. I grab a tea-towel, pull the pan off the heat and plunge it into the sink, next to a teetering pile of washing-up, clearly yesterday's, and turn on the cold tap to full blast.

'Hot, hot, hot!' I say, as plumes of smoke rise from the sizzling pan. I wave the tea-towel in front of my face, hoping the smoke alarms aren't about to go off, and run to fling open the diner door.

I turn back towards the counter. 'Hello!' I call, louder this time.

Bea appears at the doorway, clearly exhausted. 'Sorry!' she says. 'I had to . . . Oh, God! The pan!'

'Don't worry, I sorted it!' I say, wafting the smoke out of the door with the tea-towel. 'Are you okay?' She's pale. Really pale.

'I'm fine.' She collapses against the door frame for support.

'Hey, let me give you a hand,' I say, rushing forward.

'It's okay, I'm just . . .' She fans her face. 'Sorry, it's just there's so much to do, what with the Christmas fair to sort, and I haven't even started the decorations. Everyone thinks I won't be able to do it this year. But I can! Just because I'm preg—' She dips again and holds onto the door frame as if her knees have given way.

'Sit down!' I take her elbow and guide her to one of the checked wingback chairs in front of the dead fire.

She starts to protest, then concedes. 'Maybe just for a minute.' She gives in easily, looking ready to fall asleep there and then. I pick up the blanket from the arm of the chair and put it over her legs. She smiles, as if she'd like to repeat that she's fine but hasn't the energy. When I was pregnant the tiredness made me feel like I'd been hit by a bus.

I turn to the fire. I need to get it lit. I could go and look for Theo, but that would mean facing him again. And, frankly, I've had to learn to do a lot of things and this is just one more.

I look this way and that around the stove.

'There's matches in the pail, and kindling, though I need to fetch some more.' She winces and I can tell she's had a twinge in her stomach.

'I can do it,' I say.

I look in the pail and see matches, but no kindling. 'I'll go and get some,' I say, and she lacks the energy to protest.

I head to the back door and step outside. There's a wood pile, a mallet and an axe stuck in a stump of wood. I have no idea what to do. I grab the axe handle and pull but it doesn't move. I put my foot to the stump, pull really hard, and it comes away. I pick up a log, just like I watched Theo do at the cabin, and swing the axe at it. It's not as easy as it looks. I take a deep breath, ter-rified. The last thing I need is an axe injury, But I need this wood. I take a big swing and the axe lands on the log, hits it hard, and this time it splinters. *Yes!*

I drop the axe and pick up the wood fragments, then any small pieces of bark and twigs around the wood pile, and hurry back inside. I need to remember how Theo lit the fire in the cabin. Back in the diner Bea is fast asleep in the chair, her head on one side. I need to get help – find someone, her husband or partner maybe.

But, first, I need to get the fire lit.

I pull off my gloves, grab some newspaper from the pail and am about to screw it up when something catches my eye. It's a picture of the farm, the cabin I visited, and of the dead man. I tear off the page and shove it into my coat pocket. The rest I screw up and put into the stove, like Theo did. My hands are shaking with cold and nerves as I glance at Bea's sleeping face. I strike a match. It breaks. I strike another. It sparks and goes out. Come on, Chloë! I hold the next match firmly and strike. Success. I move it slowly to the paper in the stove and suddenly the back door bangs because I left it open. The draught puts out the flame. Bea barely flinches.

'Damn!' I throw the match into the stove. 'Come on!' I say, through gritted teeth.

I light the next match, quicker this time, and put it straight to the paper. It immediately takes. I start to feed small bits of wood onto the burning paper. It's like being a mum: you need to be there, encourage and not smother, I think.

Finally, the little flames flicker and build. I watch them, feeling this is what Bea needs right now. I sit back on my haunches, and shut the stove door, just like Theo showed me in the cabin. The flames rise even higher. It's a long way from turning up the thermostat at home.

The bell over the door sounds.

'Hi – Bea not around?' It's the mayor, Philippe, and the other man, Eli, I met at the barn sale. They seem always to be together. 'We met yesterday, at Harold's cabin. Chloë, isn't it?'

'Um, yes. Bea's having a rest.' I indicate her chair.

'Good. She needs it,' says the mayor. 'We've just come from sorting out the rest of the stuff from Harold's cabin. Still so hard to take in. The three of us were in school together. Been best friends ever since.' He blows into his hands. 'Hard to believe it's just the two of us now.' He's lost in his thoughts.

'Can we get some coffee and pancakes?' asks Eli.

'Is there somewhere else you could go?' I suggest.

They stare blankly at me. 'In Forêt des Esprits?'

'No, of course not. Hang on.' I slide behind the counter, pull off my coat and switch on the coffee-machine. It's not that different from the one in the campsite café at home. The fire is burning and the least I can do is make coffee and pancakes while I wait for the taxi.

'Here's your coffee, and I'll bring over the pancakes,' I tell them.

'We'll sit by the door, so as not to wake Bea,' says Eli.

The fire is blazing now and the place seems to be warming up.

'I think I should find her husband,' I say, as I deliver their plates, 'or partner.' I correct myself, as I put the pancakes down, sprinkled with vanilla icing sugar, like I had them yesterday.

'Could I get jam and maybe some bacon?'

I don't have the heart to tell them I'm not actually working here, just calling in for pancakes myself.

'Where can I find her husband or partner?' I ask, tugging on my coat and pulling out the box of matches from my pocket to light the little candle on the table just like the last time I was here.

'Bea's?' They look at each other.

'You need Theo, next door in the store.'

'Yes. You need Theo,' agrees the mayor.

'Theo next door in the store?' I repeat. The Theo who was showing me around the area in his horse-drawn sleigh yesterday? Who I was really enjoying being with, who I'd found quite attractive and thought he felt the same about me? Suddenly fury builds rapidly in me. How dare he? He was out showing me around with a pregnant partner at home! Story of my life! The older I get, the clearer it is that I'll never meet a man who's there just for me. Lucas wasn't. He tried, but he was there for Ruben. Then there are those awful blind dates people set you up on when you and your partner split and you have a small child. The last thing you want to

do is 'let your hair down', eat curry and drink lager
when you have to be up at six and will be breathing
garlic over a grouchy baby. Not one of the men I met
was there for me, a young mother. They were looking
to escape their own lives. Boring Kev talked endlessly
in monotone about his passion for real ale. Dynamic
Steve, a salesman, had five children by five different
women, loved babies but hadn't settled into family
life. And Glyn talked about his ex and ended up crying
into his beer and asking for advice on how to get her
back. I decided there and then that there would be no
more dating for me. No more being taken for a fool.
And I'd nearly let this Theo do it to me! I'm furious.

'Perhaps if more people didn't rely on Bea to do
everything, she wouldn't be so exhausted,' I say crossly.

'About the jam or bacon?' Eli says tentatively.

'There's just syrup,' I say, pointing to the bottle on
the table. Then, 'Keep an eye on things, on Bea and on
the fire, don't let it go out. *Comprenez?* ' I've dragged
out a word from school French lessons and I've no
idea why. It's not my café. They stare wide-eyed at me
and nod vigorously as I wrench open the diner door.

I stalk across the snowy terrace and find Theo outside the general store, broom in hand, Hagrid beside
him. He's wearing a baseball cap back to front. On
anyone else, that might not work but on him it does.
My treacherous heart gives a little leap, making me
even crosser. His thick checked jacket is open, to reveal

another open shirt beneath it and then a tight T-shirt across his broad chest, which I refuse to look at.

He smiles when he sees me. 'Hey, I was just coming to sweep the terrace at the diner. Fancy a coffee?'

'No, I don't!' I say angrily.

'Whoa! Someone got out of bed the wrong side this morning,' he says, holding up his hands and the broom, mocking me.

'It's got nothing to do with getting out of bed, whichever side,' I snap back, feeling everything I felt when I was a young mum on my own with Ruben after Lucas and I had agreed to go our separate ways. He got very quickly into his new bachelor life in New York, going out with friends, to the gym and to work bonding weekends, while I was alone at night, scared and anxious. And whatever I might have felt yesterday with Theo was out of the question. He's with someone! With a baby on the way! And he's been out flirting with a newcomer and showing them the countryside. I feel such a fool and also furious on Bea's behalf.

'It's Bea! Your partner! She's very pale. She's exhausted! I think she may need to see a doctor. She's pregnant. She can't do it all!'

He glares at me for just a moment, not bothering to reply, then drops the broom and in a few large strides is there, thrusting open the diner door and standing beside Bea's chair. Hagrid follows and flops down at her feet.

Theo's bending over her, holding her hand and talking quietly. She wakes, but is bleary-eyed.

'Theo?'

*'Je suis ici.'*

'It's you. For a moment I thought . . .'

'It's me. I'm here, honey. Let's get you to bed and then I'm going to call the doctor.'

She doesn't argue, but tries to stand, unsteadily. I instinctively step forward to take her arm to support her.

She's obviously too exhausted to turn down my help.

'It's okay. I remember well what it's like,' I say, and give her what I hope is a reassuring smile.

Theo nods his thanks. *'Doucement.* Easy does it,' he says, as we guide her to her feet and she leans into him. 'This way.' He points to the door behind the counter, and into the living quarters. There's a little kitchen area and a cosy living room with pink fairy lights around the mirror over the small wood-burning stove, a light pink sofa with lace arm covers and a door out to a little decking area just off the kitchen. It's lovely, cosy and very feminine. The bedroom is just off the living room and the bed is wrought iron, with a thick patchwork eiderdown, like the one in Cabane de l'Étoile. I pull it back and we ease her onto the bed. She's asleep again before her head hits the pillow.

'Do you want to get her changed into nightclothes?' I ask Theo.

'Let's leave her to sleep. I'll go and call the doctor,' he says, worried. We pull the covers over her and I'm thinking now isn't the time to take him to task on his behaviour towards his pregnant partner. Or me for that matter.

'Pre-eclampsia,' the doctor tells Theo. 'She needs rest. Lots.'

'Okay.' He nods.

'She's lucky to have you,' he tells Theo, who stares at the floor.

I harrumph quietly. That's not quite what I was thinking. As the doctor gives Theo instructions to keep Bea calm in bed and to be in touch with any concerns, I feel like I'm in some kind of bad movie.

'Do you want a coffee?' Theo asks the doctor, as we head back into the diner.

'That would be great, and pancakes if there are any?' says the doctor.

Theo slips behind the counter.

'How is she?' ask the mayor and Eli.

'She needs rest. Lots of it,' Theo says.

'This is Bea we're talking about,' says the mayor.

'I don't envy the person who has to get her to do that,' says Eli.

'You're in luck. Pancakes!' Theo holds the stack I'd made for myself when I made the others. 'Looks like it's going to be a while before we're eating any more here,' he adds, like a fish out of water behind the counter. 'Or drinking coffee . . .'

I can see the mugs from where I'm sitting and point at them. He searches for a spoon, and this time I stand up and show him, just as the bell over the door rings and a group of customers suddenly come in.

They're on a bus tour, here to see the maple forests in their snowy glory. Theo and the mayor step forward to welcome them to Forêt des Esprits. And then I'm serving coffee to them and making stacks of pancakes. While the mayor is telling them about the area, Theo comes to help me behind the counter, pouring coffee and answering questions about the syrup produced in the forest. I have one ear on what he's saying, the other on the customers' orders as we try to avoid each other behind the counter, sidestepping the very large elephant between us, namely Bea and the baby.

# 13

'Great pancakes!' call the customers, raising a hand as they leave. 'Can we buy syrup?'

Theo directs them to Nancy in the food store. 'They're good custom,' he says, gesturing towards the small group heading out into the snow, taking pictures, making for Nancy's store and the 4x4 winter tour bus. 'Especially when we're harvesting the sap during the sugaring season. This place can get really busy then. We have visitors come to see the sugar shack in action, bubbling away. We sell maple cotton candy and maple ice cream. But there's not normally many at this time of year. Especially when the rest of the country is gearing up for Christmas. It's good to welcome them when they come.'

With the rush dying down Theo pours two cups of coffee and moves around the counter to the high stools there.

'I guess I should thank you for looking after Bea,' he says. 'You're good at this.' He slides a cup of hot coffee towards me. 'I'd offer you pancakes, but they're all gone,' he says. I look at my watch, checking on my taxi's arrival time.

'And you don't seem to know your way around at all.' I take the coffee but don't move to the front of the counter. I'm in my comfort zone, behind a café counter. A barrier between him and me. There's no way I'll let his charms get under my skin again. I'm willing the taxi to come early.

He takes a sip of his coffee, then another. 'I'd better go check on Bea,' he says, suddenly tight-lipped. He stands up and goes into the back room.

I clear the counter, wiping and drying it, then filling the dishwasher with the last of the cups and plates from yesterday and the rush today. I fill the shelves with clean crockery and hang the tea-towels to dry in front of the cooker.

The door opens and a young man walks in. He's astonishingly beautiful. I'm not sure what's come over me. This doesn't happen in the Co-op back home, and the sooner I get there the better. He has beautiful dark brown skin, shiny black collar-length hair and is wearing a yellow working jacket, his hands in his pockets.

'Oh, hi!' He raises a hand. 'I was looking for Theo. I needed a saw from the store.'

'Oh, he's with his wife, partner . . .' I point to the back rooms.

The young man frowns. 'Really?'

'She's not feeling too well.'

'Really?'

'She's in bed. The doctor's been to check on her and the pregnancy.'

'Ah . . .' he says slowly. 'Bea. She's not Theo's wife. Or partner.'

'Really?' I say. This time it's my turn to tighten my lips. Maybe that's what comes of living in such a rural place.

'No.'

I don't say 'really' again but I'm thinking it. This is worse than I'd thought. What a player!

'Tell him I'll help myself and leave a note of what I've taken,' the man says. He glances at the photograph I'd put on the counter earlier, then at me. He stares at it for a split second, then says, 'Welcome,' and with that, he's gone.

'Still sleeping,' Theo says on his return.

'Okay. Well, I'd better get going. My taxi will be here any time soon.'

'So, you're definitely leaving? You didn't change your mind.'

'No. I'm leaving very soon,' I say, thinking about this man and his pregnant friend.

'I can take you to the airport, if you like. As a thank-you for helping out here with Bea and the diner.'

'No, no, it's fine. I'm staying at a hotel in the city tonight.' I hold up a hand as I gather my things, including the picture and Ruben's advent calendar. I haven't looked at today's pocket yet and will save it for the hotel.

'Oh, and, erm, a man came in. I didn't get his name. Youngish. Dark, collar-length hair. Said he was going to help himself to a new saw from the store and he'd leave you a note.'

'No worries. That'll probably have been Dakota. Dax, we call him,' he says.

I can't imagine that being no problem at home. Even the corner shop has CCTV because of persistent shoplifting. I head to the door, just as the taxi pulls up in front of the store next door.

'Hey, hang on,' he says, putting out a hand. I stop and he frowns. 'What you said, when you came to find me, about Bea.'

'Yes?' I say firmly, affronted on her behalf.

He lets out a long sigh. 'Bea and I, we're not . . .'

'I heard!' I say. 'You're not together any more. I understand.'

'No, you don't,' he says, more firmly than I'm expecting. I look out at the waiting taxi. 'Your taxi is here.'

I feel suddenly desperate to know. 'Tell me, then,' I

say. 'What exactly don't I understand? How do you think she feels knowing you're not in love with her? Or not enough to be there for her, her wingman, when she needs you. Being there because you want to, not because she's pregnant.'

He takes a deep breath. 'It's not my baby. If that's what you're thinking. Bea and I aren't in a relationship. We never were. I don't want you leaving thinking I'd misled you in some way.'

I take a moment to process the information. 'It's not your baby, and Bea isn't . . . You and Bea aren't . . .'

He shakes his head. 'No. I'm just here as a supporting arm. I'm not sure why I'm telling you this, seeing as you're off, but I didn't want you to leave with the wrong idea.'

There's an uncomfortable silence between us as I digest the information. 'You're not . . .'

'No.'

'When I said all those things . . .'

He raises an eyebrow – a very attractive eyebrow. I blush. 'I'm sorry. I shouldn't have jumped to conclusions. It's just . . . I have history in that area.'

'Ah,' he says, seemingly understanding. 'Well, it's not something I planned to say, but we all have secrets close to our chest that are better out in the open.' He waves at the framed picture I'm holding against myself again.

'I really am sorry. I assumed . . . I wish I hadn't. If I

could, I'd try to make it up to you. Try to make you realize I'm not some fire-breathing dragon.'

'Oh, that was real fire you were breathing, all right!'

This time I can't help smiling. 'I was just cross.'

'You were!' He laughs, and I find myself laughing a little too.

I look at the taxi, waiting, its red tail-lights glowing, engine running. 'I have to go.'

He bites his lower lip, glances at the waiting cab and back at me. 'You don't.'

'Don't have to what?'

'Go.'

'But my taxi's here.'

'You could stay on and help Bea for a bit. Like you say, she needs all the support she can get right now. She'll have to take lots of rest and accept lots of help.'

'Oh . . . I can't. I've changed my flight. I'm going home tomorrow.'

He searches my face. 'Okay, no worries.' He holds up a hand and drops it again.

I hesitate. 'I would stay, but . . .'

'But what? You have to get back?' He raises that eyebrow again.

'Well, I don't exactly have to right away but . . .'

'I'd say whatever you were running away from when you came here for the holidays will still be there when you get back.'

Infuriatingly, he's right. What am I going home to?

127

A cold, empty house, counting down the days until Christmas is over and Ruben gets home. I could do that from here. At least here I know what I'm doing, cooking in a café and perhaps making cakes . . . but here I'd be doing it with maple syrup.

'You'd be doing a us a big favour. Especially Bea. And it sounds like you know a bit about what she's going through.'

I remember what it was like, feeling alone, feeling I couldn't do it. But I did. With the help of Mae next door, who was a real friend when I needed one.

I can hear the taxi engine ticking over in the background. 'Okay,' I say at last. 'I'll stay. Just until after Christmas. Then I have to go home.'

'Great! Bea will be delighted she has help.' He goes into the back room again to check on her.

There are worse things I could be doing. I whip up a couple of pancakes and drizzle them with rich, sweet syrup, wrap them in foil and take them out to the waiting taxi driver. I hand the parcel to him with an apology. He takes it, filling his cab with the scent of sweetness, then checks with me that I'm sure I want to stay.

'I am.' I smile.

'Okay,' he says, clearly in disbelief that anyone would want to stay somewhere as desolate as this. He rolls up his window, raises a hand and speeds away, as fast as the snow will let him.

Back in the diner, it's warming nicely. I put the

picture I slammed onto the counter into my case, then go to check on the fire and open the stove door.

'Ouch, hot!' I shake my hand hard.

'Use a glove!' says Theo, behind me.

Another lesson learned on how to stay warm in winter in a remote Canadian town.

'How's Bea?' I ask, keeping things on safe ground.

'Awake. And cross,' he says. 'She doesn't like not being in control and busy. She hates the idea of being stuck in bed.'

'Oh,' I say.

'She's just finding it hard handing over the reins.'

'Maybe not so pleased I'm still here?'

'She will be – I mean, she is. *Merci*. Oh, and one other thing. Bea normally organizes the Christmas fair.'

'She said.'

'It's held on Christmas Eve. Sets everyone up for the big day.' He smiles widely.

'Looks like this year will be different, then,' I say, standing up from the fire. 'Unless someone else takes it on.'

'Exactly,' he says, and looks at me.

'Oh, no! I don't know anything about . . .' I flap my hands. Organizing a Christmas fair is not what I need right now. I'm here to avoid Christmas. 'There must be someone else who can do it.'

He laughs. 'It's okay, I'll help. We all will. We need to do Bea proud. Like I say, we rely on her, and it looks like we've relied on her a bit too much. It might not be how she would do it, but we can rustle up something between us if we put our minds to it.'

How on earth did I get myself signed up for this? But Bea could do with a helping hand. I remember how hard it was, realizing you couldn't do it all. I'm not here to celebrate Christmas, just give a helping hand, one mother to another.

That afternoon, I close the diner, having made coffee and pancakes for a steady stream of customers all asking about Bea. She's still not happy to be sitting in bed. She's given me instructions on regular customers and the ordering and I followed them, feeling quite a sense of achievement.

Back at the *cabane*, I let myself in. This time, I go straight to the fire and remember how I lit the one in the diner. It flares up and I close the stove door, letting the flames lick up the pane of glass at the front. Then I take off my coat and hang it by the front door. The place will warm up soon, I think. I turn on the lamps on the coffee-table and the wall lights. Then I take my case to the wardrobe and open the door. I pull out the bedding and replace it with my case. I shake out the sheets and make up the bed, properly this time, smoothing the thick quilt over it. Then I slip out Joe the Bear from where he's nestled among my clothes, hold him to my face and breathe in the smell of Ruben, then lay him on my pillow.

From my coat pocket I pull out the piece of newspaper I'd ripped out in the diner. It's a story about Harold Jones, who died earlier this year. I smooth it with my hand.

'Now that I'm staying, it would be great to get to know you better,' I say aloud. 'You're the reason I'm here, after all.'

There's a picture of him outside Maple Lodge and a short piece about him leaving the area when he went to college but returning to the house after his father died to be part of the Forêt des Esprits cooperative. He died with no family. It doesn't tell me much more than I already knew.

I leave it on the table and go to unpack the groceries I bought in Nancy's little store, including a bottle of wine. I find a corkscrew in the drawers and pour myself a glass. Next to the cutting is Ruben's advent calendar. I look for pocket number 5 and pull out the little piece of paper there: 'Have a foot spa!'

Maybe I will. I go to the sink and in the cupboard under it I find a bucket. I fill it with hot water, add some shower gel and swirl it with my hands. I put in one foot at a time, in front of the fire, and sip my wine. It may not be a bubbling foot spa, but it'll do. Looks like this is going to be home for the next couple of weeks, so I'd better get used to it, I think.

# 14

*6 December: 19 days until Christmas*

The next morning I feel like I've won a gold medal when, after a good night's sleep, I discover the fire is still alight.

Dressed, I pull out the packet of tea and the jar of Marmite I brought in my case and stuff them into my coat pocket. I take today's little paper parcel from Ruben's advent calendar, put it into my pocket with the other things, then open the cabin door and look around for signs of the moose . . . or Ike. The last few stars are still twinkling in the sky, before dawn breaks. The sight takes my breath away. With the torch from the wardrobe where the bedding was, I walk to the diner and let myself in. First I check the fire, open the vents and put another log on. Next I check on Bea.

'How are you doing?' I ask. 'I brought you some tea.'

'Tea?' she says, struggling to sit up in bed. 'Look, I'm fine. I'm sorry to have caused so much trouble, but I really don't need help. I got a little tired,' she says, pushing back the covers. 'I just need a strong coffee and I'll be right as rain.'

'The doctor says you must stay in bed and rest.'

'Oh, the doctor! What does he know? He doesn't have a business to run or Christmas to organize!'

She swings her legs over the side of the bed.

'Really, I don't think you should be . . .' I say.

'I've had a night's sleep. Women have been having babies for ever. It's nothing new,' she says, and slides her feet to the floor. Her eyes roll and her knees give.

'Whoa! Got you!' I say, guiding her back into bed. She looks as shocked and surprised as I feel. I plump up the pillows behind her. 'Here, drink this.' I hand her the tea.

She takes a sip, confused. 'I don't know what came over me.' She has another sip. 'This is quite nice,' she says surprised.

'Sometimes it's good to do things differently,' I venture.

She doesn't say anything.

'Look, I know you want to be out there, getting on with life, showing the world you can provide for your child, but you have to think of the baby. This is your body telling you that you need to put your feet up for the little one's sake. You'd never forgive yourself if something happened.' I feel bad saying it, but it needed to be said. She lowers the mug.

Slowly she nods. 'You're right. I wouldn't. I need to stay well.'

'For the baby as much as yourself.'

'Babies,' she says quietly.

'Babies? Twins?'

A couple of tears trail down her cheeks. She sniffs and brushes them away quickly.

Suddenly tears spring to my eyes too. 'It's okay to feel like that. We all do sometimes. You need to look after yourself for the babies.' Instinctively, I step forward and hug her. She leans into me, lets out a few more tears, then sits back.

She sniffs again. 'I promise, no more trying to get around the place.'

'Good!'

'But what about Christmas?' she wails.

'It's fine. I'll do it.' There, I've said it. If it helps her and the babies, it's the least I can do, isn't it? Just because I don't want Christmas this year doesn't mean I can't organize it for others.

'You will?'

I give a firm nod. 'I will if you promise to rest and take care of yourself and the babies. Christmas will happen.' I make the promise. 'I'll do the Christmas stuff and you rest.' It's not my Christmas stuff so I can do this, I tell myself. It's not like Ruben is part of it, so it won't make me miss him even more.

She nods. 'Okay. But staying in bed is so boring.'

'Well, you could make me a list of what I need to do,' I say, and plump the cushions again for her.

'Oh, yes! I can do lists. Grab me a pen and paper! And some more of this tea if you have any.'

'I packed some in my case. I always drink tea, but now I seem to prefer your coffee.' I find a pen and some paper behind the counter and take them to her.

Then I carry in one of the wingback chairs from beside the fire in the diner. 'Now you can have visitors to sit with you,' I say, hoping to cheer her up a bit.

'I'm sorry I was a bit emotional there.'

'It's fine. I told you. We all get to feel like that.'

She says nothing. Then, 'Will you sit with me? Just for a bit?' she asks tentatively and this is a different Bea from the one I first met, tired but full of bravado. This Bea has grasped that things are changing in her life, big time.

'Of course.' I sit in the chair.

'This is really good of you. Theo told me you were due to leave but are staying on to help. I'm sorry if I seemed ungrateful or rude.'

'I didn't have anything to be getting back for. And I feel a lot more useful being busy here.'

'Really? No family to go home to for the holidays?'

'No.' I shake my head. 'My son is visiting his dad for Christmas. So it's just me.'

She looks down at her swollen stomach. 'Is it hard being a single mom?' she asks.

I can't lie. 'You just have to take each day as it comes,' I say truthfully. 'Some are better than others. But it's definitely worth it.' The words catch in my throat.

'I'm scared,' she says, her eyes welling up again.

'I know it seems scary but you'll do it, I promise. And it *will* all be worth it.' I'm not sure how to show her this right now. Then I remember Ruben's advent calendar and today's little paper parcel in my coat pocket. I pull it out. 'My son made me this before he went away. It's an advent calendar to get me through the month until he's home. It's got little messages in it, with instructions. Sometimes a small gift, a chocolate or a teabag.' We chuckle. 'It's to get me through, well, a tough time.' I swallow, then say more brightly, 'I haven't opened today's yet.'

'Oh, that is so adorable. How old is he?'

I stand up, fetch a tissue from the bathroom and hand it to her. She blows her nose loudly.

'He's twelve. His name is Ruben.'

'And has it always been just you and him?'

'Pretty much.' A stray hot tear leaks from the corner of my eye and I brush it away quickly. 'I got pregnant. Lucas was a friend with benefits, as they say these days.

We weren't really a couple to start with. But when I got pregnant he vowed to stand by me, to make a go of things. We got married. A quick register-office ceremony. We rented a place with a garden, bought what we needed. But instead of growing together, we grew more and more apart. I think I was lonelier then than I was when we agreed to split and he left, just ten weeks before the baby was born.'

'Jeez, that's rough.'

'But I took things a day at a time. My dad was still alive then and helped out. He died when Ruben was five.'

'So it's been just you and him for a while.'

'Yes,' I say, not knowing what else I can tell her. 'We're each other's family.'

Bea reaches for the tea with shaking hands and I help her. She sips it. 'This is definitely interesting,' she says, with an approving nod. 'So, what does today's advent-calendar message say?'

I look at the little parcel for Day 6 and give it a prod. 'You open it.' I hold it out to her. She smiles, takes it, swathed in Sellotape. She pulls out a piece of paper and a glue stick. She reads the message and looks at me in surprise.

'It says, "Make paper chains!"'

I laugh and a couple more tears fall. I don't bother to brush them away. They feel nice. Like I'm with Ruben. She laughs too and I can tell that laughter feels good for her. 'He used to love making them as a small child,' I explain. 'There was never much money so we'd make paper chains and paper snowflakes from old newspapers.'

'He sounds like a great kid.' She rubs her belly. 'I hope I manage to do it like you have.'

'You'll be fine. You have great friends around you,' I say, thinking of Theo.

'You should hang Ruben's advent calendar in the diner. We could all do with a bit of it in our lives. Bring it in tomorrow.'

'Okay. So . . . shall I make you some pancakes?' I ask.

'I'm sick of pancakes,' says Bea. 'Literally. Nothing takes my fancy.'

'Ah,' I say. 'Wait there. I have something for you to try.'

I return with a small plate of pancakes and hand it to her. She looks at them, smells them, then puts her little finger into the spread and tastes. Her eyes widen. 'Oh, my God! What is this stuff?' she says, in awe.

'Marmite.'

'Wait! Pass me some maple syrup!'

'Maple syrup and Marmite?' I blanch. But I go to fetch a bottle.

She pours on some syrup and devours the pancakes. 'These are *soooo* good,' she says. 'Oh, *yes*! Heaven! I can see the diner's in safe hands. Thank you.'

'I know how it is to feel that you're fighting your corner on your own.'

'It wasn't meant to be like this,' she says.

'I know. But we learn as we go . . .'

I go back into the diner, stoke the fire, light the candles on the tables and in the windows, and turn on the coffee machine. The first customers are already in, wanting pancakes with crisp salty bacon and golden maple syrup. Maybe I still need to learn as I go, I think. I mean, fire-lighting was never a skill until now.

As the morning rush subsides, and the bus has taken the kids to school, I push up my sleeves. I have the urge to bake a Victoria sandwich cake. I find bread in the pantry as I look for the ingredients and think of Ruben's favourite bread-and-butter pudding. I'll use up the bread and see if anyone goes for it. Bea might like some later. I could add maple syrup. I'm happy to be back in the kitchen, wondering what to make. Maybe I just needed a shove in the right direction.

# 15

'Hey, how's the patient?' Theo is accompanied by Hagrid, and my stomach gives a little flip of excitement.

'She's good,' I say. 'Just eaten!'

'So, in a better mood, then?' he asks.

'Much!' I pour him coffee, then take a Victoria sandwich cake out of the oven and my golden, raisin-scattered buttery pudding.

'Wow! Those look great.' He leans in for a closer look and, apart from the aroma of the cake and the bread-and-butter pudding, I can smell something else, woodsmoke and pine, the scent of Forêt des Esprits. I like to think I'll remember it. 'What's that?'

'Ruben's favourite. Bread-and-butter pudding.'

'Save me some. I'm going to see Bea.' He comes around the counter and disappears into the back room.

I look at the cake and the pudding, then turn to the

big walk-in pantry to see what other ingredients there are.

Theo comes out of the back room as I'm serving in the diner. I've poured coffee and made pancakes but there's been a run on my cake and pudding. He's holding a piece of paper.

'She's feeling better,' he says, 'but she's agreed to stay in bed and take things easy.'

'That's good,' I reply. 'Would you like coffee?'

'Please.' He sits on a stool at the other side of the counter, still holding the piece of paper.

'What's that?' I say, putting down his coffee.

'She's given me a list of things to do.'

'Ah, yes,' I say. 'It was part of the deal.'

'The deal?'

'She agreed to stay put, and I suggested she make a list of jobs for others to get Christmas sorted.'

'Well, she's certainly done that.' He holds up the extensive list, which continues on the back of the page, the writing getting smaller so that everything fits on one sheet.

'Oh,' I say, staring at it. I hadn't imagined there would be so much. 'It's certainly comprehensive.'

'Don't think you'll be getting off lightly. It's a list of things for us both to do.'

I'm suddenly not quite so much in my comfort zone. 'What's the first thing?'

'We have the tree-lighting ceremony and then the Christmas fair.'

'What does all that involve?'

'Well, it starts with the Christmas-tree lighting and carols on 12 December. On Christmas Eve there's a fair, with stalls of gifts people can buy, lots of maple syrup and cakes, ready for the holiday, and a big barbecue, with roasted ribs in maple syrup, that kind of thing. And on the day after Christmas we have the race.'

'The race?'

'The sap run. People can travel however they want, on foot, skis, snowshoes. It goes through the forest along the sap trails. It's our way of celebrating the forest, saying thank you and hoping for a good harvest in the spring.'

'Bea told me about it,' I say. 'Sounds great. Who else helps to organize all this?'

He rolls his lips together.

'Bea,' I say, confirming what he's not telling me. 'Bea usually organizes it all on her own. But now she can't. She needs to rest.'

He nods.

'Well, clearly I have no idea who anyone is or where to start.'

'Maybe we should cancel,' he says, looking down at the list.

'Cancel Christmas?' I'm aghast.

'That was your plan, wasn't it, to block it out for this year?' He raises an eyebrow.

142

'Yes, but that's different. I was feeling . . .'

'Lonely?' He tilts his head, his eyes on me, and I blush.

'Out of sorts!' I say quickly. 'Like I say, this year is different with Ruben being away. But I promised Bea we'd help in any way we can.'

'Well, maybe this year is different here too. Maybe things can't go back to how they were,' he says thoughtfully. 'Everything changes.'

My heart twists. In just a few years Ruben will be making up his own mind about where to spend Christmas, where to go to college, where to live . . . 'About yesterday . . .'

He waves a hand. 'It's fine. I can see what it looked like. But Bea and I are best friends, always have been. Ever since I married her sister.'

My mouth drops open. 'Her sister?'

'Mimi and I were childhood sweethearts, I suppose you'd call it. We got married and moved to the city when I . . . had a job there. But things didn't work out. I came back. She didn't. That's it in a nutshell.'

I nod, taking it all in.

'But that's in the past.' He smiles, and I feel warm inside. He holds my gaze steadily. 'We all have a past, things we leave behind. And now,' he says, looking down at his coffee and then back at me, 'it's probably time you told me the truth about why you're actually here.'

He knows.

# 16

My cheeks are bright red and I'm flustered. 'I . . .'

He's serious.

I have no idea what to say. Of course I couldn't just hide behind the diner counter and hope to find out everything I wanted to know about my long-lost relative without anyone working out who I was. And once they do, I'll probably be run out of town anyway.

'Maybe this wasn't my best plan,' I say, feeling foolish. 'I just thought I could help out here and be a fly on the wall at the same time. Not get in the way. But maybe I should have gone when I changed my flights. Who else knows?'

'No one. It's okay. I figured it out before I persuaded you to stay.' He holds up his hands.

'How?'

'Well, like I said, we don't get many people wanting

to rent cabins out here at this time of year. I guessed you were here to sniff around, see how much land you owned.' A small smile pulls his lips, but there's tension in his eyes. 'And you share a surname with Harold, even if it's a pretty common one. The picture you bought at the farm sale was the clincher.' He jerks a thumb at the photo on the counter. 'Why else would someone buy an old picture of a stranger to take home as a souvenir?'

'I had a call from an heir hunter about a distant relative and some land and I wanted to see if it was real. I thought it might be a scam. He showed me a family tree but I wasn't sure if I believed him.'

'Oh, it's real land. And it's right in the heart of the town.'

'I didn't know anything about it or about having relatives out here. I haven't any family left at home to ask. I thought it might help to come out here. I didn't know people would be worried about losing it. Please, I don't want anyone else to know.'

He bites his bottom lip. The logs in the stove spit and spark.

'Harold,' I say quickly. 'What was he like? I really want to know. And why wouldn't he sell the land when he needed the money?'

'Maybe that's what you need to find out.'

'Look, I shouldn't be here. You're right. I'm keeping a secret. And if anyone else works it out . . .'

'You'll run away? Again?'

He looks straight at me, making me feel uncomfortable.

'You want to know how you've ended up with this land, right?' he says, getting to his feet.

I nod.

'You want to know the man behind the land?'

'Yes.'

'Well, then, staying here is exactly what you need to do. Now we have Christmas to organize, so you'll meet everyone and figure out exactly what this place is all about.'

'You're right. I can't keep running away when the going gets tough,' I muse. 'You know everyone and I can organize. I'm thinking organization isn't your strong point,' I say, remembering the boxes in the store, piled on top of each other. 'This way, I get to find out a little more about the relative I never met and you get to keep the Christmas tradition.'

'So you'll do it? We'll work together?'

'Yes.' I'm wondering what on earth I've let myself in for. 'But the town's worried. I can tell that. What if they work out who I am?'

'Don't worry. I'll keep your secret safe. On one condition.'

'What's that?' I ask.

'You won't agree to sell the land until you leave. Promise me, if this is what we think it is, that you own the land, you won't make any decisions until you've really seen the place for yourself.'

'Okay,' I say. I have no idea why he assumes that what I think about the place will change anything. The land will be sold one way or another.

# 17

*7 December: 18 days until Christmas*

'First, the Christmas-tree lighting ceremony,' I say, as we sit next to Bea's bed the following day, after the lunchtime rush. She's on her third plate of pancakes with Marmite and maple syrup.

'No, wait!' she says, licking her fingers and waving her hands over her bump. 'What's in the advent calendar today? Did you bring it in?'

'I did. I haven't opened it yet.'

'Quick! We can't do anything until we know what the calendar says.'

'The calendar?' says Theo.

'Chloë's advent calendar. Her son Ruben made it for her and every day he makes her do something to help celebrate the holidays or something she might enjoy.'

Theo smiles. 'Well, we'd better find out what Ruben has in store for us today, then.'

I slip back behind the counter in the diner. It's all quiet. I pull the Christmas pillowcase from my bag and return to the bedroom.

Just for a moment I'm embarrassed by my crafting efforts, but neither Bea nor Theo seems to notice. They're just keen to see today's message.

'Come on, come on!' says Bea, impatiently.

I reach into pocket number 7 and pull out a small wrapped present. I'm wondering if it's going to be another toffee and worry that Bea might feel let down.

I fight my way through the Sellotape and silver foil Ruben's used to wrap it and eventually I'm in. We frown. Then Bea and Theo look at me for clarification. I feel a lump in my throat. I cough to clear it but as I speak my voice cracks.

'Sorry, it's a daft one today,' I say, looking at Bea.

'It obviously means something to you.' She smiles. 'What is it?'

'It's, erm,' I clear my throat again, 'it's a decoration Ruben made at school when he was little. The first one he ever brought home.'

They peer at the toilet-roll tube with five sequins, a button (one fell off), and blue and black felt squares covered with glitter.

'What is it?' asks Theo.

'Batman on a skateboard, apparently,' I say. They're

trying to keep their faces straight, but I can't and the laughter ripples up from inside me, joyous laughter. Bea and Theo join in too until Bea is telling us to stop because it's making her stomach hurt, but every time we try, giggles erupt all over again.

'Well, I love him,' Theo announces, holding high the glittery cardboard tube.

'Me too,' says Bea. 'He must have pride of place this year. Ruben's Christmas decoration!'

'I love him too,' I say, 'even if he looks nothing like Batman on a donkey.'

'Skateboard!' Bea and Theo correct me, and we let ourselves enjoy the laughter all over again. Then Bea claps her hands.

'All we need is a tree to hang it on,' she says. 'No good having a tree decoration without a tree. We need one for the diner and one for the town square.' She starts a new list with gusto. 'The lights are in your storeroom, Theo.' She points the end of the pen at him as she talks and writes.

'Check,' says Theo. 'Although I'm not sure where.'

Bea rolls her eyes at me. 'Then there's the decorations to make and put up,' she goes on.

'Okay,' we say.

'Talking of which,' I say, and hand her a pile of newspapers from the basket beside the fire in the diner. 'Paper chains, remember?'

'I haven't done this in years.'

'It might stop her writing lists,' says Theo, quietly.

'So where do we go for Christmas trees around here?' I ask, clapping my hands together. 'I'm guessing we don't buy one in the supermarket.'

They laugh. Theo shakes his head. 'We're in a forest. We'll go out early in the morning, see how the trees are looking, where they need thinning out and where we'll take them from. I'll need one for the store as well.'

We stand to leave.

'Have you everything you need for now?' I ask Bea.

'Yes,' she says, 'thank you.' She looks down at the piles of newspaper I've left her.

'Oh, and hang up the advent calendar in the diner so we can all see it,' says Bea.

In the diner I find a hook behind the counter, used for hanging long tongs, take down the tongs and hang the advent calendar there. A little bit of home is with me now.

Outside dusk is falling. 'Finish up here and get an early night,' Theo tells me. 'We have trees to introduce you to tomorrow. It's Sunday. The store and the diner will be closed.' He leans in. 'Time you met your ancestors,' he whispers, 'and picked out a Christmas tree.'

I remind myself that this is nothing more than a fact-finding mission. Nothing more.

# 18

*8 December: 17 days until Christmas*

A shuffling noise is coming from the front porch and this time I know it's not the moose or a wolf. The fire is lit and I'm dressed. I open the cabin door as Theo sweeps away overnight snow from the porch.

'*Bonjour!*' He's in his navy working jacket, with thick gloves and a hat.

'*Bonjour!*' I smile back, wishing that my attraction to him would stop nipping at my heels every time I see him.

Beyond and around him, it's barely daybreak. The light is just starting to arrive, shiny streaks creating shadows through the branches as the moon reluctantly takes her leave.

'What are those?' I ask, pointing.

'Skis!' he answers. 'For our outing!'

This time I don't return his smile. 'I can't ski. I was never one of the wealthy parents who took their kids to the Alps in the school holidays. I was more trips to the cinema, with fish and chips as a treat afterwards.'

'It's cross-country skiing. It's different. You'll be fine. It's like walking but you glide.'

'I've never done anything like it before.'

'It'll be fine. It's how we get around out here.' He holds out a pair of skis to me. Another pair is resting against the porch.

'Can't we take the horses?'

'Not where we're going.'

'Okay,' I say slowly, taking the skis from him. 'Where are we going?'

'Over to the other side of the lake where the good pines grow.'

I'm excited and terrified at the same time.

'But wait! What does your advent calendar say today?'

'Oh!' My heart drops. 'I haven't got it. It's at the diner.'

'Good thing I brought it with me.' He pulls it out of his rucksack and hands it to me. I'm touched by his thoughtfulness. 'Go on. Bea was adamant that we can't set off until we hear what Ruben wants you to do. She told me how much it means to you. And now to her.'

I take out the piece of paper from today's pocket: 'It

says, "Take a picture from somewhere you've never been before."'

'Well, I know just the place. Come on.' Theo puts the advent calendar into his rucksack. 'I'll hang it back where it was later. Oh, and you'll need this. It's a head torch. Wear it over your hat.'

I do as I'm told, then let him help me on with my skis and wonder why on earth I've said yes.

'These are the lines I was telling you about, how we collect the sap.' He points.

I'm still confused. 'How does it actually work? How can you collect something just though tubes?'

'So,' he explains, 'the change between cold nights and warmer days is what makes the sap start to flow. Traditionally people would hammer a tap into the tree and collect the sap in a pail. Like I told you, we still do that with some of the older, harder to reach trees. But mostly we collect it like this, through these plastic tubes. They work either by gravity or vacuum and take the sap directly to the sugar shack. So, when the warm weather comes, the snow starts to melt and the sap starts to rise. That's when we get the sap boiling in the sugar shack, so the water evaporates, to make into syrup.'

'So that's where the expression comes from?'

He smiles and nods. 'When the weather warms, the sap rises and everything just gets a bit more exciting around here.'

I give a little shiver of anticipation. 'How much sap does it take to make syrup?'

'About forty litres will produce a litre. This whole place comes alive then. There's steam from the sugar shack, people helping to tap the older trees, and we barbecue by the *cabane* where you're staying. It's a real community time. Someone usually brings a guitar so we sing as the sap boils. It's a shame you won't see it.'

The sun continues to reach through the trees, dazzling us as it bounces off the settled snow. Part of me wishes I'd be here to see it too.

'And here is where we tap it.' He's pointing to a tree a little out of the way. 'We drill a hole into the tree, just big enough, bang in the tap and the tree gives us the sap. Like I say, we look after them and they look after us.'

I'm standing on my skis, poles in hand, and so far, he's right. I'm doing fine, sliding along the tracks behind him, through the trees, along the cleared trails.

'How long has your family been here?'

'About as long as yours,' he says, and I feel almost envious, wondering how it must be to belong in a place. To feel you have roots. 'Four generations. And this is yours now, I suppose.' He holds out his arms.

'Not yet it isn't.'

He puts his hand to the tree on which he showed me where to tap. I see a very faint engraving on it. They look like initials and a heart with wings on it.

'These trees are about where our families have come from and what we're leaving for the future. Here.' He grasps my gloved hand and places it on the tree on the engraving. 'Here,' he says again, and pulls off his glove, finger by finger. Then he pulls off my glove, leaving my hand bare in the wind, and places his over mine, guiding it back to the engraving. Like the lines around us connecting each tree, his fingers on mine make me feel the connection I've suspected was there all along. I reach out my forefinger, the smell of cold in the air, the smell of snow on its way, with his hand over mine, and we trace the initials there, J and N, and the little winged heart shape.

'N?'

'For Namid,' he says gently.

I snap my head round to him. 'Namid?'

He nods slowly.

My mouth feels dry. I hesitate, then say, 'That's my middle name.'

'It means "star dancing",' he says, then adds, 'A First Nations name. These were Joseph and Namid's initials.'

I'm suddenly desperate to know more. 'But how?'

'Look, all I know is that Harold's grandfather took over this land from his brother, who went back to the UK.'

'My great-grandfather? Joseph?'

'I only know what my parents told me. How the

different families came to be here. I assumed you knew all this.'

I shake my head.

'The brothers came out here to make better lives for themselves, grab the opportunities that the country was offering. But your great-grandfather went back to the UK, so I understand, to look after their father who ran the local shop and was ill.'

Some of the pieces of the jigsaw are fitting into place and I feel some sort of connection. 'I knew my family ran the local shop. My grandfather took it on. Kept it going as long as he could until the supermarkets moved in. My father had to sell it when I was a child.' The memory scratches at the back of my mind. 'My friend Mae said something about my great-grandfather having a brother. But she didn't know much more.'

'Well, he did. Your great-great-uncle. He took over the land, handed it on to his son. And then to Harold.'

'So the heir hunter was right. We were cousins.'

He nods.

'And Harold had no family?'

'Not . . . not when he died. None to speak of. Never married. So no official heirs. Until now.' He seems to be holding back. He looks at me, as if willing me to understand. 'As I said, he had a stroke some years ago. We all pitched in to help. Bea organized us all, as she always does.' He says no more, just stares at me.

Suddenly I get it. 'It's Bea, isn't it? The babies are his.'

He seems to breathe a sigh of relief. 'Bea seems to want to keep this to herself. But we all know that they fell for each other.'

'So the land belongs to the babies?' I say, almost relieved.

He drops his head. 'Harold and Bea weren't married. Unless we can find a will, you're still the only official heir.'

My head and heart swoop and swirl with confusion. 'So why wouldn't he sell the land, after his first stroke? When he couldn't work it any more?'

'That's where things get complicated,' he says, letting his hand go. 'It would be better to ask someone else rather than me about that part of the story. I just helped out with the trees when Harold couldn't.'

'And what will happen now?'

He shrugs. 'That depends.'

'On what?'

He looks me straight in the eyes.

'You told me everyone had been looking for the will at the cabin the other day, the day of the barn sale. And if they can't find it?'

'The land goes to whoever claims it as the rightful owner. It'll be sold, no doubt, and the profits passed on.'

To me, I think, feeling the weight of all this on my shoulders and wishing it didn't fall to me. Part of me wishes I'd never known about Forêt des Esprits. But looking out through the trees, the other part of me is very grateful to have had the chance to come here.

'Star dancing,' I say quietly, looking at the engraving.

'There is something you might like to do before you leave.'

'What's that?'

'Hug the tree.' He nods towards it.

'Sorry?'

'Hug it. Get energized by it.'

'Oh, no! You're fine. That's not for me.' I wave a hand.

'Sure? Okay. Come on, then, let me show you more of this place and why it matters to us.'

The information swirls in my head. Harold, Bea, the babies and how I come to be connected to this place. This is what I wanted to find out, isn't it?

'Let's head up the mountain a bit. You can see the lake from there.'

I follow him on the skis, one foot in front of the other, leaving a trail in the snow, a mark of where I've been that I know will fade, when more snow falls, and will soon be gone.

# 19

'I thought you said it was easier than downhill skilling,' I pant, the cold air stinging my throat.

'It's different. You okay?' He stops.

I shake my head, breathing even deeper. The cold air seems to be stripping my lungs.

'We're here. The tabletop.'

I turn to look. It's breathtaking in both senses of the word. I'm out of breath, but wow, I'm speechless too. It really does feel like we're on top of the world looking out over the snowy trees and lake below. There is snow in the air up here. I remove my gloves with my teeth to take a photo with my phone, then shove it back into my pocket and pull my gloves on quickly, not taking my eyes off the view, the snowy treetops, the rooftops of the cabins dotted among them, curling smoke rising from the chimneys.

'Here.' Theo taps my elbow as he pulls a silver hip flask from his rucksack.

'What's that?'

'Something to give you energy for the journey down.' He unscrews the lid and hands it to me.

It hits the back of my throat and burns. 'What is it?' I croak, as it warms me inside, making my cheeks glow and bringing a smile to my face. I take another swig.

'Maple moonshine.' He grins. 'Made in the woods. Come on. Let's eat.'

He swishes snow away from a fallen tree and puts a blanket on it. Then from his backpack he produces packages: turkey wraps with salsa, maple sticky ribs and wings, coleslaw, and slices of cake, soft, sweet and crumbling.

'This is amazing. When did you do all this?'

'Last night.' He bites into the cake. 'I may be a bit disorganized, but I know how to cook.' He hands me the maple moonshine. 'And that's your cake. I bought it from the diner.'

'*What?*'

'I paid for it!' He puts his hands up. 'Dropped the money into the till. It was Bea's idea.'

'If the boss said it was okay, it's fine by me.'

We gaze out over the trees, both smiling. It's like they've been sprinkled with icing sugar. I think, *This is the picture I want to send to Ruben.*

When we finish eating, I help pack up and get ready to ski again.

'That was lovely. *Merci*,' I say.

'Come on, I've still got to show you the sugar shack and then, over there, the pine trees.'

The view is amazing. A winter wonderland. Like something off a Christmas card. Suddenly a huge bird swoops down in front of us.

'What was that?'

'An eagle,' Theo tells me.

'An eagle?' My eyes widen.

Delight is evident on his face. I watch as the eagle swoops and circles, eventually dropping lower down the valley.

'Yup, a bald eagle. Gets its name from being piebald because of its white head. Probably heading down towards the lake.'

I'm blown away by its size. 'We have cars that size where I live!'

'Look, over there,' Theo says quickly, and I follow his pointing finger.

'What? Where?'

'Over there!'

I look down in the direction he's pointing, and then I see it.

'The moose again. With her young.' We watch her working her way through the forest on the other side of the lake.

'We'll stay well clear of them.'

'Okay, but how are we going to get down from here?' I say.

'Ski.'

'But . . .'

'Don't worry.' He positions his skis. 'Put your skis inside mine. Your hands around my waist. We're heading towards the lake where the best Christmas trees are.'

I do as I'm told. 'Can't we just take one from here?'

'No, you'll be fine. These are good but not as good as they are on the far side. Do you need more maple moonshine?'

'I might when this is over.' I'm holding on tight around his waist, screwing my eyes up.

'Keep your eyes open – this is gonna be good! Something to tell Ruben when you get back.' He tips his skis over the ridge of the hill and I cling tighter, eyes still shut. I force them open.

I can smell pine trees, the cold snow and Theo, my face to his back as he gently zigzags down the hill. I'm clinging to him, but we're travelling slowly and steadily and I start to loosen my grip and lift my head. It's incredible. I can hear the swooshing of the skis and the call of the eagle, taste the snowflakes in the air, and all I can see is trees, all around us. It's stunning. Like I'm travelling through a postcard. Finally, in a big swoop, and a spray of snow, we come to a stop at the bottom of the hill.

'I loved that!' I say. I'm out of breath, but just from the beauty of it all.

'Good. Now, this time, you think you can do it on your own?' He indicates a small slope, the last down to the main track that will take us back to the town.

Right now I feel I could do anything.

'Head right between those two trees at the bottom. I'll be just behind you. Watch out for that root,' he says.

I focus on the trees ahead and push off down the short slope, steady and straight.

Yes! I feel totally alive. I can do this. I can help at the diner and put on the Christmas fair and light a fire and ski. I can do all of this.

'Just head for the gap between those two trees,' I hear Theo call behind me.

I'm focusing on the trees he's talking about and can see the ground climbing upwards again beyond them. I'm smiling from ear to ear.

Just then a squirrel bolts out in front of me and I lean to the left to avoid it, nearly topple and lean sharply to the right. Hit the tree root, take off over it, leaving the snowy ground for a moment, and land face first in the snow. I lie there for a split second, wondering how to untangle my skis and stand up when there's an *oomph* and I'm winded again. Theo is behind me, right behind me, well, on top of me now, and we're in a heap, a tangle of limbs and skis.

'You okay?' I hear him ask, from the muffled depths of our hoods and scarves.

'Yup,' I manage. 'You?'

Just for a second we say nothing.

'Sorry, I must have tripped you as I fell.'

'I was close behind you.'

Then he says, 'You made it! You got there!'

'It wasn't pretty,' I say, looking up from the snow I'm lying in and starting to smile, 'but I did it.'

'May have been a bump along the way, but I'm proud of you. You did it!' he says.

'Thank you.' I turn to see his face close to mine and want to stay there for ever, examining his features up close.

'Better get you up. Can't have you lying in the snow, as much as I'm enjoying the view.' We hold each other's gaze for just a little longer, then roll apart and he stands, holding out a hand to me.

I take it and he pulls me up, then lets me go a little, and I collapse backwards, with a shriek. He's teasing me again.

'Hey!' I shout, grabbing snow with my free hand and throwing it at him. It lands on his shoulder, and he laughs as he pulls me to my feet, with certainty this time, and close to him. I feel helpless, like I did on the ski run. My feelings are running ahead of me, leading me to somewhere I haven't been for a very long time.

'Come on. We have trees to look at before it gets dark,' he says, and the moment that had us frozen to the spot passes. 'This way,' he says, and leads me past the lake and into the pine forest on the other side.

We look at the trees, picking out the best and marking them with bits of ribbon tied to the branches. 'And we'll take one back for the diner,' he says, getting out his saw from his rucksack. He takes off his jacket, to reveal the flannel shirt underneath, and rolls back his sleeves to his elbows. 'Which one takes your fancy?' He beams at me, and a little bubble of fun ripples up inside me.

'How about that one?' I suggest.

He frowns. 'Too small.'

I laugh. 'This?' I point to a taller one.

'It's uneven.'

We wind our way through the trees. I run my hand along their needles as I go, breathing in their scent.

'Chloë?' he calls. 'How about this?' I navigate the trees and see him standing next to one the same height as him and just as broad.

'It's perfect.' I admire its bushy green branches.

'Sure?'

'Sure,' I say. I imagine sending Ruben a picture of it with his decoration in prime place on a branch.

Theo pushes back his sleeves again and whips off his hat to reveal his dark brown wavy hair. He bends and holds the blade to the trunk and begins to saw. The muscles ripple up and down his forearms with each stroke. His large shoulders under the checked flannel shirt move in time with the saw. I can't help looking at his wide thighs under denim jeans. He's using all of his body to fell the tree. Eventually, he stands up, his face hot and red with exertion, curls of dark hair springing down across his hot forehead. 'Ready?'

'Ready!' I shout back.

'Timber!' he calls, and gives the tree a final push with his hands.

He steps back and there's a crack, then a whoosh, and I practically squeal as the tree hits the snowy ground between its upright neighbours. Everything around us falls silent. He looks back at me with a huge smile. 'Okay, let's get this tree home.'

And I feel as excited and alive as a star dancing.

Theo ties the tree with rope, puts on his jacket and slings the other end of the rope around himself, ready to drag it home behind him on the skis.

'All done,' he says, and reaches into his rucksack, offering me another swig of maple moonshine before we head for home. I take the hip flask, putting my lips where his have been and feeling the thrill of a connection. In fact, I'm feeling a thrill about everything that's happened today, the skiing, the eagle, the moose, the trees. Spending the day with Theo. The sight of Theo felling the Christmas tree and dragging it home. I'll never forget it.

As darkness falls we reach the town and stop outside the diner.

My legs are killing me. I need a bath and a glass of wine.

'At least you have something to show Ruben for today,' says Theo. 'I took a photo of you skiing too. I'll send it to you if you give me your number. First, let's check in on Bea. Then . . . I was thinking maybe we could have some dinner.'

'Great! Where do you go for dinner around here?'

'We cook it ourselves.'

I smile. 'Perfect!' And it really does feel like that. I'm enjoying the now. Nothing more. Just this. Some grown-up time. Ruben was right. I'm having fun.

We take off our skis, prop them against the porch and let ourselves into the diner.

'I'm going to do it. I'm going to organize the Christmas fair!' I say. 'We can do this. We've got a tree. We're on our way.'

'I'm glad,' says Theo. 'Your cousin would be glad too.'

I smile, feeling that strange sensation again: I have roots here.

'Come on, let's check on Bea. And then have dinner.'

I follow him as fast as my aching legs will allow to

the back room. He knocks on the door and stops. I stop behind him.

'Hey, Bea,' I call. 'You'll never guess what I did and where I've been. It was amazing.'

'Ski trip through the woods?' says a voice similar to Bea's but with a heavier French-Canadian accent. 'I remember it well.' I squeeze next to Theo, who is standing stock still, gazing at the woman sitting next to Bea, who's in bed, surrounded by paper snowflakes. Bea is not looking happy.

'*Bonjour*, Theo!' The woman smiles.

'Mimi! What are you doing here?' he asks, clearly surprised.

'I came to check on my little sister.'

# 20

'Hi, I'm Mimi, Bea's sister,' the woman tells me. 'She tells me you've been a great help.'

Her smile is certainly not warm or friendly, and definitely doesn't reach her eyes. She's sitting by the bed in the chair I put there, in her coat, clearly with no intention of taking off the coat or letting go of her expensive handbag.

'It's fine. I'm happy to,' I smile warmly back, but am met by more coldness. Even Theo seems frozen to the spot.

'Well, thank you, but I can take it from here.'

I'm being dismissed.

'Oh, right.' I glance at Theo, then turn to Bea, who seems really uncomfortable.

'Theo, it's okay if I stay with you, isn't it?' says Mimi.

'It's not like there's many places to stay around here and there's no way I'm going to Cabane de l'Étoile.'

'It's fine,' Theo says quickly, as he turns to me and opens his mouth to speak.

I interrupt him. I don't need to hear that he can't make it for dinner now. I can see that for myself and I feel a bit of a fool for looking forward to it.

'It's fine,' I repeat his words. But clearly none of this is fine. I'm not sure what's going on, but it's not my business. I'm just here to help out in the diner . . . and organize the Christmas fair. My bubble of excitement and positivity pops. 'I'll get going,' I say, and turn away, my legs stiffening and seizing up on the spot. 'Ouch! Just need a minute to get moving.' I'm willing my joints, sore from the day's skiing, to move faster with less pain.

'Ah, yes, I remember days out skiing, searching for the best trees,' says Mimi, with a tight smile.

I feel like I've been slapped.

'Have a warm bath,' Theo says to me quietly, touching my elbow. 'And the best thing you can do is get back out on the skis again tomorrow.' He attempts a smile. 'Sorry about dinner. I had a great day.'

I wave a hand, putting the other out to the wall to support me as I go. 'No problem. Another time.' I wish I hadn't sounded so disappointed.

'*Au revoir*. Nice meeting you,' says Mimi, from her

chair. The one I sat in to keep Bea company when she needed it.

'Come by in the morning, Chloë – I have to know what tomorrow's advent calendar message is,' Bea calls after me.

'And you'll open the diner?' says Mimi. It's more of a statement than a request. 'I'm not really here for that.'

I nod and leave, out through the diner. The tree we brought back with us is leaning against the porch. My legs hurt so much I could cry. At least I think that's why I'm feeling so alone and sorry for myself.

Back at Cabane de l'Étoile I take in the blanket of stars above me as I heave myself up the steps to the front door. Maybe dinner wouldn't have been such a good idea anyway. Inside, I have a bath, as Theo suggested, and head straight for bed, skipping the glass of wine and the toasted cheese sandwich I'd promised myself. I'm just dropping off when I hear a tapping noise. I lift my head to listen. It's not snow falling. I hear it again.

Tap, tap. It's at the front door.

'Hello?' I call, knowing the moose isn't going to be knocking at my door at this or any other time, but I'm not sure who else it would be.

A voice makes my heart do a little skip. 'Chloë?'

'Theo?' I struggle out of bed and shuffle as fast as I can across the floor, my legs as stiff as tree trunks. I make it to the door, unlock and open it. 'Theo? What are you doing here?' I say. 'Is everything okay? Is there a problem with Bea?'

'Bea is fine. Just cross that Mimi has turned up and is telling her what to do. Stopped her eating pancakes and banned her from making paper snowflakes in bed because of the mess.'

'But she loves the snowflakes and the pancakes. And it stops her worrying about the things she can't do.'

'Or making lists.' Theo laughs.

'Exactly! We'll all be run off our feet if she keeps making lists like she was!'

Our laughter tails off. I look at him in the silver moonlight, Hagrid just behind him. It's cold but not snowing. Just silver strands of moonlight reaching through the trees to the clearing in front of the cabin. And Theo is here, not in his own cabin with Mimi.

'I wanted to see if you were okay. And say sorry about Mimi. She can be a bit . . . direct.'

He's come to see if I'm okay and it feels good. Like maple syrup on pancakes, making you feel someone cares.

'I'm fine. Well, I would be if my legs worked,' I say, laughing again and wincing. 'Do you want to come in?'

He shakes his head. 'Just wanted to check in on you. Apologize again. And remember, get back on the skis tomorrow.' He jabs a forefinger towards the instruments of torture leaning up against the wall by the front door.

I groan.

He smiles. A smile I've come to like so much.

'I'm going back to cut down more trees tomorrow, if you fancy it or can spare the time. I'll drag them up to the main path and take the horses to pick them up. Oh, and there's the wreaths and mistletoe bombs for the tree-lighting ceremony to make too. People will want to start decorating their homes.'

'Are they on Bea's list?'

'Of course!' he exclaims. 'Thank you, Chloë. I wasn't sure if Christmas was going to happen in the town at all this year but Bea is much happier. This is down to you. *Merci.*'

He leans forward and kisses my cheek. I feel the warmth of his skin on mine, smell the scent of woodsmoke and pine from his jacket, and know exactly how I would have liked tonight to end.

'I had a great day. Now I have to get back,' he says quietly. 'See you at the diner in the morning.' He steps back, raises a hand and turns to walk away.

'Good night. And thank you for a lovely day. *Merci*,' I say after him.

He turns back slightly. 'Just so you know . . . What Mimi said, I don't take every passing stranger out to the forest.'

I smile. 'Just the ones you marry!' I joke, then want

to die of embarrassment! 'I'm sorry, I don't know what I was thinking. I mean, no, it's fine!'

'I'll hold you to that!' He laughs, and my embarrassment ebbs away.

He goes back down the porch steps, clips on his skis and I watch his head torch go off into the night, Hagrid by his side. They disappear into the dark night-time shadows. What I really wanted to do was ask him in and climb back into bed with him. And I know he's feeling the same, but he has a house guest, his ex-wife, which makes this even more complicated than it is already.

# 21

*9 December: 16 days until Christmas*

The next morning, I step out onto the porch, shutting the door behind me. A family of deer is there, standing ankle deep in the snow. They're as surprised to see me as I am to see them and, for just a moment, we stare at each other. Their long necks, big brown eyes and cara-mel fur make them look almost regal as they assess me. Then one moves off and the others follow. That was a beautiful start to the morning. Better than getting caught up in the school-run traffic that uses our road as a shortcut, clogging it up.

I pick up the skis and lay them on the ground, aching with every movement. I know Theo's right. The only way for this to stop hurting is to try it again. I clip on my skis, pick up my poles and slowly straighten.

There's a rustle in the bushes and I turn to see if it's the deer returning. Instead, Ike appears, waving his wings, and I smile, pulling on my gloves. 'Come on, Ike! Let's do this!' I say, as I push off, nervous, my legs practically screaming with pain. Ike waddles behind me, as if urging me onwards. Each stride is an effort, but the pain seems to ease the more I take. When I look round, Ike's following.

'Keep up!' I push on, harder, through the pain, but Ike doesn't catch up until I arrive at the diner, legs sore and aching, but working as they should. Looks like getting back into the saddle was exactly what I needed to do, however much it hurt.

I unclip the skis and carry them up the steps, lean them there and slip off a glove to reach into my pocket for the key to the diner. With it comes Ruben's ornament, ready for the tree. I look about for the pine we brought back yesterday. It's not where we left it outside. Maybe Theo has taken it in, ready for decorating. I plan to use Bea's paper chains and snowflakes. Give it a rustic homemade feel to match the homemade ornament.

'*Bonjour!* Morning!' I call, as I let myself in, so Bea doesn't have to get out of bed, and see the tree, standing beside the fire, fully decorated in red and gold. It looks like it's had the professional touch. Still eyeing it, I walk towards the wood-burning stove, put a log on the fire and open up the vents. The flames suddenly shoot up from nowhere, big and bold, exploding into life after a night lying dormant.

Mimi appears from the back room, looking out of place. 'Oh, good, you're here. Could I have coffee, please, and something to eat? I have no idea how this old machine works. And Theo's is just as bad. I'd forgotten! I can't find anything in his house. It's so untidy.' She shudders.

I bristle, but tell myself it's not my business. 'I can do pancakes?'

'Hasn't this town moved on from pancakes and syrup? No wonder the place is dying on its feet. The sooner someone new comes in and shows it what's needed the better!'

I bite my tongue. I say nothing about how I've come to find it utterly charming and don't want anything to change. Apart from the tree, which looks so out of place.

I head to the counter. 'I could do French toast instead, or there's bread-and-butter pudding with maple syrup, Victoria sandwich cake . . .'

She tuts and folds her arms. 'Don't worry. I can wait until lunch.'

I look down and see bags, packed, beside the counter. Lots of them.

How long is she staying? Is she moving in with Bea? Maybe I'm not needed in the diner. She'll start serving sushi or whatever else she thinks the place 'needs'. I bristle again, and tell myself to stop overreacting. It's not my diner, and not my home.

'Bea is getting dressed,' Mimi informs me.

'Getting dressed? But the doctor said she had to stay in bed. She has pre-eclampsia. She needs to rest.'

'I'm taking her back to the city with me. Far better for her. Theo is driving us.'

At that moment Theo appears through the back-room doorway with a cross-looking Bea leaning on his arm. I can see he's worried.

'I'm sorry to leave you like this. Will you be okay?' Bea has concern written all over her face.

'Dax will be in the hardware store, taking care of it, so if there's anything you need . . .' Theo says.

'Erm, what about the tree-lighting ceremony? It's in three days.'

'We need to get going before it starts snowing again,' says Mimi. 'Around here, that won't be long.'

Bea looks at the decorated tree with dismay.

'It was the least I could do to help,' says Mimi, following her gaze, and I see Bea bite her lower lip.

She turns to me. 'What's in the advent calendar today, Chloë?'

'What's this about an advent calendar?' Dax has come in from sweeping the porches.

'Chloë has an advent calendar her son made for her

to count down to Christmas. Things to remind her to have fun when he's away. Things she has to do or little gifts that mean something. It's lovely! We should all be doing it.'

I'm blushing.

'Sounds great!' says Dax, swinging a leg over one of the bar stools. 'What's in it today?'

'We were just about to look.' Bea raises a smile as Philippe the mayor, still on his crutches, and Eli come into the diner, wearing what looks to be a homemade knitted hat over his wild hair.

'*Bonjour!* Ah, Bea, good to see you up and about,' says Philippe.

'Actually—'

'She's leaving with me!' interrupts Mimi, tartly.

'Mimi, you never could wait to get away,' says Philippe.

'Gosh, Mimi, we haven't seen you in these parts since—' Eli stops abruptly, as Philippe nudges him in the ribs.

'We came in for coffee and some of your Ruben's bread-and-butter special, Chloë,' says Philippe.

Mimi raises her eyebrows. 'We should be going,' she says.

'Not until we've seen what's in the advent calendar,' says Bea.

'What's this?' asks Philippe.

'Chloë's son made it for her to count down the days until Christmas. It's messages and gifts to remind her to have fun. Apparently Bea thinks we should all be joining in,' says Dax.

'Sounds fun!' says Philippe. 'Maybe we all need to be reminded of that right now. What with this being . . . well, with Harold not here. What is it today?'

I turn to the calendar, hoping this hasn't been too built up now, but loving that Ruben has done this. I must FaceTime him later and tell him how everyone is interested in the calend—

'It's gone!' I say, staring at the empty hook.

I look around. When my eyes rest on Mimi she shuffles uncomfortably. My eyes narrow.

'Well,' she lifts her chin, 'I really didn't think it was in keeping. Looked a bit amateurish.'

My hackles rise. 'Where is it, Mimi? Where's my advent calendar?'

'Okay! Have it your way. I was just trying to smarten things up. I threw it in the garbage.'

Everyone looks aghast at her as I march over to the bin, open it and pull out the pillowcase. I dust off the remnants of coffee grounds, leaving stains on it, and hang it back on the hook, giving Mimi a fierce glare.

'We should be going,' she says. 'Theo!'

'Not until we've seen what's in the advent calendar,' says Bea, tired but determined.

It's another little tree ornament, a new one Ruben must have bought, a little heart, saying, 'Home is where the heart is,' and Bea bursts into tears.

'It's the hormones,' Mimi barks.

Theo is still supporting Bea and I rush to her other side.

'It's not just that,' says Theo. 'But maybe Mimi's right,' he tells Bea. 'A bit of time away from here might do you good.'

She sniffs, running her hand under her nose, then takes his arm again and he leads her out to the waiting truck. Dax follows with the bags.

'Chloë,' Theo calls, 'could you take care of Hagrid? Dax is allergic to his hair.'

'Of course,' I say, looking at the big dog standing on the porch.

'*Reste ici*,' he says to Hagrid, who seems to understand. 'You're in good hands.'

'If you need anything, just call.' He waves his phone at me. 'Oh, and take Dax with you to get the tree for the town square. You know the ones we've chosen.'

I'm feeling weirdly tearful. I wave to Bea, who waves back. Mimi gets into the front of the truck and Theo gives me one last look, then climbs into the driver's seat.

I feel just like I did when Lucas got into his car, piled high with cases, and drove out of my life for good: the door on that chapter of our lives had been shut and bolted. I have no idea how long Theo will be gone. I'm just here for the next couple of weeks, but while I am, I want to do this for Bea.

I look at Hagrid, who seems to give me the permission I need, and I go back into the diner, put my new decoration from Ruben in pride of place on the tree, and his homemade one next to it. Actually, I may have to redecorate the whole thing – with Bea's paper chains and snowflakes from her bedroom. This place is perfect as it is, and I plan to help Bea keep it that way, no matter what her sister says.

Theo's ex-wife, I remind myself, and wonder if she wants to get him to stay in the city too. Was this all part of her plan? Does she mean to wait until they're back in Montréal and suggest they have another go? She seems so territorial over Theo that I'd say she still had unfinished business. And what was it that Eli said? That they hadn't seen her back here since . . .? I look at Ruben's little heart and his homemade decoration. I have no idea what Theo is thinking, but I'm not running away from this, not this time. I have a tree-lighting ceremony to organize, I tell myself. 'Haven't we, Hagrid?' His big sad eyes gaze up at me. 'Yes, I know. Don't tell anyone, but I'm missing him already too.'

# 22

*10 December: 15 days until Christmas*

The next morning, after Hagrid and I have spent the night in the cabin and I've skied in with him and Ike for company, Dax comes into the diner with a huge box of tangled outside lights. 'I'm guessing Theo didn't put these away quite as well as he should. For an untidy guy, his heart is in the right place.'

It is, I think. His heart is absolutely in the right place. Just a little tangled, like the lights. Not that I want to be a complication in this. I don't. I can't be part of his life. I have one to go back to, and right now, his seems to be with Bea and Mimi. I chew my bottom lip and push any nagging thoughts to the back of my mind. I walk towards the counter, looking at Ruben's little heart on the newly decorated Christmas tree, with homemade paper chains and paper snowflakes, each one individual. It makes me smile.

Instead of thinking about Theo and Mimi, and any suspicions I may have about her motives in getting him to drive her and Bea to the city, I start baking, new ideas I've had overnight. A basic maple cake, but also pastries, pecan and maple, maybe pistachio and more of Ruben's favourite bread-and-butter pudding, with raisins soaked in maple moonshine. They're all based on things I haven't thought of making for ages. I'm going back to the classics but with the addition of maple syrup, like banana cake and maple, carrot cake and maple . . .

After the early breakfast rush, the girls' ice-hockey team come in for hot chocolate and cookies before the bus arrives to take them to an all-day tournament. I'm surprised by their glum faces. 'Cheer up!' I tell them.

'What do *you* know about ice hockey?' asks one of the girls. I think she may be the team captain.

I'm stumped, and a bit taken aback. But I right myself. I'm used to cheeky not-quite-teens. 'Well, nothing. But I do know about standing on the side-lines at rugby.'

They look at me as if they're waiting for some kind of advice. I think about Ruben's advent calendar and the tree decoration. 'I know that home is where the heart is, and today you lot are representing your home.'

For a moment they don't say anything.

'Just something my son reminded me of, in the advent calendar he made me.'

They look at me, unsure, and then at the advent calendar on the wall by the tree. Philippe, who is also the team's coach, stands up on his crutches juggling his coffee cup.

'Here, let me take that!' I say.

'Good words of advice your boy gave you,' he says.

'Well, it's only what his decoration said in the advent calendar yesterday.'

'He seems like a great kid. I hope to meet him some day.'

'I'd like that,' I say, but it'll never happen. Once I leave here, and the land is sold, there will be no coming back.

'Right, let's go, gang! The bus is here.'

And there it is, waiting outside the store, just as it does in the mornings to take the local children to school.

'What's in today's advent calendar?' asks Philippe.

'I don't know – I haven't opened it yet.'

'What's this about an advent calendar?' asks the team captain.

'Chloë's son made it for her, little things to do every day that remind her to have fun,' Philippe says.

The girl who challenged me says, 'What kind of things?'

'Just ways to be kind to yourself.'

'Like a spa day?'

'Hmm, kind of.' I think of the foot spa and the teabag. 'Just things that'll make me smile and get me doing stuff I might not have wanted to do but turn out to be fun.'

She nods slowly, as if she's deciding whether or not this is interesting.

'Open today's pocket, if you like,' I say to her, gesturing at the slightly coffee-stained pillowcase. I'm still holding Philippe's mug.

She stands slowly and turns to her teammates, in tracksuits, woolly hats and coats, getting ready to leave. She walks over to the advent calendar. 'December tenth,' she says.

Only two days to the tree-lighting ceremony, I think, with sudden panic. I need to look at Bea's lists.

She reaches into the pocket and pulls out a piece of paper. ' "Start the day with a song! Sing like no one is listening, except Mae through the thin walls, and you know she'll be joining in!" '

The girl is clearly deflated and tosses the scrap of paper onto the table.

The others gather their bags and trail towards the door, beaten before they've even got to their game.

I stare hard at the paper on the table, trying to summon all the bravery I have. Mums are supposed to be embarrassing, aren't they? You can do this, I tell myself. Ruben would be cringing, but this is what he's told me to do. I screw up my eyes and pretend it's just me, in the kitchen, with Mae on the other side of the wall. Then I open my mouth, just a little.

'On the first day of Christmas, my true love gave to me . . .' My throat tightens and I croak to a stop. I can feel my toes curling. I open my eyes, to see everyone staring at me. But I've started – I can't stop now. I'd look even more foolish. Come on, Chloë. Start the day with a song!

I clear my throat and glance at Philippe and Eli, who's just come into the diner, for support. 'On the second day of Christmas, my true love gave to me . . .' I'm still on my own with a load of young girls gawping at me as if I'm a madwoman. Some lift their phones to film me and I cringe, but I struggle on.

Then, just when I couldn't feel any more ridiculous, I hear another voice joining in. It's the girl who opened the advent calendar. She's singing and starting to smile. She turns to the girl standing next to her, nudges her to put down her phone and gives her a stare. The girl shoves her phone into her coat pocket and starts to sing. Others around the table, bags over their shoulders, ice-hockey sticks in hand, join in too. Philippe and Eli pick up the tune.

'Five gold rings . . .'

One voice stands out, beautiful and angelic, a quiet girl at the back of the group. The others turn to her, and she looks as if she might stop, but the girls carry on, and she sings even louder. At the end, when we finally manage twelve drummers drumming and count down to 'a partridge in a pear tree', they all whoop, cheer and pat each other on the back.

'Come on!' calls the team captain.

Suddenly they're all in high spirits, shaking their ice-hockey sticks and helmets.

'Let's go!'

One by one they file out.

'Come on, Océane!' the captain calls to the small girl with the lovely voice. 'You can sit by me. Let's sing another song.' And they start another Christmas classic. As they pass me, each one high-fives me. Ruben would be dying with embarrassment right now. '*Merci*, Ruben's mum!'

As Océane passes I hand her another cookie. 'For *plus tard*,' I attempt, 'later.' I smile and she beams back at me, as if she's been accepted into a popular and exclusive club. Tears prickle my eyes as she turns back to wave, then joins her teammates on the bus. I remember the days Ruben came home from school having fallen out with friends, not enjoying school, missing his dad. Although he never told me, I know he wished we were like other families who had a mum and a dad at home.

'Good going, Ruben's mum,' says Philippe, as he follows the girls out to the waiting bus. 'You should speak to the choirmaster at the church – I bet he'd love you to join.'

'Will do!' I call after him. The choirmaster: I need to speak to him about the tree-lighting ceremony. I make a mental note.

The bell pings over the door as it shuts, and the diner is quiet. I wave the bus off through the window, hoping that, no matter what happens today, they have fun.

Dax and Eli are watching me, as if they're wondering what just happened. I'm wondering that too. All I know is, I feel good. And, hopefully, so do the girls on that bus.

'We'd better go get the tree for the square,' says Dax.

'Yes,' I agree. I turn the sign on the door to 'Closed' after Eli lets himself out and fetch my coat and skis, as if it was the most natural thing in the world.

## 23

Suddenly the door of the diner flies open, the bell ringing for all it's worth.

'It's you, isn't it? I knew it! I should have worked it out before Theo fobbed me off. Good job I bumped into his wife who said she'd ring me if she heard anything.'

It's the man who came into Theo's store a few days ago. Thomas, I think his name was.

I raise my eyebrows. 'Sorry?'

'Theo's wife. Mimi. At the diner. Said she'd be in touch if she heard anything. I went in there to find Theo, but it was closed last night. She answered the door. Told me to keep the noise down, her sister was sleeping. She messaged to say someone from out of town was staying in the cabin in the woods.'

'Ex-wife,' I feel the need to add, looking between the man and Dax, who is trying to untangle the lights.

'Is it you? Chloë Jones – Chloë Namid Jones? You're here for Harold's land.'

'Er, no.' My mouth is dry.

'Or, rather, to see what it's worth.' He chuckles and I feel sick.

'No!' I insist, feeling Dax behind me, steadily untangling the lights but hearing everything that is taking place.

'Look, I'm Thomas Tremblay, from Tremblay Syrups, a cooperative over at Ville de Chasse, a neighbouring town. We're looking to expand. You might have heard. Your land could be very useful to us. Forêt des Esprits could do worse than think about joining us.' He hands me a card. 'I've written down the price we're prepared to pay. Like I say, it could be very valuable to us. And to you.'

I look at the card he's still holding out.

'Ring me, as soon as you've made your decision. We're very keen to do a deal with you.' He stares intently at me and I'm cross.

'It hasn't come to me yet,' I say, my cheeks burning. I'm wishing I hadn't said anything. I could kick myself.

'We can wait. And if you have interest from anywhere else, let us know.' He places the card on the counter in front of me, just as the door flies open.

'Theo!' I say, thrilled and hugely embarrassed at the

same time. The card flickers up in the wind from the open door. It flutters across the floor and Dax stands on it, trapping it.

'Theo,' says the man. 'From the store, right? We met before.'

Hagrid jumps up from his position in front of the fire and barks in delight at the return of his boss. The man jumps back.

'Hi, Thomas. How can I help?' Theo says tightly.

'Just a bit of business,' he says. 'Nice advent calendar.' He points, and I don't know whether to feel pleased he's noticed it or insulted by his sarcasm. He gives Hagrid an unsure glance and leaves, the bell ringing, as he heads over the porch for the big SUV parked outside the diner in the snow.

'Theo!' I repeat in amazement, wondering what just happened but also how Theo has just appeared. 'What are you doing back? I thought you'd be away for a few days, a while anyway, with Mimi, getting Bea settled.'

'Seems someone couldn't bear to be away and was desperate to get back.' Theo steps aside to reveal the heavily pregnant Bea.

'Well, I couldn't miss the tree-lighting ceremony, could I?'

'Bea! I thought you were going to stay in the city!' I can't help beaming at the sight of her and Theo.

She shakes her head. 'I realized everything I needed was here. I just had to say it to Mimi, stand up to her.

If you don't mind helping me a bit, I could sit over there by the fire. The doctor checked me over and said it was fine if I stayed quiet.'

'Mind? Not at all! I think we need paper snowflakes hanging from the ceiling – I mean, if you do too. It's your diner!'

'That sounds great!' She claps her hands. 'And I love what you've done to the tree.' She leans forward to hug me over her belly. 'Between you and Theo, I have everything I need right here. And it's where I want to be,' she says, more quietly. 'At home.'

'They say that running away is never the answer.' I look at Theo. 'What about Mimi? Did she mind?'

'She wasn't happy, but I explained we were perfectly capable of looking after Bea. And that I had no plans on spending any more time in the city than I have to. I wanted to be home too.' He holds my eyes and my insides melt, like cheese on toast, bubbling excitedly.

'That's . . .' I clear my throat '. . . that's good news.'

Bea looks at me, then Theo, and smiles.

'But Mimi plans to keep an eye on Bea from the city, and we're to call if we need her. So let's get you back to bed. Doctor's orders,' says Theo.

'I have plenty more newspapers for you to make paper chains and snowflakes,' I call after her.

'And would you have any Marmite left, for the pancakes with maple syrup?'

'Of course!'

'And Ruben's special, the bread-and-butter pudding?'

'I'm making it every day. And I've tried a few other ideas I want to run past you.'

'Bring it on!' She heads for the back room.

As Theo guides her by the arm, Dax hands me Thomas Tremblay's card.

'Thank you,' I say, then slowly turn it over to see the figure written on the back, my eyes widening as I read and reread it to check and recount the zeros.

I'm wondering what Dax makes of it.

'Have you ever lived anywhere other than here, Dax?' I ask.

He shakes his head.

'Do you ever want to leave? Wonder what's out there?'

He shakes his head again.

'This is where I was born, where I belong.'

'I wish I felt the same. I wish I felt I belonged somewhere. Somehow, since my dad died, my home has changed. I don't feel like I belong. It's just somewhere I live.'

He settles down to untangle the lights once again.

'You knew why I was here, didn't you?' I say quietly.

'I had a feeling. It felt like you were here for answers.'

'But I can't get them. All I know is who Harold Jones was, not why the land matters so much that he wouldn't sell it.'

'What I know is that you're here, trying your best for the community. I'd say you definitely belong,' he says, with a smile.

'Thank you, Dax,' I say, feeling a warm glow.

'Now, we need to get the amplifier from Theo's house,' says Dax, moving on, and I'm grateful.

'What about the tree?'

'Maybe Theo will want to get it. Let's find the amplifier first. I've got the key.'

'I can go,' I say. 'You finish the lights.'

He hands me the key. 'Be warned. He's not the tidiest of people.'

It's a lovely little cabin, set back down a driveway behind the store and the diner, nestled among the trees there. I let myself in. There's a huge dog bed in front of the fireplace, where presumably Hagrid sleeps. Dax was right: there is a chaotic charm to the place, to the smart but untidy kitchen.

I make my way down the corridor, turning on the lights as I go, mostly so I don't trip over anything. The cabin isn't what I expected. But maybe this is more Mimi's taste than his, I remind myself. I find what Dax described as 'the den', with a dartboard, a big television and a desk in the corner. Beside it I see the amplifier and bend to pick it up. I just need to move a box out of the way first. I give it a tug and a tear opens up down one edge as I try to shift it and some of the contents spill out. I give it another tug, then reach forward for the black box amplifier and lift that. It's heavy. I hoist it over the box and into the middle of the room. Then I attempt to push the box back. This time it collapses. I try to push everything back in as it spills out. I stare at the box's contents, then look more closely at them. I frown. But it's not my business. I push the box back against the wall and hope Theo doesn't notice it's been opened. With all the tools and boots lying around, he probably won't. Even so, I'm curious and can't stop thinking about what I've seen and wishing I hadn't. It's not my business. But maybe I'm not the only one with things I'm keeping to myself around here.

I carry the amplifier to the diner, ready for the music at the tree-lighting ceremony tomorrow night. Then I wonder what I should be cooking for the event. Canapés? Muffins? Something special that celebrates the place. Something from here.

As the evening draws in, I go to lock up the diner, having checked in with Bea, who has been making paper chains and snowflakes, and is now creating snowmen and -women, happy and settled. Theo is out with the horses, collecting the tree for tomorrow's ceremony. Just as I put the key into the lock, a set of headlights comes down the road towards the square. It's snowing again. They're getting closer. The vehicle is tooting its horn and flashing its lights. Dax is with me, smiling.

Jo Thomas

'Who's that?' I'm interested. As the vehicle gets closer I recognize it. It's the school bus bringing the girls' ice-hockey team back from their tournament. It pulls up in front of the diner, and I can feel the excitement coming out of it as the girls grab their bags, coats and sticks to file off.

Instead of spreading out for home, as they do after school, they come to the front porch.

'We won!' shouts the team captain. 'We won!' She's waving a cup. 'It was Océane! She scored the winning goal!' She pulls the small girl towards her. 'And we sang all the way there and back!'

'Whooo-hooooo!' the girls shout, dancing and still singing.

'Fantastic!' I say, clapping.

'What's this?' Theo comes into view, out of breath, dragging a large pine tree behind him, his head torch throwing light onto the team's faces. I wonder whether to mention what I saw at his cabin today, but with the noise coming from the girls, now isn't the time.

'We won!' they shout, and lift Océane over their shoulders. 'She's small but mighty!'

I wonder if this is the first time the team has noticed the small girl waiting in the wings for someone to pass her the ball. Now they have, there'll be no stopping her. 'I'm delighted,' I say. 'Well done!'

'The singing really set them up as a team for today,'

198

says Philippe, waving first one and then both of his crutches in celebration.

'Well, in that case, I want to see you all here tomorrow for carols around the Christmas tree,' I shout, over the rowdy bunch.

They put Océane down.

'*Oui!* See you then!' they call, as they set off for home.

'Océane?' She turns to me. 'I don't suppose you'd like to sing a solo, would you? No problem if you wouldn't,' I say quickly.

Theo is smiling.

'I'd like that, *merci*.' She beams and the shy little girl at the back of the group is replaced with this happy, confident one. I hope she's here for good, long after I'm gone.

'*Merci*,' says Theo, coming to stand beside me. 'Sounds like you made a big difference here today.'

Once again, I feel that warm glow. I have no idea if it's because I'm standing next to Theo or because this place is making me feel I belong.

# 24

*11 December: 14 days until Christmas*

'Light a candle,' says the note in today's advent-calendar pocket. So I do: I light a few and put them along the counter and beside the wingback chairs and on the hearth, a little distance from the stove.

I spend the day baking in the diner, carols playing on the radio. Bea stays put and creates a mountain of paper snowflakes. I speak to the choirmaster at the church and introduce myself to some of the other locals. Theo and I snatch glances at each other as he and Dax work to string lights, and as the tree is placed on the town square ready for the ceremony. As I FaceTime Ruben from the front porch and show him the activity around me, the air is filled with contentment, light snow and anticipation.

\*

*12 December: 13 days until Christmas*

The next morning I'm up early, putting on my boots. It's cold, and my breath swirls around and upwards. My fingers are freezing. My porch has been swept clear, as has the path leading to the town square.

'Okay, Ike, I'm coming.' I look up from tying my boots. But it's not Ike, waiting to race me to the diner. It's a red squirrel. The snow is falling gently but steadily around the clearing.

'It's cold out here,' I say, then turn back into the cabin and pick up the remnants of the bread I brought home from the diner last night. I go back out onto the porch, but it's gone. I crumble the bread and leave it on the balustrade in the snow, then put on my skis.

'Come on, Ike! Let's go!' There's a rustle from the bushes and Ike is with me, running awkwardly but not giving up, chasing me to the diner where he stands, looking hopeful.

'Okay, I'll get some crumbs for you too,' I say, panting, my hot breath making plumes in the cold, fresh, clean air. I pull off my gloves and unlock the diner. 'Only me!' I call.

I listen for sounds of Bea, but it's quiet. She must still be asleep. I go straight to the wood-burning stove and open it. It's like a game of Russian roulette, wondering if the log I put on last thing at night has stayed lit.

It has!

I open the vents, put on another log and close the doors, watching the flames start to grow. I smile, with huge satisfaction.

Then I go to the back of the counter and switch on the coffee machine, just as I would if I was in the café back home. Now all I need to do is work out what to bake for the tree-lighting ceremony this evening.

But first I gather some crumbs for Ike. As I go to the door to open it and throw them out for him, I see a figure hiding in the shadows at the bottom of the steps.

'Océane?'

She looks at me nervously.

'Is everything okay? Problems?'

She shakes her head.

'It's okay, you can tell me if something's bothering you.' I start down the steps. She doesn't move. I hope she hasn't come to pull out of the tree lighting. I throw the crumbs to Ike. 'He's waiting for these,' I tell her, trying to make her feel more comfortable.

She smiles as Ike pecks at his breakfast.

'Did you want to come in? Have a hot drink?'

She shakes her head again.

'I . . .' I'm willing her not to lose the confidence she'd grown yesterday. 'I just came to give you this,' she says, and reaches out a hand to me. It's a small parcel and smells amazing.

'Thank you!' I say, surprised.

'I mean, you probably don't need, want . . . You

have lots of cakes. You're a great baker.' The words tumble out of her mouth.

'This is lovely of you,' I tell her, opening the parcel of baking paper, tied with string. It's a little tin. I open it to reveal shiny dark brown sweets in the shape of snowmen.

'It's maple taffy, my grandmother's recipe. They usually make it when the syrup is being boiled in the sugar shack at harvest time. The boiling syrup is drizzled into the snow to make candy. I thought you could take some home for Ruben. It's a thank-you,' she says, 'for what you did yesterday, before we played the game. It helped. And thanks to Ruben, of course.'

I'm admiring the lovely shiny shapes, each one strung on a red ribbon, ready to hang on a tree. 'That's a lovely idea! Thank you so much! Come in, come in,' I say, as all the warmth from the fire disappears out through the door. 'This is really kind of you.' I head back behind the counter.

'I wanted to. I've always loved singing, but never been brave enough. Never felt brave about anything, really. But the singing, well, it just helped. I felt part of the team. We all did! And we won our first game!'

'How long have you been playing with them?' I ask.

'Oh, I've only been here for just over a year. It took a bit of getting used to at first. This is my second Christmas in Forêt des Esprits.'

'And how do you like it?'

203

'It's hard, without my parents. They died.' She swallows. 'But I know I'm in a good place. I feel safe here. The trees seem to protect me.'

We fall into silence. I don't want to ask any more about her life before she arrived here. It's enough to know she's happy and safe now. 'These are great!' I look down again at the sweets, suddenly feeling quite tearful. 'Thank you!'

'No – thank *you*. Charlene, the captain, says it's been a long time since anyone took any real notice of our team. Bea used to be great at supporting us but she's tied up now. And Coach has twisted his ankle. Though he's never been very interested in the girls' team. I don't suppose . . .'

I frown.

'I don't suppose you fancy coaching us, do you?' she finishes.

'Me? I don't know anything about ice hockey! I can't even skate!'

She shrugs. 'It was worth asking. I told Charlene I would.'

'I'm flattered. Thank you. But I really can't. Besides, I'm only here until the end of the month. Then I have to go home, to Ruben.'

'You really can't skate?' Her smile lights up her face.

'Nope,' I say.

'Ever tried?' she asks, with a little glint in her eye.

'Er, no,' I joke back. 'Well, I did once. Fell over, got a

bloody nose! Why would I do something again that hurt the last time?' And suddenly I wonder if I'm talking about skating or relationships. 'I'd be terrified. It's a long way to fall, you know!' And I'm still not sure what I'm really talking about, so I change the subject. 'Now, would you like some hot chocolate?'

She hesitates.

'On me!' I add.

'Thank you. *Merci.*'

I start to make it for her and she slides onto one of the stools. 'You could help me out today if you're not busy?' I say, with my back to her. 'I have to bake for the tree-lighting ceremony and I think more maple . . . maple . . . What did you call it?'

'Maple taffy!' She giggles.

'Maple taffy could be just the thing to hang on the tree after the lighting ceremony. What do you think?'

I slide the hot chocolate towards her, with extra cream and marshmallows. Her eyes widen. 'I think they'd be great!' she says, her confidence returning, with a sweet smile. 'And I'd love to help after school, before the tree lighting. I just have to let my grandparents know.'

'Okay! Well, you drink that, then let them know after school and tell them I said I'm delighted to have the help. And, of course, I'll have to pay you.'

She blushes and takes her first sip of the hot chocolate through the cream. 'What's in the advent calendar today?'

'Morning, y'all! Have we missed the opening of the calendar?' Philippe hobbles in with Eli, wearing his knitted hat and a zipped-up gilet over his many layers. 'Hey, Océane. Great game yesterday!'

She practically bursts with pride. 'Now all we need is proper practice sessions, like the boys have,' she says, making me proud of her. 'And a full-time coach.'

'I know, I know,' Philippe says, ordering coffee and some of Ruben's special, the bread-and-butter pudding, with syrup.

'What's all this about an advent calendar?' Nancy from the store comes in with her reusable cup for filling. She glances at Eli, who harrumphs, as does she. They clearly don't like each other.

'Chloë's son Ruben made it for her. It's to help us all get into the Christmas spirit. Little things we have to do and say. Things that make Christmas Christmas.'

'Sounds great! What's today?'

'You do it, Océane,' I tell her.

They all look at me, coffees in hand, the scent of pancakes and frying bacon filling the air. The best marriage ever, I have discovered. Not one I'd have expected to go together, like chalk and cheese, but it works so well.

Océane goes to the calendar and pulls out the paper from today's pocket.

'What does it say?' I hear, as more of the hockey team come in, dressed in big coats and hats, dropping their school bags and ordering cookies to go.

'It says . . .' She hands it to me to read aloud.

I look down at the folded piece of paper. 'Go dancing! Well, that one's not going to happen.' I read on: '"Dance like we used to dance on a Friday night in the kitchen!"' Every Friday night, we'd turn up the radio for *All Request Friday* on Radio 2 and I'd cook chips and we'd dance to all the great tracks we heard. 'And eat chips!' I say, with a croak in my voice and a pain in my heart where I'm missing Ruben.

'Poutine!' they all say at once.

I look up from the folded paper. 'What?' I ask.

'Poutine!' says Océane, smiling. 'That's what you should serve after the tree-lighting ceremony tonight.'

'My favourite!' says Philippe.

'My mum used to make it for me,' Océane says quietly.

'Haven't had it in years,' says Eli.

'It's best eaten in the snow,' Nancy joins in.

The excitement in the diner is building.

The door opens again.

'Morning! What's in the advent calendar?' It's Theo and my stomach does that fizzy flipping thing again, like a new skater flailing before they fall.

'Dancing!' they chorus. 'And poutine!' They're clapping now.

Once again I look at Theo and, for someone who does so much for his town and community, I'm surprised he's packed away such an important part of his life in the box in his cabin. I wave a tea-towel. 'Right, well . . .'

'We can make that happen! Did you get the amplifier from my house?' he asks me, and I wonder again why all those trophies are boxed up, or if he noticed I'd been in and disturbed them.

'I did.' I gesture to it in the corner by the Christmas tree and blazing fire.

'Then we're all set. Dancing it is.' He beams. 'Right after the tree-lighting ceremony!'

'And the poutine!' they say and laugh.

'Okay, poutine for everyone. And maple taffy for the tree.' I say, and the crowd disperses. Philippe and Eli move to the table in the window where I light the candle. Nancy scowls at Eli and leaves.

Theo laughs. 'They've been like that for years.'

'Why?'

He shrugs. 'They were childhood sweethearts, but they broke up. Nancy ended it after a row and Eli was asked out by another girl. He ended up marrying her, and Nancy . . . I don't think she ever forgave him. Even after he was widowed.'

'That is sad. And what about the mayor, Philippe?'

'Philippe never married. His heart is with the town. He'll do anything for Forêt des Esprits. That's his life-long love.'

The ice-hockey team grab their cookies to take out.

'Didn't you want a cookie too, Océane?'

She shakes her head. 'I don't have the money right now.'

I see Theo reach into his pocket.

'It's no problem,' I say. 'This one's on me. Just come back and help me later. I told you, I plan to pay you.'

Theo joins Philippe and Eli.

Océane beams. 'I will!' She's about to leave when she turns to me. 'Oh, and about the skating? No problem. We'll teach you. Come and meet us at the next practice.'

'I think we can say that's one thing I *won't* be doing!'

The bustle in the diner has helped me through missing Ruben, and Ruben's advent calendar has helped again.

# 25

'I declare this the start of Christmas in Forêt des Esprits,' says the mayor, and flicks the switch. The tree lights up. The maple taffy sparkles amid the decorated pine cones we've hung there too. We're all buoyed up after the singing we've done with the choir and I'm delighted to see all the ice-hockey girls there, the boys too.

Bea is wrapped up warm and sitting on the porch of the store, a blanket over her knees.

'You okay, Bea?' I put a hand on her shoulder.

'It's beautiful. Thank you!' she says.

'It may not be how you'd do it . . .'

She holds up her mittened hand. 'I love it,' she says. 'Like I say, it's being at home that counts. It's okay to let others help, I'm realizing now.'

I wish Ruben was here to see this.

And then the crowd goes quiet, the ice-hockey girls

shushing each other, and music starts from the speaker. Theo is by the amplifier, handing Océane a microphone. The choirmaster is there too, standing close by to support her. She looks at me, and for a moment I wonder if she's going to disappear back into her shell. I nod to her, keeping my eyes focused on her. Then I see her look at an elderly couple bundled up against the cold, holding on to each other: her grandparents. And then, as music builds, the introduction leading into the verse, she looks up at the tree and opens her mouth.

'Silent night . . .' It's as if she is singing to her parents among the stars.

When she's finished there is a hush across the square, as the final note hangs in the air, the lights sparkling in the tree and the snow, like glitter, falling. I hand Bea a tissue to wipe away the tears, Océane's grandparents use their mittens and the girls from the ice-hockey team sniff. Then there is rapturous applause. Once again little Océane has blown us away with her talent. She rushes forward and hugs her grandparents, who hug her tightly back.

There is cheering and clapping, then more music as the ice-hockey girls join in with Océane, arms linked around each other.

I see her grandparents kiss her on both cheeks, then turn. It might be getting cold for them. But they're walking towards me.

'Océane's grandparents,' Bea says. 'They don't come out much these days. It's good to see them. They haven't been out since Océane's parents died in a car crash. Awful business.'

'Oh, no! How dreadful.' I bite my lip. They're still walking straight towards me.

They nod at me and I come down the steps to meet them.

'I'll check on things inside,' says Bea, excusing herself.

I want to tell her to make sure she sits down, but I can't turn away from this pair. 'Can I get you something to drink, or maybe you'd like to come in to get warm?' I say.

They shake their heads but they're smiling.

'We wanted to thank you.' He nods and so does she, her plaited dark hair streaked with silver grey. 'Océane is very precious to us and you have helped her settle in. It's taken her a long while to get used to her new life. You've helped so much. Thank you.'

'It was my pleasure. Actually, it was my son Ruben, his advent calendar.'

'So we heard. We have heard a lot about the advent calendar. He seems like a caring boy.'

'He is.' It catches in my throat. 'And Océane is a lovely girl. She's helped me too, being new around here.'

'We just hope she feels she belongs now. It's where

her family grew up, before moving away to find work, and now she is back with us.'

We turn to where she's laughing with the girls.

'You are a very welcome member of the community,' he says, and then quietly, 'as was your great-grandfather, Joseph Jones, many years ago.'

My head snaps back to him. 'You know about my family?'

'Dax is our other grandchild. He told me who you are.'

'I'm Chloë Namid Jones.'

He pauses and takes a deep breath. 'My grandmother was Namid. Star dancing.'

I stare, not sure what to ask next.

'They were very much in love from what I know. Your great-grandfather Joseph and his brother came out here to find work and new lives. Joseph fell in love with Namid. They were due to be married. They carved their initials into a tree they planned to marry beside.'

'I know the tree,' I say, with rising excitement.

'The land was given to your great-grandfather by my family, as a wedding gift.'

I catch my breath. 'And what happened?'

'Joseph was called back to Britain because his father was ill and, good man that he was, he returned to help his mother look after him and the shop he ran. He vowed to return for Namid.'

'And did he?' I'm wide-eyed, listening to Océane's

grandfather, hanging on his every word, wanting to remember it.

He shakes his head. 'Joseph planned to keep his word, I know it. But Namid died.'

'Oh, no!' My hand flies to my mouth.

'His brother gave him the news. Joseph never returned to Forêt des Esprits. His brother took over the land and handed it down to his son. So it went until Harold, who had no descendants.'

'So that's how the land came to be in our family. A wedding gift for a wedding that didn't happen,' I say.

'I hope this helps you,' he says, 'in your time here.'

'It does, thank you.' I'm moved by hearing this.

'You have helped Océane and our family. I wanted to return the kindness.'

I feel a strange sense of peace in talking to this kind couple. 'You've explained the picture I have of him, standing next to his wife-to-be, and her father, maybe, in their traditional dress.'

'Joseph Jones with my family, in their ceremonial clothes, I expect,' he says.

'Joseph looks so much like my son Ruben.' I manage a watery smile.

I'm feeling our conversation has come to a close when his wife tugs at his arm and nods to me. He looks at her, her face stern and then back at me. 'One other thing you should know . . .'

'Yes?'

'Namid died in childbirth,' he says.

'Oh, no . . . How sad.'

'But . . . the child did not.'

'Pardon?' I ask him to repeat it.

'The child didn't die.'

'So,' my mind is whirring, 'why is this land in my family?'

He sighs. 'Your great-grandfather, Joseph, was never told of the baby. His brother just told him his love had died and, heartbroken, he never returned. Nor did Jack return to Britain. He stayed here, took the land as his own and it has stayed within his family.'

'So it doesn't actually belong to my family at all,' I say, suddenly indignant on behalf of Dax and Océane.

He shrugs. 'It was passed on to the children who were born in wedlock. Only legitimate heirs can inherit.'

'But that doesn't seem fair!'

'What matters is that this land is as much a part of the community as the people. As long as it stays within the community, it is in the right hands,' he says.

'And that's why Harold wouldn't sell it. He sounds like a good man too. If only he'd left a will,' I say.

Suddenly there's a whistle of feedback from the microphone, crashing in on my tangled thoughts.

'Thank you for all you have done with Océane, and here,' the old man says again.

I don't know if it's the done thing, but I lean

forward and hug them both, feeling we're sort of connected. It's a lot like family.

'Okay. Now, the dancing!' says Theo, over the microphone, his eyes dancing with fun as he stares at me.

'Oh, no!' I say. I want to ask Océane's grandparents more, but the moment has clearly passed. They turn towards the tree and the music.

Everyone claps. I look at Theo and smile, although his timing was terrible.

'No one gets their poutine until they've danced!' Theo laughs. 'Nancy, over to you!' He runs over and grabs my hand.

Nancy stands on the snow-covered bandstand, wearing a hat with earflaps and a Stetson on top. Her hands on her hips, she pulls her slightly bent body as straight as she can and everyone lines up behind her.

'Come on!' the girls from the ice-hockey team call to me and I blush.

With a shove from Bea, Theo leads me down the steps to the tree in the snow. He starts the next track from his iPad and Nancy calls out the moves.

'Line dancing! In the snow?' I shout, over the music.

'Yup!' says Theo. 'Nancy was our line-dancing queen! Come on, keep up!' The line moves to the right and I follow. All the ice-hockey team are there, with their parents, the mayor, barely leaning on his crutches, other families, and the boys' ice-hockey team. Snow flies up in little arcs as we all follow Nancy's lead.

'Haven't done this in years!' yells Nancy over her shoulder, with a twinkle in her eye and a whoop.

'I've never done it!' I bellow, over the festive rendition of 'Jingle Bell Rock'.

Even Eli is joining in, smiling at Nancy as she shuffles and flings her arms into the air in sheer delight.

Theo takes a picture and joins me.

'For Ruben,' he says. His eyes, twinkling in the lights, hold mine.

Thank you, Ruben, I think.

I'm out of breath and laughing as I make my way back up the steps onto the porch of the diner where Bea is sitting again, eating poutine.

'These are the best chips, gravy and cheese I've had in ages,' she says. 'They're going back on the menu.'

'I'll have to take the recipe home with me. Right, let's serve.'

Everyone stands around eating from cardboard bowls, steam rising. Children are having snowball fights. I've put candles along the porch to light the steady fall of sparkling snowflakes. I take photographs and send them to Ruben to get smiley faces back.

'Good to see everyone tonight and share news. Word has it that the neighbouring town is getting ready to start tapping,' Theo says, handing me a bottle of beer and coming to stand next to me looking out over the tree. 'Seems to get earlier and earlier every year,' he says, as if I understand the land, the trees and tapping.

'Warming temperatures?' I ask.

'Not that you'd know it right now. But, yup, spring seems to arrive sooner every year. It's good for the trees to hibernate, take some time out to rest before we start to harvest again.' He swigs from his bottle. 'It's good to rest and rejuvenate.' He looks out over the square and I'm not sure it's just the trees he's talking about.

'Theo,' I say. He turns to me. 'I've . . . made a decision.'

He says nothing, holding my stare.

'About the land.'

'I thought you might mean that.' He takes a breath. I watch his chest rise and fall as he gazes over the trees beyond the square. I turn. We're standing side by side, not looking at each other.

It's stopped snowing and the clouds are passing to reveal a big dark sky. One by one, the stars appear, like diamonds scattered on a calm sea. We stand and stare upwards. Bea has gone to bed, happy and full.

Families are wandering home. He turns to face me.

'I'm not going to sell, Theo. If or when the land comes to me, I won't sell it. It's not mine to sell. It's not right. This land belongs to the community here. However it's come to be in my family, it needs to stay here, within the community.'

All at once he wraps me in his arms and hugs me. And when he lets me go, just a little, I don't want it to end. I breathe him in and store his scent with other special memories I want to hang on to for ever.

I scan his face. I can't fall for him. I can't. This can't be for ever.

But the draw is so strong, pulling me towards him, as someone shouts for one more dance and Nancy's name is chanted. I lean in closer, examining his face, his close-shaved beard, his slightly crooked nose and his large eyes, which seem to be scanning my face, like I'm scanning his, under the starlit early-evening sky.

I can't think of anything else right now, other than his lips on mine.

We hold each other, savouring the moment, knowing it's what we both want, as if our stars have collided here and now. Me arriving here, him being here, the land, finding out how I'm connected to it: it all feels right. Our bodies push together, there in the shadows of the porch.

He reaches down and I reach up, my heart racing, my knees trembling and my insides on fire. He curls his finger under my chin and draws it to him tantalizingly slowly. My lips quiver with anticipation.

'Well, you lot certainly know how to party around here,' says a voice.

Hagrid jumps up and barks, startling us. A man is getting out of an SUV and walking up the steps to the diner. Suddenly I feel as though cold water has been poured onto the fire inside me and step back, the flames hissing and spitting.

'We do!' says Theo. 'You looking for someone? Can I help?'

The man's smartly dressed, with short, neat hair and a skiing jacket. 'Yes,' he says. His accent is Canadian but not French-Canadian, I notice. He's not from round here. 'I'm looking for someone.'

'Who? Maybe I can help. We all know each other and each other's business around here.'

'Her name is Chloë Namid Jones.'

'That's me.' My insides turn to panic now. 'What is it? What's happened? Is Ruben okay?' I stare at his face for signs of tragedy – frowning, cheek twitching, biting his lower lip.

'What is it? What's happened? Where is he?' I say, my voice high-pitched. Theo steps forward to stand behind me, supporting me.

Suddenly the man laughs and I'm confused, still trying to read what he's trying to tell me on his face and in his body.

'I have no idea where Ruben is.'

'No idea?' I'm down the steps and pulling out my phone. 'What's happened?'

'Nothing that I know of,' he says. 'But, boy, you go from zero to a hundred fast! I'm looking for Maple Lodge. I'm Harold Jones's relative, Jed Anderson.'

I stare at him. 'Maple Lodge?'

'Yes.'

'Harold Jones's relative?'

'Yes.'

I'm processing all the information. I frown. 'I'm Harold's relative,' I say, forgetting I was keeping this to myself.

'Well, in that case, I think I may be your cousin,' he announces.

# 26

'Well, a distant cousin by the sound of it.' Jed Anderson is smiling, a very white smile, the colour of fallen snow. He's quite attractive in a smart, neat way. He shivers. 'Boy, this place is cold!'

'So, how do we . . . how are we related?' I stumble over my words, trying to take in the information.

'To be honest, I'm not really sure. Got a call from an heir hunter. Says I'm a relative of someone called Harold Jones and I'm in line to inherit some land. So I guess that makes two of us.'

'Why are you here?'

'Thought I'd come out and see what it was all about. You?'

People are wandering over to the porch, putting empty poutine bowls into the bin and taking an interest in the new arrival in the smart car, dressed like he's ready to hit the slopes in his brand-new ski jacket.

At that moment, I notice Bea standing in the door of the diner with a quilt around her, holding a pancake dripping with Marmite and syrup.

'Bea, you'll freeze!' I say. 'What are you doing out here?'

'Got up for a snack,' she says, frozen to the spot. Hagrid is doing a good job of licking up Marmite and syrup, apart from the drops that land on his soft black ears.

'Come on, in you go!' I say bossily, wanting her out of the cold and not wanting her to hear what's going on. But she doesn't move. She looks at the man, Jed, then back at me.

'Did you say you're related to Harold?' says Bea, frowning at me. 'Because I'm pretty sure that, in all the time you've been here, you would have mentioned something as big as that.'

The little crowd has turned to me. Nancy, Philippe, Eli, the girls' ice-hockey team, Océane's grandparents. My toes curl, my cheeks burn, and I wish the ground would open up and swallow me.

I can't think of anything to say so I nod slowly.

'And you came here in the first place because of Harold and the land? Because you're a relative?'

Again I nod slowly.

'And how did you come to know about him?' she asks, a distance in her voice that I haven't heard before.

'An . . . heir hunter contacted me.'

There's muttering around the group gathered at the bottom of the porch steps, the earlier happy atmosphere turning chillier by the second.

'So, you're here to sell the land? Here for the money?'

There's a ripple in the crowd.

'It's not like that, Bea,' Theo wades in, but Bea's face is thunderous.

'No, it's not like that. Really,' I say to her. 'I'm not like that.'

'What is it like, then?' says Philippe, stepping forward.

I spin round. 'I came to find out more. Find out who this relative was. How I was connected to him. To see if I might . . . just might . . . belong.' The words catch in my throat.

Bea's face softens and a fat tear runs down her cheek to match mine. She turns slowly and goes back into the diner, the quilt dragging behind, her shoulders sagging, sadness weighing her down.

No one says anything. The chilly atmosphere is broken by Jed Anderson. 'Is there anywhere to stay? I need some accommodation while I'm here.'

Theo glares at him. 'Only Cabane de l'Étoile, and Chloë's in that,' he says, unplugging the amplifier and winding up the cable. The party is clearly over. People start to wander home, heads low, shoulders rounded, and I feel I've let them down somehow. Maybe I should have been upfront from the beginning. Or maybe I shouldn't have come at all.

I look around the disappointed faces as they turn to leave. I have no idea how to make this better or what another heir turning up means. I need to make him understand that this land can't be sold to anyone outside the town.

'I can take Maple Lodge,' I say. 'It's empty. I'll be fine. You take the *cabane*,' I say. 'I'll move my stuff. Bit warmer than Maple Lodge, I expect.'

'You sure?' Jed claps his hands together. 'Tell you what, I'll flip a coin for it. Heads wins.'

'It's fine,' I say. 'You take the *cabane*.'

'Maple Lodge?' says Theo, clearly concerned.

'It's fine. Perfectly habitable, if a bit dated.' I attempt a smile.

'You sure there isn't a hotel or guesthouse around here?' Jed cuts in.

'There isn't,' I tell him, keen to get the situation sorted quickly.

Theo looks at me. 'If you're sure. I'll help.'

I rummage in my pocket for the key, my big gloves making me clumsy. I pull out the big chunky wooden key-ring and the business card from Thomas Tremblay flies out. It lands on the wooden floor between us. I freeze as Theo bends to pick it up and looks at the figure written on the back.

'Really, Chloë?' He hands me the card. 'Did you mean it when you said you weren't going to sell the land?'

'You have to believe me! Yes, Thomas came to the diner, but I meant what I said earlier.'

'Well, it looks like you and your cousin have things to talk about.' Theo storms off the porch into the night.

'No, Theo, wait!'

I want to run out after him. The snow has started to fall again.

'Everything okay?' asks Jed, as the dejected figures head home.

'It's . . . complicated,' I say, watching Theo. I have no idea what to say to him if I go after him.

'I'll get my things sorted and show you Cabane de l'Étoile,' I say, feeling that nothing will be okay now.

## 27

'There really isn't a hotel or something nearby?' Jed repeats, peering into the simple, but now warm *cabane*. He comes inside and closes the door.

I shake my head. 'This is it. It's used in the spring, once the harvest begins.' I pull my case out of the wardrobe.

He frowns.

'They keep the syrup boiling all through the night in the sugar shack, just across the way.' I point, as I pack my belongings. 'They use this place to catch naps, make food and hang out.' For a moment I wish I could be here for the harvest, to smell the sap boiling in the sugar shack and see the smoke rising from the chimney through the trees. But I won't. I pack quicker, pushing down the lid of my case and zipping it up.

I slide it off the bed. 'Keep the fire lit, or it gets cold quickly,' I tell him. 'Oh, and don't mind Ike if he turns up in the morning. He's a turkey. And I was leaving crumbs out for the squirrels, if you could . . .' I trail off.

He's smiling at me. 'You seem quite the local.'

'If only,' I say quietly, and head for the door.

'Do you need a hand?'

'No, I'm fine,' I say, switching on my head torch and stepping out into the darkening evening.

'Okay,' he says. 'Let's find out what we've got here, then get the hell out of this place and back to civilization as soon as we can.' He laughs. 'See you tomorrow.' Without waiting for an answer he closes the door and I take a look around the little porch of the place that has been my home for almost the past couple of weeks.

And then the outside light goes out. I follow the beam from my head torch back to the town square, and to Maple Lodge beyond it, dragging my case in the thick snow behind me. I find the key under the wood-pile on the front porch, where Nancy has told me it's kept, and let myself in. The first thing I need to do is get a fire going.

I leave my case propping open the door to the little wooden house, tired, sad and cold, a bit like me, I think, feeling hugely sorry for myself. How could things have changed so quickly back there? One minute I was exactly where I wanted to be, living for the now, enjoying a newfound sense of belonging, a feeling I had roots here. Now I've never felt more like an outsider, an interloper.

I pick up the axe outside the door on the woodpile, swing it and split the first log I put there, then a second. By the third, the swinging and splitting seem to be lightening my mood.

'I'm guessing you don't need any help, then,' says a voice, which is still as frosty as the frozen icicles hanging over the front of the house. I swing round, axe in the air.

'Woah!' Theo steps back.

I look at the snowy porch, the old barn where the sale took place. 'No, I don't,' I say, with a grateful smile. 'But thank you.'

Theo isn't smiling. Hagrid is beside him, his thick black coat getting covered with snow. He resembles a badger, or maybe a skunk. Do they even have skunks out here? I have no idea. In fact, there's a lot I don't know about this place still. It's not my home. I'm just passing through.

'What about your cousin? Is he settled in?'

I frown. 'I had no idea about him.' I swing and split another log on top of the big trunk it was sitting on. Hagrid takes a sensible two steps back. 'I promise I didn't, Theo. But now the whole community knows about me and why I'm here, and they probably hate me for it.' I take a swing at another log, which splits. 'I wanted to do my best for you all, keep the land for the town, like I told you.'

229

He takes a moment. 'I believe you. I'm sorry I reacted like that.' He takes a deep breath. 'But does your cousin have the same best interests as you do?'

'Could you stop calling him my cousin, please? I'd never met the man or even knew he existed before now. I don't even know how we're related. I've gone from having no relatives to having Harold and now this Jed. I mean, where does he fit into it?' I swing the axe again.

'I think you've probably got enough kindling now,' he says, as I split another log.

'I don't know anything about him or what he wants. But,' I turn to Theo, 'I intend to find out, and get him to understand our thinking. Leave it with me. I'll show him all the best bits of Forêt des Esprits. I had a very good instructor.'

He gives me a smile. I put down the axe and lean on it. The snow tickles my cheeks and nose and I brush it away.

'I promise, Theo,' I say again. 'I'm going to do my best to make him understand that the land's owner needs to be in the town.'

He's clearly worried. 'And you think he'll go for it?'

'Well, I don't know him but who wouldn't fall in love with this place once they get to know it and the town? I'm sure he'll see it too.'

'Look, I'm sorry about that, back there. I don't know what I was thinking, blowing up at you like that. This isn't your fault.'

'It's okay. You're just looking out for the town. They're lucky to have you. You're all lucky to have each other.'

'I could say we're lucky to have you too,' he says, and a small smile pulls at the corners of my mouth. There's one on his lips too. Around us I can hear snow falling from the branches.

At least it looks like we're friends again. My only problem is that this feels a lot more than friendship and that is a whole other complication. But I know I care. I care about him and I care about this town, and I'm determined to make sure nothing happens to it. I need to pull on my big-girl pants again and show my cousin – if that's what he really is – how things work in this neighbourhood.

'Do you want to stay, have a coffee?' I have no idea if I have the makings of such but he holds his hands up.

'I have to get up early and bring in Christmas trees to sell. Bea is going to make mistletoe balls.' I feel a pang as I remember Bea's hurt face as she realized what I'd hidden from her.

'They'll be all over her bed!' I try to laugh but it catches in my throat.

'Along with the cuttings from the paper snowflakes,' he adds, trying to help me out of the hurt I'm feeling.

We smile.

'I'm glad she came back.'

'Me too. Nothing beats home.' He shoves his hands into his pockets and stares at the trees.

'And Mimi?'

He looks surprised.

'Sorry! Not my business!' I pick up an armful of kindling and head for the porch.

'No, it's fine!' He follows me with more kindling. 'There's nothing about her that I'm keeping to myself.'

'Really,' I say firmly, 'it has nothing to do with me.'

I push my case from in front of the door. A huge dump of snow falls from the porch and lands between us. Hagrid jumps back, barks, then throws himself into the pile of snow and rolls.

'See? Who wouldn't love this place? Hagrid certainly does!' I chuckle.

Theo looks at me and, more than anything, I want to go back to where we were earlier this evening and kiss him. But I can't. I won't. Whatever happens now, I'm leaving at the end of the month. And I won't be back. Our stars didn't so much collide as come close and miss. But there is one thing I can't help thinking about.

'If we *are* talking about keeping things to ourselves, though . . .' I find myself saying, intrigued and wondering whether to go on. He cocks his head on one side.

'Yes?'

'You didn't tell me . . .' I walk inside, lay the kindling

beside the stove, and stack it on newspaper with my back to him.

'Tell me what?' I hear from behind me.

'That you used to be an ice-hockey champion,' I say, and wait.

There's a moment's awkward silence and I turn slowly to see him eyeing the floor. Then he says quietly, 'It was a long time ago.' He lifts his head. 'In the past. Like most of the big things in my life. Now, if you're sure you're okay, I'll get going.'

I decide not to push it. 'I am, *merci*.' I put a match to the fire, shut the door, then watch the flames catch and lick up the glass.

'*De rien*,' he says, and calls Hagrid from his snow bath.

I watch as they walk down the drive. Theo stops, looks back, and raises a hand before picking up his skis. I hear their swoosh as he heads back to his own cabin in the woods, alone, like me.

I shouldn't have mentioned it, I think.

I pick up my case, carry it into the front room and put it down. Out of my bag I take the picture I bought at the yard sale and put it on the mantelpiece.

'Back where you belong,' I say, not expecting to feel the twist I get in my chest. Maybe we need to remember the past to find out where we should be going next, I wonder to myself.

# 28

*13 December: 12 days until Christmas*

'*Bonjour!*' Philippe, Eli and Nancy troop into the diner, with the girls' and boys' ice-hockey teams, now all sitting together, laughing and joking.

'We've come for the calendar,' says Charlene, the girls' captain.

'And Ruben's special!' says one of the boys. Suddenly I'm run off my feet, making hot chocolate and warming the bread-and-butter pudding I made earlier that morning, until the school bus arrives, its lights bright in the dark snowy morning. Even the driver comes in for coffee.

'The kids have been telling me about the advent calendar. I hope I'm not too late,' he says, sitting at the counter, hungrily tucking into the bread-and-butter pudding with added cream and syrup.

Bea shuffles out of her room with extreme bed hair, yawning. *'Bonjour!* Morning!' she says, as I hand her a cup of tea and her breakfast pancakes, with Marmite and syrup, and she sits by the fire in the checked wing-back chair and pulls a blanket over her legs.

I wonder how to start putting things right between us. But she's first to speak. 'What's in the calendar today? Have I missed it?' she asks.

'No, you haven't,' I reply. And I'm glad that last night's revelation hasn't ruined everything. It looks like Ruben's calendar is keeping us all together.

'Open it!'

'Yes, do! I've got to get these kids to school,' says the bus driver, his big belly hanging over his belt and his shirt stretching across it, threatening to pop a button, as I top him up with coffee.

I sling my tea-towel over my shoulder and head for the calendar by the Christmas tree. I pull out the piece of paper in today's pocket and unfold it. I can feel all eyes on me, Bea's in particular, and I know I must talk to her and explain.

'It says . . .' my hands are shaking a little, '. . . "Once again, say yes to something."'

'Hey.' One of the lads sitting next to Charlene turns to her. 'Do you fancy going snowboarding after school with me?'

She glances at him in surprise, then smiles. 'Okay, *oui*. Yes!'

235

'Great!' He high-fives her.

Océane sidles up to me. 'My music teacher has asked me to sing at the end-of-term concert.'

'And what did you say?' I hand her another cookie.

'That I'd think about it.'

'So what are you going to say now?'

She looks up at me, cookie in hand. '*Oui!* Yes!' We grin at one another.

'Eli, I have a stew for two slow-cooking. Would you like to come over this evening to share it?' says Nancy.

Eli is totally surprised. '*Oui, oui!*'

Charlene comes and puts her mug on the counter. 'How about I give you that skating lesson, Chloë?' She's beaming too.

'What? N—'

'Uh-huh. Remember the calendar!'

I tut.

'Okay, okay, yes!' I put up my hands in surrender and the girls cheer and clap. 'Now, go on, off to school with you all!' I shoo them and they gather their bags and coats and make for the door.

'*Au revoir!*' they call to me, and to Bea, who smiles and waves them off from her chair by the fire.

Finally, the school bus leaves, with a friendly toot on the horn. And I'm waving once again through the glass at the window.

I turn back to see Philippe, Eli, Nancy and Bea

watching me and the happy little bubble that was inside me just a moment ago has burst.

'Er, more coffee, anyone, tea, Bea?' I grab the coffee pot and top them all up, negotiating my way around the elephant in the room.

'Sorry I'm late.' The door flies open and Theo comes in. 'Couldn't find this morning's delivery list.'

'It's okay, we haven't started. But I think we should,' says Philippe. Theo pulls off his hat and gloves and pushes his hair off his face. They all gather at the table by the fire where Bea is sitting.

'Chloë, grab a coffee. Come and join us. We have a suggestion to put to you.'

Feeling ridiculously nervous, I do as I'm told and join them at the table.

'What kind of suggestion? You want me to leave town – that's it, isn't it?' I feel wretched.

'We have a proposition for you.'

I study the piece of paper in front of me with a figure on it. 'But that must be all of the sugar-shack equipment fund!'

'We've spoken to all the other farmers in the cooperative and we agree that this is the best use of our money. Theo has done a great job in keeping the sugar shack going this year and it looks like we'll have to limp on for another year, do some more fundraising. It's more important that we buy the land so it doesn't go out of the cooperative.'

I feel dreadful. 'I don't want the money!'

'But if you sell it to us, it stays in the cooperative. Safe.'

'And gives you something for Ruben's future,' says Bea, rubbing her belly and letting out a little burp. '*Excusez moi*,' she says. 'It's important to think of their future, I can understand that. You're just doing what's right for future generations, a gift from the past, laying down roots. That's what we do around here.'

I look at the paper. 'But it's not just me now, is it? There's Jed Anderson.'

'All you have to do is say yes,' says Theo.

'Then get Jed on board to agree to it too,' says Nancy. 'But how?'

'Show him why it matters,' says Theo. 'To all of us. Like you said you would.'

'Yes,' I sniff and wipe my nose. 'Of course! I mean *oui*!'

'We're relying on you, Chloë,' says Philippe. 'It's a solid offer. We all get what we want. And in the new year we can start to prepare for the spring and put the taps into the trees, ready for the sap to rise.' He lifts his coffee cup.

'Here's to that.' We all clink our cups, except Bea who raises hers.

'Yes!' I just hope I can achieve what they need me to do.

'I gotta go. I've got a stew to warm through,' says Nancy, with a smile to Eli as she stands and, still looking surprised, he smiles back.

238

# 29

The fire is lit and I'm on the sofa with a rug pulled over me in Maple Lodge, nursing hot chocolate with a slug of the maple moonshine that Nancy slipped into my bag at the diner. 'To help warm up your cousin and make him see the right thing to do.'

I'm curled up, looking at the photographs I took this morning and am sending to Ruben. I've just FaceTimed him and told him about my day, and he told me about his trip to an ice-hockey game, making me think of the girls' team here. I'm tired after all the skiing I did today, but at least I stayed on my feet and didn't make a fool of myself, like I did a few days ago with Theo. My cheeks blush at the memory of his face close to mine as we lay in that heap in the snow. I could feel his hot breath on my lips. I'm remembering his face, his eyes and how I felt, lying there, wanting more than anything to press my lips to his.

Today went a lot quicker. Jed wanted to see every-thing, all the land. There was no time for picnics on the tabletop. He was on a mission and continually wanted to race me. 'Race you to the lake! Last one has to buy the drinks!' I tried to explain there wasn't even a bar in town and there was no need to race, but it seems that Jed adds a competitive element to every-thing, and likes to win. I think of him standing on the tabletop, barely taking in the view before he was 'racing' me on the downhill slope and standing grin-ning at the bottom. It seemed that winning was more important than taking in the view, the trees, the wild-life I tried to point out. It was exhausting. I wondered what Ruben would make of Jed. At some points I tried to find out how we are both related to Harold, but he wasn't interested in going over the family tree. I just need to know for myself how we're related and how we've both ended up inheriting this land. He was clearly more interested in finding out how much land there was and covering as much of it as possible in one trip.

After I'd left him, I'd agreed to meet Charlene, Océane and the other girls by the lake for my skating lesson. I'm so tired I can barely keep my eyes open now. I'm aching, sore and I'll have a bruise on my backside as a souvenir of my first attempts. *Thank you, Ruben*. I smile to myself.

There's a shuffling outside on the porch, breaking into my thoughts, and my cheeks are glowing from the fire and the moonshine. It's probably Ike, staking out my new place.

I put down the hot chocolate and walk over to the door in my socks, my thighs and calves throbbing.

There's another shuffle from the porch. Surely Ike can't be waiting for me at this time of night just to catch me out in the morning. He'll freeze out there.

I put my hand on the door to shoo him away, when there's a knock. I wonder if it's Jed. I've told him about the offer on the land and he's taking some time to think about it. Let's hope this is it.

'*Bonjour!* Hi!' I'm sounding more French-Canadian by the day.

It's not Jed, it's Theo, and instead of being disappointed, my stomach does an excited flip. He's smiling bashfully, having dragged a small misshapen tree behind him up to the porch.

'Hi! This is for you!' he says, holding it in front of him. 'It's to say sorry. And thank you.'

I look at it.

'I know most people bring flowers. Round here we do things a little differently.'

'I can see that!'

'His name is Sid. He was the last one left today at the store. No one wanted him.'

'Well, I certainly do! Come in, Sid!' I stand back as Theo comes in, carrying the tree in one hand and something wrapped in a sleeping bag in the other. Hagrid follows and flops onto the floor, taking up most of the space.

'On your own? I don't want to interrupt.' Theo looks around.

'Are you checking up on me?' I look at him sideways.

'No . . . not really. Just seeing how things were going,' he says, sheepish. 'And to bring you a tree. You can't be here for Christmas and not have a tree.'

I look at it, sorely out of shape, and giggle. 'Thank you . . . and, yes, I'm on my own. Jed had some calls to make or something and is mulling over the offer for the land. But the weather's bad again, so he might have trouble with his calls.'

'Good!' I think I hear Theo say. He goes on hastily, 'I mean, good . . . that you're here, that he's not . . . Just good.' He's unusually flustered and even a little nervous. But I know how much this deal means to him and everyone else. I'm nervous too.

I reach for the little tree. 'Ouch!'

'Watch out for spikes!' he says, as an afterthought.

I can smell it already. Beautiful pine. It's what the forest on the other side of the lake smells like. It's a beautiful tree. 'I've never had a real one before,' I say quietly.

'What – never? Not when you were growing up?'

'Dad used to bring out the family artificial one when he was still alive,' I say.

'I'm sorry.'

'Don't be.' I put up a hand, not wanting pity. 'But after he died I just kept doing the same thing.' I give him a wry smile. 'And now it's just me and Ruben at home, well, we have an artificial one too. It's done us okay.'

'Until this year,' he states.

'Until this year. You've ruined me! I'll need a real tree every Christmas now! To remind me of Forêt des Esprits, if nothing else.'

'Do you miss him?' he asks softly.

'My dad? Yes, very much.' My throat tightens.

'Actually, I meant Ruben's dad.'

'Oh. Erm. I'm not sure. I'm not sure about anything right now. After he left, I wondered if I'd done the right thing. I was numb for a long time. Especially after I'd had Ruben. Just getting through each day with a baby depending on me for everything. I was angry. I needed him there. Well, I thought I needed him.'

'But you clearly did a good job,' he says gently.

I blush. 'And then, well, I just wanted things to stay the same, for Ruben. So he felt his dad was still in his life. The town, the school, the routines, it was as if I built Lucas into our lives even though he wasn't there.'

'And now?'

I swallow. 'I think I was keeping Lucas in our lives, not letting him go, for myself.' I take a deep breath. 'I might do things a little differently from now on.'

He looks straight at me, and that's another memory I want to take with me.

'What about you and Mimi? Do you ever wonder if you did the right thing, splitting up?'

He sighs, a long one.

'Mimi and I grew up here, in the town. I played ice hockey . . . as you know. I captained the team and a scout came out to see us. Philippe organized it. Someone he knew. I was picked up and played professionally. Mimi came with me to Montréal and we married. We had what a lot of people would think was a great life. But I always missed it here. Even built the cabin after my parents died. We'd come here for holidays and weekends, but she never enjoyed it. She couldn't wait to get back to the city.'

The fire crackles behind us.

'But you wanted to stay here? Tough decision.'

He sighs again. 'I . . . There was this one match.'

I can tell he's back there, thinking about it.

'I was coming to the end of my sporting career, but I wanted to go out on a high. I went for the final shot, made the decision to go out in glory. But I missed. We lost the championship. It was down to me.' I watch him take another breath. 'I never played again.'

'Never?'

'They tried to get me to stay on, coaching. Mimi was furious. Couldn't understand why I'd just lost all trust in my instinct. I couldn't do it. Scared of letting everyone down.'

'And that's why you still won't coach now,' I say, understanding.

'Mimi and I split up. I wanted to come back here. She wanted to stay, and got together with a teammate . . . a friend of mine, or so I thought. But it didn't end well. I knew it wouldn't. I was worried for her.'

'And do you still love her?'

He takes a moment. 'No. I wish her happiness, but I'm not in love with her.' I think back to Eli saying they hadn't seen her since . . . Clearly this was the 'since'. Since she and Theo had split up.

I reach out to take the tree again, feeling its spikes, but also a shockwave between us. A connection so strong that I snatch away my hand again. I can't let this happen! I cannot fall in love with this man or this place. I'm leaving. But at the same time I know I'm in love with him. And there isn't anything I can do about it. Here we are, standing in the cabin's front room, him in his coat, holding a Christmas tree and a sleeping bag under his arm, sharing our innermost thoughts. And there is nowhere right now I'd rather be.

'Right,' I say. 'You'd better show me what to do with

a real Christmas tree.' I can't take my eyes off his, rubbing my hands down my thighs, feeling hot all over.

'Oh, and I brought this in case you were busy and hadn't had time to cook.'

He hands me the very heavy sleeping bag. Inside I find a warm casserole dish. 'By way of another apology,' he says. 'Beef stew, with—'

'With maple syrup!' we say together, and laugh.

'I'm learning!'

'Must be in the blood!' Theo jokes.

'No one's ever brought me a casserole before,' I say.

'Another first! Come on, let's eat!' he says. 'If you're not too tired. And then we'll decorate the tree.'

'Yes! I'd like that very much.' I'm unable to resist the food, the tree or the man who's brought them to me, his face lit by the fire and the soft glow from the lamps.

At which point Hagrid snores loudly, helping to break the moment.

That night as I lie in bed, listening to the hoot of the owls, I realize I've been standing at a crossroads in my life for far too long. When Lucas left, I never really moved forward. I've been standing there all this time, wondering what would have happened if I'd gone with him, if he'd loved me enough to stay, if I'd loved him the way I'm in love with Theo. Was it just that I was scared of being alone? But, as scary as it was, I did it. Staying put had meant he was still there with me, in some way, where we had left each other. But he just didn't love me enough to stay. And I didn't love him enough to go with him. He was, and is, a great father. Maybe it's time to leave the crossroads, pick a new path. I feel something so different now, warmth and excitement, and I swear my frozen heart is thawing.

# 30

*14 December: 11 days until Christmas*

It's snowing hard, and Ike has trouble chasing me in the snow this morning. Even though I've moved into Maple Lodge, he's found me!

Jed is waiting on the diner's porch, shivering, hands in pockets and, despite his ski jacket, without a suitable hat. Everyone knows around here that the right hat is important.

I pull up on my skis and turn to check for Ike. He's some way behind.

'Come on, keep up!' I call. He seems to take that as encouragement and gives a final push to catch me up. I turn back to Jed.

'Jed, *bonjour*, good morning.' I smile. 'How did you sleep?'

'Dreadful! How do people stay in that place? It's cold, dark. The Wi-Fi is dreadful and there are all kinds of noises at night. As for trying to keep the fire going . . .'

'Come on in. I'll put the coffee on, check on Bea, then make you some maple-syrup pancakes.'

'No more pancakes. This place seems to run on sugar.'

'It does,' I agree, moving behind the counter to switch on the coffee machine and the oven. 'It's what gives people the energy to work through the cold.' I'm smiling.

'But I'll take a coffee, thank you. Black.'

He checks his phone and stamps his feet. I head to the wood-burning stove, load it with logs, open the vents and the fire leaps into life. It reminds me of the firelight last night as Theo and I ate the delicious beef stew with maple dumplings from bowls at the little table in front of the fire, with a candle on the table and another on the windowsill as the snow fell silently outside and Hagrid snored. Then we decorated the tree with paper chains and snowflakes that Bea had made that day and, finally, a string of lights as white and bright as the stars in the sky at night. Afterwards, we finished the bottle of wine Theo had brought and I'd opened. We talked, him about Mimi and how coming back here had seemed the best solution after they'd split up, and me about how I'd stayed put when Lucas left. I'd hoped that would make Ruben feel safe and secure, even though his dad wasn't there. We sat side by side on the sagging sofa until finally the wine was gone. Much as I wanted to reach out my hand to his stretched along the back of the sofa, I was dead on my feet – well, falling asleep on the sofa. After a round of yawns, we knew the evening had come to an end. He stood to leave, put on his coat and hat, Hagrid standing and stretching, and he kissed my cheek. After he'd gone, I kept my fingers on my cheek where the kiss had been, glad we hadn't suggested going to bed, knowing that that answer would have been 'Yes. *Oui!*' But that I really couldn't have stayed awake, never mind how much I'd have liked to.

I pour Jed coffee and he sits at the counter. I take a deep breath.

'So,' I say, hoping to have good news for everyone when they arrive in the diner.

He says nothing.

I pull out the family tree that Nigel Berry gave me and lay it on the counter. Jed barely glances at it.

'This is a turn-up for the books. You're related to Jack, my great-grandfather's brother.'

He sips the coffee. 'So the heir hunter told me. To Jack's wife, her sister or something like that.' He waves a hand.

'Looks like we really are related, then.' Just for a moment I wonder if we're going to have some big hug, but there's nothing. He's peering into his coffee and grimacing. 'So,' I take a deep breath and clap my hands together, 'the offer from the cooperative. What do you think?'

'Oh, I see. Well, it's an offer,' he says, with a tight smile.

'So can we say yes? I know it's what I want to do. Let the heir hunters know. We could get this wrapped up before the Christmas fair and you could be home for the holidays. It's really important to the community. That's why I wanted you to see it, the trees, meet everyone. So that you'd realize how important to them this parcel of land is.'

'I know how important it is to them. You told me,' he says, with an edge to his voice that is making me uneasy. 'But this inheritance is also important to me.'

'Okay. Well . . . there's still more of the place I want you to see,' I tell him.

'I've seen all I need to, thank you.' An unpleasant smile hangs on his lips.

'You could stay for the fair, at least? It's just ten days away.'

'Well, I'm sure you'll enjoy it, but Christmas for me is a little more . . . civilized.'

I bristle.

He checks his phone. 'I'll let you know my thoughts when I'm back at home,' he says. 'I have a taxi on its way. Big poker game with the boys tonight.' Clearly that's more his idea of fun. The snow is getting heavier and piling on the steps up to the diner's porch. Theo is out there, sweeping. He's leaving me to it.

'Can't you tell me now? As I say, it's a decent offer and it would be good to get this agreed, then let the heir hunters do the paperwork. All sorted in time for Christmas.' I'm looking out at Theo, who is clearly desperate for news – good news.

'Damn it!' Jed says. 'My taxi's cancelled! The road to the airport is blocked by snow. Looks like I'm stuck in this godforsaken place for a while longer.'

I frown. 'I'd hardly call it that. If anything, I'd say this place is really rather special, if you just look.'

'Whatever. Could this be any worse?'

'Well,' I say, 'now you can try the new maple and carrot cake I've been working on. Made with the local syrup.' I put on a smile and pull a bottle from the chiller. 'Whole maple syrup from the trees right here. I bet I could get a few sent over to you every year if you agree to the deal today.'

He sighs loudly. 'Don't you have *anything* without maple syrup?' He's frustrated.

'Absolutely nothing!' I hold up my cream-cheese-frosted maple and carrot cake. 'Absolutely nothing at all!'

# 31

*23 December: 2 days until Christmas*

'What's in the advent calendar?'

The schools have broken up for the holidays, and everyone is out and about, organizing themselves for the Christmas fair tomorrow. Each day for the past nine days the town has popped in to find out what the advent calendar has said. At its instruction, we had a games evening, everyone bringing board games to the diner and taking turns to play different ones, the boys and girls mixing instead of sitting at opposite ends of the room. Nancy and Eli faced each other down over a game of draughts. Jed got rather competitive over Happy Families when he lost Mrs Bun, and Theo had to remind him that it was just a game.

Then there was cinema night, when we all watched

*A Muppet Family Christmas* on a makeshift screen, made from a sheet, and ate popcorn and hotdogs, just like Ruben and I would do at home, though these were maple drizzled. Theo and I shared popcorn and glances, but neither of us has taken the next step. We know we can't. Why let ourselves go there just to get hurt again? This is fine. This is warm and comfortable. This won't hurt as much when I have to leave. We'll be left with the what-if, a few happy memories and smiles.

Another day the calendar told us, 'Say hello and happy Christmas to everyone you see.' The town buzzed with '*Bonjour*' and *joie de vivre*. There've been baking days in the diner and pizza nights. 'Go for a walk', and we went on a lantern walk through the trees at dusk. Everyone, the whole community, was carrying lanterns, following the trails that Theo has kept clear all this time, listening to the owls and large lumps of snow falling. Suddenly the trails and pathways weren't scary to me. There was peace in them. We stopped at the clearing near the tree that has the heart carved into it and, yes, I finally hugged a tree. Wait until I tell Ruben that one. There was 'Tell a Christmas joke' day, and, yes, there really was 'Why did Santa go to the doctor? Because of his bad elf!' and my favourite, read by Océane, 'What's the difference between a snowman and a snow-woman? Snowballs!' And Theo's 'My wife just gave me a telling off for throwing a snowball at our son. And on top of that I've just been banned from the maternity ward!' Bea laughed so much I thought she was going to go into labour there and then. But the laughter that filled the diner was joyous. And every day since, people have been dropping in to find out what's in the calendar.

'So what's in it today?' asks the mother of one of the ice-hockey girls, as I hand her a coffee to take out. 'My daughter's told me all about it!'

I unfold the message: ' "Do something for yourself." '

'Ooh, what?' she asks.

'Um,' I say, and wonder what it might be. 'Maybe a hot bath later with bubbles from Nancy's store after we've got everything sorted for tomorrow's Christmas fair.'

'Good plan. I will too! Been ages since I've had a relaxing bath with a good book.'

Bea has got out of bed against the doctor's orders. She's rubbing her big round belly, sitting in the armchair by the stove, with a patchwork quilt over her knees.

'I promise not to interfere with anything,' she says, holding up her hands. 'I'm just going to sit here and listen.'

'Well!' says Theo, like a strict older brother.

'I can't sit back there when all the excitement is going on out here,' she pleads.

'Okay, but you're not to get involved in organizing or overdo things, promise?'

'I do, Theo, really!'

She really is glowing, I think. Such a difference from when I first got here and she could barely think about giving up the reins on the business or the Christmas fair.

She's making more paper snowflakes and paper chains. We can't move for them. They're hanging from the ceiling, the porch and in the store. But you can't have too many paper snowflakes, I think, and plan to do them again next year at home. Next year, I think, this will all be a distant memory. I pull another bread-and-butter pudding from the oven and drizzle it with syrup. The smell is amazing: caramelizing, browning, toasting bread and plump raisins soaked in maple moonshine. It's definitely become a favourite at the diner. I have to remember to write down the recipe for Bea before I leave . . . I quickly push the thought away.

We all sit at the big table in the middle of the diner, apart from Bea who stays on the wingback chair. The candles in the window are lit and the snow is banked up in the square panes there.

'So how are things looking for the fair?' I start the meeting.

'I've got paper chains and paper snowflakes for the stalls!' says Bea, holding up the latest one proudly.

'I've got some more trees and mistletoe balls to sell,' says Theo. 'Goes without saying all the cash will go to the fund.'

They thank him.

'And, of course, there's plenty of syrup to buy,' says Nancy.

'I'll make cakes,' I say. 'Lots. Ruben's special, chocolate logs and fruit cakes, and Christmas puddings, like the new one I made last night. Anyone want to try?'

'*Oui!* Yes!' They dive into the plate I've put in the middle of the table. I take a slice over to Bea. She puts down her paper snowflake and lifts the cake to her nose. She sniffs, then looks at me and bites. Her eyes close and she chews slowly. Then she opens her eyes. 'It's fantastic. It's Christmas, spice and maple trees all in one bite! It's Forêt des Esprits! We're certainly going to miss you and your cakes around here!' she says, and a lump catches in my throat. I give a little cough.

'I'm going to miss around here too.' I put my hand on hers.

'It'll be back to waffles and bacon!' she says, and we laugh. Then she gives a pained grimace, as if she felt a twinge in her stomach.

'You okay?' I ask.

'Yes, just kicking,' she says, rubbing her sides. 'Reminding me of what's to come! I think these boys love the cakes too.'

'You sure it's boys, then?'

'I think so. I just have a feeling. Did you know?' she says, taking another bite, and letting her eyes shut in

257

delight at the rich, fruity, sticky cake. Dark sultanas, candied peel and glacé cherries are crammed into it.

'Yes, I think I did,' I say, hands on hips. 'And, of course, the ultrasound confirmed it. But my instincts were right.'

'It's all we can rely on in life, isn't it, our own instincts?' she says thoughtfully, and I wonder if she's going to tell me about Harold being the father. But she says nothing more and I'm not going to bring it up. It's for her to tell me if she wants to. I turn back to the table and Theo suddenly looks down at his feet.

'What else do we need to get ready for tomorrow?' I ask.

'The ice-hockey teams are organizing skating on the lake for anyone who wants to take part, hoping to get a few donations for the sugar-shack fund.'

'And Nicole and Nicolas, the horses, will be giving sleigh rides around the trails. We'll put the lights up along them this afternoon. The snow should be stopping about then.'

'Eli and I will be doing the barbecue, maple-drizzled ribs and burgers,' says the mayor. 'Goes without saying that the profits will go to the fund.'

These people have become my friends and I feel wretched.

'I'm sorry, guys. If it was just me, I wouldn't be taking any of your money.' I feel bad. If Jed agrees to the sale, they'll still have to raise more funds for new sugar-shack equipment.

'We know,' they all say. And it makes me feel even worse that they're so understanding.

'At least you've given us this opportunity to keep the land in the community and we're grateful for that,' says Philippe.

'Let's hope we get visitors from the nearby towns,' says Nancy, and I can't help noticing that she and Eli are sitting close to each other.

'I've posted on all the tourism websites around,' says Dax. 'Should be a good turn-out.'

'People will come for miles just for this pudding!' says Eli, clearing his plate.

'And the band is organized,' says Philippe.

'And I have the bar ready to set up in the store,' says Theo.

We regard him with interest, wondering how he's made space among the boxes.

'Océane is going to help me make hot drinks and serve in here,' I say. 'So we're looking good.'

I can see Jed Anderson outside, kicking around in the snow while he's on the phone. Why hasn't he given us an answer yet? Surely there is only one: *'Oui!'* And it can't come soon enough.

I spend the whole day baking and cooking. Big batches of bread-and-butter pudding, Christmas puddings, chocolate logs and gingerbread ponies, based on Nicole and Nicolas. I'm just pulling out a batch of chocolate-chip cookies from the oven when the bell goes over the door. My heart gives a little leap. I hadn't noticed until now but it's getting darker out there. Nearly time to lock up for the day. But the candles look so inviting in the window and the fire is cheerfully flickering. I could stay here all day and night. I love it.

'Wow, the smell is amazing in here. How's it going?' Theo comes in and shuts the door behind him.

'Fine,' I say, shattered, rubbing a floury hand across my forehead. I haven't spoken to Jed Anderson all day, and I've enjoyed not having to think about him for a bit.

'Nearly done?' he asks.

Cakes and puddings cover every available space. Bea has gone to bed, tired from the comings and goings in the diner as stalls set up outside, more lights going up along the maple trails and signs pointing the way. 'Just got to get things away and be in early to finish setting up.'

'I'm going to check the lights on the trails, and wondered if you wanted to join me.'

I smile. ' "Do something for yourself!" ' I say aloud, reminding myself of Ruben's advent calendar.

'Ruben's right. Come on, you've been working hard. Everyone needs a break.'

'I'd love to! I'll just tidy away and grab my coat.' I feel a tingle of excitement.

# 32

Nicole and Nicolas are waiting outside, their ginger coats groomed, blond manes brushed with red ribbons plaited into them, dark hoofs polished and glistening, as the snow gently settles on their hindquarters.

'Ready?' Theo holds out a hand to me. I take it and he pulls me up onto the leather bench seat of the sleigh. Our eyes connect, holding each other's gaze, and there is so much unsaid that could be said. But, right now, I'm happy to be here, beside him, with the snow falling, as if we're being showered in icing sugar. He smiles, not taking his eyes off me, and hands me a thick woollen blanket to go across my knees. I pull it over myself and nod. I'm feeling very much ready.

Hagrid jumps up into the sleigh behind us, sitting up tall, clearly looking forward to the ride.

Theo clicks to the horses from the corner of his mouth, giving a little flick of the reins, and they move off. The trails are wide and he's worked hard to push back all the snow and clear them. Along the route down towards the lake, where the lines connect the trees ready for the sap to rise and be harvested, festoon lighting shows the way.

'It's beautiful!' I breathe, looking up at the snow-laden branches. It's a long way from Mae's inflatable snowman at home and the electronic snow machine throwing patterns at the wall, keeping half the street awake at night. This is peaceful. An owl hoots and Theo turns to me. I feel myself light up, like the snowy trees around me, in the white glow. I don't think I've ever felt more alive than I do in this moment. Whatever else happens in my life, I will always remember this, with the mountaintop picnic, the lantern walk, linking arms and sharing popcorn at the cinema night, and the evening when we decorated little Sid the Christmas tree together.

I'm beginning to know this trail now, the turns and dips, leading towards the lake and the mountaintop on the other side, overlooking the fields where the cattle graze in summer and the best Christmas trees grow. Where I fell, and where we had our picnic, and where we walked with the lanterns. These are really special memories I'm taking home with me.

'What's on your mind?' says Theo, steadying the horses as they make their way through the forest slowly.

'Just thinking about going home.'

He raises an eyebrow. 'Homesick?'

'No. Grateful that I have all these memories to take with me. Thanks to Ruben.'

'Still a couple more days to go. Wonder what he's got planned.'

'Wait!' I say, as we near the tree in the heart of the forest.

He slows the horses.

I slide the blanket off my knees and jump down, then make my way to the tree. I reach up and touch the heart engraved there. 'This was him declaring his love for her. They thought they'd found what everyone is looking for. But it was whipped away from them. I guess a bit of me will always be here while this is.'

He nods. 'While the trees are here, part of you will be here too. It's where your roots are.'

I pat the heart on the tree one more time, then put my arms around its trunk for one last hug, shut my eyes and take in the moment, how it smells, fresh and clean, with snow in the air. How it feels, rough and patterned. What I can hear: snow falling from branches. I open my eyes and try to commit it to memory, the trees around it. Like Theo said, you start to get to know them. I just wish I could be here for the maple harvest and know how the syrup tastes straight from the sugar shack. Then I turn back to Theo, climb onto the sleigh and pull the blanket over me. I'm saying hello and goodbye to my ancestors who planted trees here but never knew what their future would be.

'You ready?' Theo asks.

'I am.' Here, I feel right. I have roots. I have a past connection to this place and I wish it could be in my future too, all of it, I think, glancing at Theo. But it can't. I have to say goodbye. As the horses move off, I brush away the tears that have filled my eyes. As I do, the lake comes into view. The sight is breathtaking. 'Beautiful!' I'm staring at it, illuminated by lights hanging from the trees there.

'It is, isn't it?' he says, as if he's seeing it for the first time too.

He pulls up the horses.

'Where is everyone?' I ask. 'Where are the ice-hockey teams?'

He slides down from the sleigh, securing the horses' reins. They seem to understand and stand. 'No idea.' He seems puzzled. 'I left them here when I came to fetch you, I told them we'd be back.'

There, by the frozen lakeside, on a snowy bench, are two pairs of skates.

'Looks like we're going to be their first customers.' He grins at me. 'Fancy giving it a go? I mean, you probably don't want to. I know you don't skate.'

'Erm, actually, I do!' I smile.

'What?'

'I do want to, and I do skate!'

'I thought you said you didn't.'

' "Say yes!" That's what Ruben said. So I did. Océane and Charlene taught me.'

'Well, in that case, let's do it!' He beams.

We pull off our boots and put on the skates. I'm nervous. I've only done this once before, for all my bravado. Theo sees my apprehension and holds out a hand. I take it gratefully and he leads me onto the icy, frozen lake. I wobble at first, think about turning back, but he holds my hand firmly, then guides me over the ice as if it's the most natural thing in the world. Holding Theo's hand feels like that too. We skate in time with each other, snatching glances, and I feel like a schoolgirl with a huge crush. That was the glorious bit. The crush, the kiss, the dating. Maybe this is just the same but backwards, the dating, the kiss and the crush . . . not that we've actually kissed, but nearly.

Suddenly I stumble, trip and, although Theo tries to catch me, I fall. I'm not a schoolgirl with a crush any more, I remind myself, feeling stupid. I'm a mum with a life to go home to. A school Ruben is happy in. He has friends, stability, and I have those too, plus a job, a house. More than anything, I want to try to buy that house so Ruben can have a future, knowing there is something solid I've left behind. I've spent my life trying to keep things the same, so Ruben would feel safe. I look at the ice where I've fallen, the trees, the sky. I know now that it was me who needed to feel safe by staying put. I've been living in the past. I've never wanted to be with anyone else, not after Lucas. I've needed to make a change. Isn't that what Ruben's advent calendar's done? Forced me to make a change? And have I found I like it!

'Come on,' says Theo, holding out a hand to me, smiling that lopsided smile. He pulls me to my feet, and I find myself in his arms. I slide mine around him and, finally, our lips meet. They're exactly where they're meant to be. Home. And, inside me, it's like all the festoon lighting has come on at once. I feel lit up from the inside, as if anything is possible.

*Clunk!*

Something hits the ice beside us. We break apart, still with our arms around each other.

'Maybe not as alone as we thought!' says Theo, gesturing at the snowball that's landed at our feet.

Another swiftly hits the ground. 'Cut that out!' he calls, and I laugh. I'm looking too, and can't see anyone but I know the direction it came from.

'Seems there's no privacy, even out in the forest,' he says, leaning his forehead against mine.

'I'd better get back to the diner. This was lovely. Thank you.' I lean in to him once more, taking one more kiss with me, when something catches my eye and I watch as an ice-hockey stick slides across the ice and stops at his feet.

This time I hear a snigger coming from the bushes beside the lake. He looks at the stick, then back at me.

'Did you do this?'

I hold up my hands. 'I had nothing to do with it.'

He glances left and right, then bends to the stick and picks it up, holding it in both hands, as if he's feeling the weight of a newborn baby. Then he drops it to his side and does a practice swing, as if he can't help himself.

Suddenly, a puck whistles past me. He catches it cleanly, instinctively. My eyes are wide open. That could have done some damage. I step back and shrug. 'You never know what will happen when you just say *oui*!'

He hesitates, looks at the puck and the stick, and I think he's about to throw them both to the ground. He grips the handle of the stick, then raises his chin. 'Okay! Come on out! If you want to play, I'll take you on! Whether it's clean or dirty!' he calls, and suddenly from behind the bushes come the girls' team, led by Océane and Charlène, cheering and yelling.

'Océane, you did this?' I stop her, as she skates up beside me.

'Sometimes people need a push, or a great big shove in the right direction! And to say, "*Oui.*"' She beams and is back on the ice with Theo as the puck is passed to and fro and shots to goal are taken and scored with shouts of excitement!

I sit on the bench in the sleigh, watching, the horses waiting patiently.

It's just like being at back at home, waiting on the sidelines at rugby, only there it would be raining, not snowing gently.

Finally, they all high-five each other. Pink-cheeked, glowing and out of breath, they skate towards me.

'I want to see you back here for training next week. We've got some moves to work on and fitness to sort out,' Theo calls.

'*Oui*, Coach! Yes, Coach!' they shout as one, and high-five each all over again.

'So, Coach, is it?' I say, as the team take off their skates. 'I'll meet you in the diner for hot chocolate, girls!' I call after them.

'Well, they could do with a little help,' he says, rolling his head from side to side. 'And it was good to be on the ice again.'

In the sleigh he drives the horses, one hand on the reins, the other holding mine. No matter how hard I try to stop this, my instincts are taking me in one direction towards a night with this man. I want to remember every minute of it.

We pull up at the diner. The lights are on. I wonder if Océane has let them in already.

'You go in. I'll put the horses away and join you. Perhaps we could take dinner and a bottle of maple moonshine to Maple Lodge later.'

'I'd like that, very much,' I say, leaning in and kissing him softly on the lips. My body thrills with anticipation for what's to come. This may not be for ever, but I'm living in the moment, doing something for me, because right now I'm just me. Not a mum, or a daughter looking after her sick father, or an ex of Lucas, just me. And tonight I want to have the memory of spending the night with a man I've fallen for, however much it will hurt when I have to leave.

I slide from the sleigh and find myself humming a Christmas tune. 'Three French hens, two turtle doves and a partridge in a pear tree . . .' I sing, with a smile in my voice and a spring in my step, even though I ache from the ice skating and the bump from where I fell. I feel really happy.

I open the door to the diner to see just two people sitting at a table. They look up at me.

'Mimi!' I say, in surprise. 'What are you doing here?' And then I see the person sitting opposite her. Jed Anderson is smiling at me.

'I've come to check on how my sister is doing, of course. It's Christmas, after all, and I'm helping Jed to get to know more about the area, the land . . .' she pauses '. . . and its worth.'

All thoughts of a romantic night ahead melt like the snow making puddles at my feet. And I suddenly feel cold, very cold indeed.

# 33

*24 December: 1 day until Christmas*

'Buy something and wrap it up from me,' instructs the note in the advent calendar, early that morning. I hold it to my lips, thinking about Ruben, and I intend to do exactly as he says. Later in the afternoon I walk around the fair and stop at a stall selling silver jewellery. I buy a small silver maple leaf on a chain and plan to wrap it up from Ruben, a reminder of my time here. My heart squeezes. I wish he was with me right now.

By six o'clock that evening, the fair is in full swing and I'm so busy in the diner I haven't time to think about how much I'm missing Ruben. Hot chocolate and maple-syrup cookies are flying off the counter. 'Thank goodness I've got you to help me, Océane.'

Outside on the decorated bandstand, next to the Christmas tree, which is lit with white festoon lighting, Philippe and the doctor are playing jazzy Christmas songs, and Bea is singing from a stool on the stage. The doctor is on the saxophone, Philippe on the slide trombone. His boot and crutches are nowhere to be seen. He doesn't even limp.

The horses, with Theo driving them, are giving families rides on the sleigh through the forest while the snow falls. The lake is busy with skaters and Eli is cooking up a storm on the outdoor barbecue, serving ribs and burgers, with Nancy's help, while I make portions of poutine in the fryer to go with them.

'Two coffees and poutines, please.'

It's Jed.

'Jed, you're still here. With Mimi arriving, I assumed the road would be open and you'd be on your way home.'

'Thought I'd hang around a little longer. Check on my . . . our inheritance. I want to make sure we're getting everything that's owed to us.'

'But nothing's owed to us—' I start to say.

'We'll be sitting right over there!' He cuts across me and points to where another man is sitting with his back to us.

I freeze. 'Isn't that Thomas Tremblay from Tremblay Syrups?'

'That's right. He's keen to see how things are done around here.'

'Really?'

'Yes. You know, a lot of businesses could learn a thing or two from one another. And he's a keen poker player too. Might get a game in.'

'Right. I suppose so. Here's your coffees. I'll bring over the poutine.'

'It was you who made me realize what we have here and think about what's really valuable.'

'That's great!' I say. Does that mean I haven't ruined everything? He could be about to accept the locals' offer . . . 'Look, if you don't have anything planned for tomorrow, perhaps we could have Christmas lunch together. Bury the hatchet, so to speak,' I offer.

'Where?'

'Here, at the diner?'

He shrugs. 'Okay,' he says, matter-of-fact, making me bristle. 'I mean, it's not like there's anywhere else to eat around here, is there?'

'I meant if you don't have anywhere else you'd rather be. The road's open now. Don't you want to go home?'

'What? Back to all that family stuff?'

'Yes!'

'No, thanks, not for me! Last thing I want to do is spend time with people I've got nothing in common with.'

As the fair begins to wind down, I make some hot chocolate, then stand on the porch to drink it. The band are finishing their tunes. People are picking up their Christmas trees, wreaths and mistletoe balls from Dax, who's manning the store. He waves from the neighbouring porch and I wave back. 'You want some hot chocolate?' I ask.

'Yes, please.'

And I go inside to make him some.

Jed and Thomas Tremblay are pulling on their coats, laughing and joking like old friends, patting each other's shoulders.

'Did you get to see the lake? Try skating?' I ask, as I go over to their table, trying to hear what they're talking about.

'I did. It's great!' says Thomas.

'And the best views are from the mountaintop, where you can see the eagles in daylight. Jed should show you.'

'You sound as if you've been living here all your life,' says Jed.

'It sort of feels like that.'

They wish me good night and Jed says he'll see me tomorrow.

Just one last meal with him. Try to leave on a good note, I tell myself. I don't want anything to ruin the memories I've made of this place. Perhaps tomorrow we can agree on the sale of the land to the town and finally celebrate everyone getting what they wanted.

I take the hot chocolate outside and hand it over the

porch to Dax, his hands in thick working gloves for carrying trees. 'Thanks,' he says, watching Thomas Tremblay and Jed say goodbye to each other and go their separate ways.

'Jed says he wanted to understand the value of the place,' I say, 'so maybe tomorrow we can agree on the sale to the community.'

'Well, there's been a fair contribution towards the fund tonight,' says Dax. 'People have been really generous.'

'It means a lot,' I say.

'And what about you, when you get home?' Dax says, between sips of hot chocolate.

'I'm hoping to buy my own home.' I tell him. 'Put down some roots for Ruben.'

He nods thoughtfully. 'It feels good to know you have a home.'

We stare at the snowy square in front of the store.

'Well, Happy Christmas!' says Dax.

'Thanks, Dax. And to you.'

Theo walks up the steps, back from having put the horses to bed.

'Happy Christmas, Theo.'

'Thanks for all your help, Dax,' he says, pulling off his gloves and reaching into his pocket for a small roll of notes.

'No problem,' says Dax.

'I'll lock up,' Theo tells him.

Dax waves and is gone. I have no idea where home

is for Dax or what his Christmas will be, although I assume he'll see Océane and his grandparents at some stage. But that doesn't matter. What matters is that all these people come together when it matters.

'Why isn't Philippe on his crutches this evening?' I ask.

'It would appear that his foot isn't nearly as bad as it seemed. Once I agreed to help out and coach the girls, he was back on two.' And we laugh.

'Theo? Will you come for Christmas lunch tomorrow, here at the diner? I'm cooking for Bea. I expect that means Mimi too. And Jed is coming now too.'

'Sounds like an interesting mix.'

'Will you?'

'Wouldn't miss it,' he says, leans in and kisses me, 'but I'd much rather spend Christmas morning with you.' He kisses me again and I feel like all my presents have come at once. It may not be what Ruben thought he was giving me, but I couldn't feel more excited and happy.

Finally, as we lock the store and the diner, and turn off the lights, except the ones on the Christmas tree, I lead him away from the square and up the snowy lane, Hagrid following, towards Maple Lodge where he kisses me all over again on the front porch and we let ourselves in. Hagrid sprawls in front of the fire and Theo leads me upstairs to the bedroom. Christmas on my own doesn't seem half as lonely as I thought it would be.

# 34

*25 December, Christmas Day: 6 days until Ruben comes home*

'Make bread sauce!' I read the note from the star pocket on the advent calendar. I always did a present for 25 December, tucked into a star-shaped pocket. Usually sweets or chocolate. And there's a PS: 'Happy Christmas, Mum. Thanks for everything you do for me. You're the best. Hope you enjoyed your advent calendar. You're going to have to take it from here! Just six days until I'm home.'

'Bread sauce? With turkey?' says Theo, kissing the back of my neck as I read and reread the note. I turn and kiss him, long and lingering, then remember I really must turn on the oven. We're in the diner in the dark morning light, trying not to wake Bea, who is sleeping in the back bedroom. Theo has lit the wood-burning stove and the candles along the counter and I prepare the turkey Nancy delivered yesterday. It's substantially bigger than the crown I usually cook for me and Ruben.

'What would you be doing at home right now?'

I tell him how Ruben and I would get into bed together, me with a cup of tea, him with his stocking, which he'd open. Then we'd go downstairs and open presents under the tree, eat chocolate and get the lunch ready. We'd make bread sauce and lay the table, and he'd speak to his dad on FaceTime. And we'd go to Mae's after lunch for games.

Theo's laughing as I tell him about Twister and charades, which, every year, include *Gone with the Wind*. Mae always laughs so hard that she farts every time. Every year!

'I hope I'm not interrupting!' A cold wind blows into the diner, accompanied by Mimi.

'You're not. Merry Christmas, Mimi,' says Theo, his arm around my shoulders, making no secret of the fact that we're enjoying the last of my time here together. I can't think about that today. Today I'm going to enjoy myself.

'You didn't come home last night,' she says stiffly. 'I can see you were otherwise engaged.'

'I was,' says Theo, and nothing more. No need for explanations, I like that, and no hiding either. No secrets. It may not be for ever, but it is for now and we're happy.

She looks at the Christmas tree, bright and light and crowded, as we've pinned all of Ruben's advent-calendar notes to it, and tuts. 'Don't tell me we're having some kind of British Christmas dinner today,' she says.

'We are, Mimi. Because if we don't make a change, no one else will,' says Theo. And for me everything has changed.

I spend the next few hours in the kitchen with Theo helping me as we listen to the radio and cut and chop and enjoy that time whilst the turkey is cooking to laugh, joke and chat.

Finally, I turn to check the bread sauce.

'Okay, I think we're ready,' I say looking around the kitchen. 'Let's eat!' I say, with a smile for Theo, who grins back.

The turkey is just as I wanted, golden skin with crispy bacon laced across the top, falling into soft white slices as it's carved. There are pigs in blankets drizzled with maple syrup, and parsnips. Everything I asked Nancy to get for me has been delivered. Brussels sprouts, covered with melting butter and a sprinkling of bacon bits. And, of course, there's a huge bowl of golden crispy-edged roast potatoes, fluffy inside and steaming as I put the dish on the table.

'Everyone, tuck in,' I say, putting down bowls of sweet, bright carrots and mashed, buttery swede. There are jugs of gravy, made from turkey stock, with a hint of bay, and a slug of boozy maple moonshine.

'Crackers!' I say, and hold up the one on my place setting.

*Bang!* goes the first, making Bea squeal. *Bang!* goes another. Paper hats and Christmas jokes tumble onto the table.

It may not be my usual Christmas dinner. It's different without Ruben ... but different is fine. Bea is loading her plate, covering it with gravy, then adding a dollop of bread sauce, tasting it and giving it the nod of approval. Jed seems happy to tuck in too. Theo takes his time, checking I've got some of everything on my plate, and handing me the jug of gravy first. Mimi takes some turkey, asking Theo to pass her a few carrots, and declines the bread sauce and parsnips. Tentatively she takes a potato, then another, saying she wouldn't usually eat carbs but because it's Christmas she will. Wine is poured from the bottles Theo has placed on the table and there's a feeling of contentment, despite our rather disparate group, as people discuss their introduction to bread sauce, the merits of the gravy and the roast potatoes. Finally there's the scraping of cutlery on plates, as people mop up the last of the gravy with a Brussels sprout or a potato. A loosening of waistbands. Even Mimi looks like she enjoyed it.

'Hope you've all left room for dessert,' I say. 'I couldn't get a Christmas pudding made in time, so we've got Ruben's boozy bread-and-butter maple-syrup pudding.' With the plates cleared away I bring it out. It's golden on top, and as I spoon it into bowls, it's soft, light and fluffy. I can smell the raisins soaked in maple moonshine.

Theo stands and fills everyone's wine glass, then holds up his own. 'To the chef!' His eyes are fixed on mine and I feel happy and content. For a moment I wonder if this is how Mae feels, with a happy, contented table, and remember how much she enjoys bringing people together for the day. I sip my wine, deep, rich, peppery and red. I like this a lot, I think, gazing at Theo smiling in the soft candlelight.

It's getting dark outside.

'Well, thank you for lunch,' says Jed, draining his glass and pulling off his paper hat. He had a second helping of bread-and-butter pudding and a large glass of brandy. He stands and puts on his coat.

'Thank you for coming. Merry Christmas,' I say.

'I enjoyed it,' he says, as if surprised.

'I did too! We'll have to exchange Christmas cards next year, what with us being family now,' I joke, the wine from lunch making my cheeks glow.

'Sure. We'll swap addresses along with all the paperwork when I get back. Put our heir hunters in touch with each other.'

'Oh, that's great news!' Suddenly I feel a rush of joy and as if I could hug him! 'Fabulous! Do you hear that Bea, Theo?' I call over to them excitedly.

'What's that?' says Bea, looking sleepy, her paper hat listing to one side.

'Jed's ready to accept the town's offer on the land. We're going to tell our heir hunters and get the paperwork sorted. That is *great* news!' I beam at him.

'Yes, yes, it is!' says Theo, standing and holding out a hand for Jed to shake. '*Merci! Merci* indeed!'

'I'm glad you saw sense, Jed,' I say.

Bea is looking happy, even though she's clearly uncomfortable in her chair.

'This means a lot to us all,' says Theo.

Jed looks at Theo's outstretched hand and then at me. 'Sorry?' He frowns. 'I'm not sure . . .'

'About selling the land back to the community. It's the right thing to do,' I enthuse, and this time I actually hug him.

He doesn't hug me back.

I pull away, waiting to see him smile. But he doesn't. A cold shiver runs up my spine.

'Jed?'

'I'm not agreeing to sell to the community. I was going to tell you tomorrow, before I left. I've got us a far better deal with Thomas Tremblay. Way more than he offered you when you first got here.'

'But . . .' I stare at him.

'Wait. What?' Theo pulls himself up to his full height.

'You're planning to sell to *him*, after all this?' I say, red mist rising around the edges of my eyes.

Jed shrugs. 'It's the best deal. For both of us.'

'Not for me!' I retort. 'It's not only your decision.'

'Well, I'm sorry, but I won't be selling for a pittance. Let me know what you decide in the morning before I leave.'

And with that he strides out of the door.

Mimi hiccups, clearly having overdone the red wine. 'Shame. He was nice,' she says. 'Theo? Do you think there's a chance of you and me getting back together? I mean, now you're playing ice hockey again . . .'

'Coaching.'

'Still, there's coaching jobs all over! Back in the city.'

'Mimi.' He turns to her. 'You and I are not getting back together. Ever.'

'But your new girlfriend will be gone in a few days.' Mimi pouts.

'Whatever this is, it's more than I ever hoped for.' He looks at me, then back at Mimi. 'But it means you and I don't have a future.' He puts a hand on my shoulder.

'Fine. I'll leave tomorrow. Let me know if Bea needs me.' She staggers to her feet and slams out of the diner.

Theo's hand is still on my shoulder. 'Okay if I stay at yours tonight? Not sure I haven't been locked out of my own home.'

'Of course,' I say, tears filling my eyes.

'I'm off to bed,' says Bea, wearily, rising from her seat stiffly, and both Theo and I step forward to help her. She doesn't object.

'You tried, Chloë. That's all we could ask of you. You're one of us.'

'I'm sorry, Bea,' I say, and fat tears fall down my cheeks.

We help Bea to bed. Then, as we're clearing up, Theo pours us two large glasses of maple moonshine, puts them on the table in front of the fire and beckons me to one of the wingback chairs. There in the firelight we sip the moonshine, sweet yet fiery.

'So, he's really not going to sell it to the town. He's gone for the better offer.' I look at Theo, his jaw tight. 'I've ruined everything! I should've done more.'

'Someone's going to have to tell Philippe,' he says, swigging his drink.

I drop my head into my hands and in no time he's kneeling in front of me, holding my hands, his forehead touching mine. 'You haven't – you really haven't. You did your best. Like Bea says, you're one of us. I wouldn't have missed this time we've had together for the world.'

'Nor me,' I say. 'I just wish I could have got him to agree to the deal, for all your sakes. I'm sorry.'

And he kisses my cheeks where the tears are still trickling.

# 35

*26 December: 5 days until Ruben comes home*

I look up at the door of Cabane de l'Étoile and the sugar shack beyond it, wishing I could see the harvest in action. But I won't. I think about Ruben's note from yesterday. 'You have to take it from here, Mum.' And that's exactly what I intend to do. Ruben may not be guiding me now, but I know what I have to do.

I raise my hand to knock on the door, but before I can it flies open.

'Chloë! It's you,' says Jed, ready and packed, his case by the door.

'We need to talk,' I say firmly.

'Do you want to come in?' He's taken aback, then slightly amused, which irritates me.

I shake my head. 'No. I'm just here to tell you that

I'm not selling to Thomas Tremblay,' I state flatly, folding my arms.

'Right.' He hesitates. 'Well, I'm not selling to the cooperative.'

We glare at each other.

'But the land needs to be claimed and sold,' he says, making me feel patronized.

I lift my head and my chin. 'You wanted to know the real value of this land,' I tell him.

'Yes – and it's way more than you're expecting me to accept.'

'That isn't the value of the land,' I say crossly. 'It's about the community, their roots, where they're from and the generations to come.'

'Well, maybe for them, but not to me.'

'Don't you care about how this land came to be given to our ancestors?'

'No.'

'How they fell in love with each other and everything about this place?'

'No.'

We stand in silence. Stalemate.

'Well, if that's your position, there's only one thing for it,' says Jed.

'What's that?' I say, my spirits rising slightly.

'We split the land!' he exclaims.

'We what? We . . . You can't do that?!'

'Why not? You sell your half to the community. I'll

sell my half to Thomas Tremblay and Tremblay Syrups. But being as how you're looking to put down roots of your own for your boy Ruben, I'd say it was his future you were jeopardizing.'

I glare at him. But I have a shred of doubt. Is he right?

I think about the advent calendar and narrow my eyes at him. 'I'm not doing it. It wouldn't be right!' I couldn't live with myself if I just went for the highest offer and left these people high and dry. 'I'm not selling to Thomas.'

'Fine. Keep your half! I'm selling!' And with that, he shuts the door in my face. I'm furious. I turn and storm back to the diner.

There's a gathering of people in hats and gloves, and lots of chatter – apparently about the land and me.

'What's going on?' I ask Theo.

'It's the trail race. The sap race? Remember?'

'The what?'

'Remember, I told you? On the twenty-sixth of December, we run off our Christmas lunch – well, run, ski or use snow shoes – along the trail, the sap run, and hope we'll have a good harvest when the sap begins to rise.'

Philippe is there, with a flag and a starting gun.

'Oh, yes.' I'm not really taking things in, and Theo notices.

'Did you speak to Jed?' he asks nervously.

I nod. 'He wants to divide the land in half.'

'*What?*'

Other members of the town turn to look at Theo and me. Philippe comes over to join us.

'He can't do that!' Theo says angrily. 'Jed wants to divide the land,' he tells Philippe. 'But he can't just split it in half.'

'He can,' I say, feeling as if all the wind has been knocked out of me. 'I can sell my half to you and he can sell his to whoever he wants. There's no reason why he shouldn't.'

'They'll be looking for a new mayor if that happens!' Philippe says. 'I can't be mayor of this town with the Tremblays at the heart of it. I can't be a part of that.'

Eli joins us. 'Split the land? How?' he asks.

'And what about the lake? You can't split that in half. Where will the teams train?' Nancy joins the group.

They look at Philippe, his head down.

'There is another way,' says a voice, from the back of the gathering crowd. It's Jed. He's clearly followed me.

I swing round and sigh heavily. 'I've told you, I'm not selling my half of the land to Thomas Tremblay.'

'You did. And you don't want the land to be split in half at all?'

I shake my head.

'Then race me for it.'

'Huh?'

He lifts his head and juts out his chin. 'Race me for it. Bet on it. Winner takes all.'

'Don't be ridiculous!' I snap.

The crowd are murmuring. Even Ike puts in an appearance at this suggestion.

'We'll do the sap run, the winner gets all the land and they can sell to whoever they want.'

'So if you win you'll sell the whole parcel to Thomas Tremblay.'

'Correct.'

'And if I win, the land isn't split and stays in the community.'

'Exactly!'

'But why? Why would you do that?'

'Some things in life are worth taking a gamble on. You just have to say yes!' I think about Ruben and the advent calendar.

I look at Theo, uncertain. It's snowing, heavier and heavier. I can smell it in the air, cold and crisp. It's darkening, like the mood around me. The snow is blurring my vision through the trees, just a white swirl. More than ever I wish there had been an advent-calendar note this morning. What would it have said? What did the last one say? 'Over to you, Mum. You've got to take it from here.'

Theo puts his hands on my shoulders and talks quietly to me, staring straight at me. 'It's up to you but you can do this. You know the trails. Your skiing is great now.'

'Thanks to Ike!' I say.

'Believe in yourself,' says Dax, behind me. 'We all do.'

'You can do it!' shouts Bea, standing up from her rocking chair on the porch. Then she remembers she's not supposed to get overexcited and sits down again.

'You can do it.' The crowd start to clap and cheer.

'Wait, wait!' I try to stop the gathering momentum. 'What if I can't?' I look at Theo in panic.

'What have we got to lose?' says Philippe. 'If he sells to Thomas Tremblay the land will be broken up anyway. We'll already have lost part of it, the heart of it. Our town will be broken up. This is a chance to keep it together, Chloë,' he says. 'You have this chance, so why not go for it?'

'Do it!' says Nancy.

'With our blessing!' says Philippe, nodding.

'What would Ruben say?' says one of the girls from the ice-hockey team.

'We need an advent-calendar note this morning.'

'He'd say, "Take a chance!"'

This is the closest to family I've ever felt, and Ruben is a part of it. I want to do it for them.

I touch the little maple-leaf pendant I bought for myself from Ruben and think again about the message he sent me. 'You'll have to take it from here!'

I have to try for them, for Theo and Bea and Philippe and all the others in the town. Or for Ruben. I can't leave here knowing I did nothing to try to save this land. I have to try everything.

'Okay.' I take a deep breath. 'I will.'

And a huge cheer goes up. I feel excited, terrified and sick all at once. But it's better than feeling nothing, I think, as I look at Jed. I know who's richer and it's not him. I have to take a chance.

# 36

My teeth are chattering so loudly, they sound like the set of wind-up toy teeth Ruben once had in his stocking. Whiskey the cat hated it.

I'm standing on the start line, in skis, hat, and some glittery purple goggles Nancy's lent me.

I briefly think of Mae and wonder what she would make of this. It's a long way from Boxing Day leftovers and her favourite films on the telly. Ruben usually loved that. I wonder if he'll still love it after Christmas in New York or if everything will have changed. Everything *has* changed, for both of us. We have memories to take home. New customs to add to our Christmas traditions, like maple syrup and bacon and a love of ice hockey.

I look across at Jed next to me, pulling down his skiing goggles. He's clearly used to the slopes and has had more practice at this than I have. I feel the snow shifting from under my feet.

'But he doesn't know the trails like you do,' I hear Theo beside me, whispering in my ear. 'Trust your instincts. They're usually right! It took someone special to remind me of that.'

Behind us are the rest of the skiers: they've decided not to race to give us a clear run at it.

'Come on, Chloë!' shouts Bea, holding her bump. 'Do it for Forêt des Esprits.'

The Forest of Spirits. I'm doing it for all of them.

'Do it for Ruben!' I hear someone else call.

Everyone is there, including Ruben in spirit, and I touch the little necklace again.

'The weather's getting worse. Are you sure you want to continue?' Philippe asks.

'Yes,' says Jed, not even looking up.

'*Oui!*' I say, determined to win.

'In that case, skiers,' Philippe takes a big breath, 'are you ready?'

Ike appears out of the bushes. I smile. Like a good-luck charm, or even a training partner, he's with me.

'Come on, Ike, we can do this!' I say.

Jed laughs. 'You and the overgrown Thanksgiving dinner there?'

My hackles rise in the freezing air, like my curling breath in the cold. I grip the handles of my poles, turn to the mayor, nod, and feel a focus I have never felt before.

'*Un, deux, trois! Allez!*' he shouts, and lets off a loud bang from the starter's pistol, making Ike squawk, Hagrid bark and me jump.

Jed is off first, but I'm right behind him, with Ike behind me.

I push the sticks into the snow. I'm rushing and panting, flailing about. What am I doing out here? Jed starts to pull away from me. Focus, Chloë! I tell myself, and suddenly I remember being on the ice rink with Theo, one and two, left and right, and I settle into a rhythmic routine, making up a little ground, but keeping a steady distance behind Jed. I keep counting, and imagining myself on the skates. I keep going, settling into my stride.

I can smell the snow as my legs push forward and back and my arms pull in tandem to move me along the familiar trail.

Ike puts a push on, flapping his wings.

Feeling more confident now, I speed up. I'm right behind Jed, on his tail. And he knows it. There's a wide turn in the path coming up, and I move to one side, hoping to overtake him. But he veers across the snowy trail to block my path. I falter and am unbalanced. I tip back and forward as I try to stay on the path and not crash off it.

Jed glances back at me, to my fury, to see me flailing, poles waving, and skis off as I try to right myself. I untangle my ski from the thick banked-up snow over bushes and back onto the path.

I see him smile, which fuels my determination. I sort out my skis and find my balance. As I do, I push on harder and faster and I'm even closer on his tail this time. I can hear his rapid breathing. And I know he can hear mine too. He hasn't got away from me. He hasn't got this in the bag yet.

We're coming to the downhill slope, where Theo and I collided, and I'm not going to tumble there again.

He goes first and I follow, practically beside him. We're coming up to the two trees fast. The gap between them is narrow enough for only one of us to make it through at a time. I go wide and avoid the root I hit last time when I fell. Jed takes a more direct course and hits the root, knocking him sideways, not off his feet but just enough to let me pass and make it between the two trees first. Now I'm ahead of him.

I grin, and although my calves are starting to ache like they never have before, I push on. I need to get over that finishing line first and know now that I can do it.

He's right behind me as we ski through the forest, around the lake, then through the pines on the other side. At one point I take off my skis and carry them, finding it quicker on foot than trying to ski uphill. It felt like the right thing to do. He follows.

I hear him panting behind me. Close on my tail.

Ike has given up long ago, leaving me to it. I'm supposing he reckons I'm doing okay on my own, like Ruben does: they're letting me take it from here.

My lungs are dragging in the air, my mouth dry and thirsty.

Now we turn back towards the maple trees, careful not to get caught in the lines between the trees there. Another corner's coming up and Jed could take me on this one – except I hear a stumble and a mutter. I glance over my shoulder to see he's gone wide and run into one of the lines.

Swearing, he rights himself and drives on, making ground again. Clearly his battered pride is urging him on.

I'm slowing, I can feel it. I'm dragging in breath, and my chest hurts. But we're on the homeward stretch. I know it! I just have to follow this path to get out of the forest and we'll be heading towards the main road and back into the town to the square where, with luck, I'll collapse into the cheering crowd.

There's still a gap between us, but it's closing. The more we push on, the slower I'm going and the faster he is. Even though I'm wearing gloves, my hands, gripping my poles, are paining me with each push propelling me forward. I can feel him getting closer. I just have to get down this last narrow path in the lead and sprint for home down the road.

*Come on!* I shout to myself. I have to do this!

Something rustles in the bushes behind me, distracting me. I look around. I know it's not Ike – it sounds much bigger than a turkey. I turn back, not to be distracted, and keep focused on the end of the trail, now in sight.

'Whoa!' I hear a shout from Jed. I ignore it at first. 'Whoooaaaa!' I hear again, this time louder. I glance over my shoulder, then do a double-take. It's definitely not Ike. I stop and turn. It's the moose, standing right across the middle of the trail, taking up the full width of it. She's between me and Jed and isn't moving.

'Yah! Yah!' Jed is shouting, waving his arms. And then I spot it. She has her young one with her, tucked safely behind her back legs, barely visible.

I take a deep breath. Looks like luck is on my side. I turn back towards the trail and the finish line. I've nearly done it! I've nearly bloody well done it!

I fill my lungs with a huge breath of Forêt des Esprits air.

As I push towards the finishing line, I can hear the crowds in the distance. But over them I can hear Jed. 'Go on! Geddaway! Shoo!'

I try to block him out. I try to push on. But I can't. I slow. I stop again.

I want to tell Jed not to shout. Just to move around her quietly. A new mother will do anything to protect her young. An older one, too, for that matter.

*Come on!* I tell myself. *Push on!*

'Get away! Get back!' Jed's calls are more urgent. 'Gah! Chloë! Help!'

I take another deep breath and turn back.

## 37

'Don't shout!' I hiss at him, from a little distance. 'Don't upset her! Just let her go on her way. She mustn't feel threatened.'

'I am threatening her! If she comes near me, I'll—' He's waving his pole like a sword at her, and she flinches. 'Get back!' he shouts again. She's snorting now, tossing her head and kicking at the snow, her huge antlers waving. 'GET BACK!'

'Sssh! It's okay.' I try to soothe them both, despite being out of breath, my cheeks burning with exertion in the cold. 'Sssh! Jed! Put down the pole, for Christ's sake!' I say.

'You must be joking!'

'Just do it!' I command, and he slowly does as he's told, lowering the pole. The moose is starting to calm.

'Now, just back off and let her pass,' I tell him.

'No way, I'm not going backwards here so you can get a head start on me again.'

'Just do it!' I snap.

The moose turns towards me and snorts, her big round nostrils flaring, her dark eyes focusing on me.

I drop my poles and hold out my hands to her.

'It's okay. You're fine. No one's going to hurt you or your little one.'

She doesn't move and neither do I. I'm holding my breath. The crowd at the finish line have gone quiet. They must be wondering where we are. We should have appeared from the forest by now.

She looks as if she might have calmed again. She looks from me to Jed and back at me. Then, very slowly, she puts one foot in front of the other and the little one follows her. I still hold my breath and I don't know how long it's been now. For ever is how it seems. Stuck in the same place, hoping everything will turn out right. A bit like at home, with Ruben: me refusing to make any changes that will disrupt things, too scared to do anything that might cause a reaction. She takes another step forward and another, the youngster right behind her. She's crossing the trail, moving into the forest. Slowly I bend to pick up my poles.

'Go on! Rah!' Jed shouts, spooking me, the moose and her calf. Grabbing his pole, he pushes off and darts around the calf behind her causing her to lunge at him. Head down, he thrusts the poles into the snow and dodges around me, shoving me with his shoulder right into the path of the moose. After the collision, I hit the ground, crash into a tree and fall, over and over again, down a ravine. Everything goes black.

# 38

'Chloë!' I hear a shout. Theo?

'No, no, I can't . . . this can't . . . I have to catch him up. I have to do this on my own.' I'm trying to get my bearings. It's not far up the bank to the trail. There's no sign of the moose and her calf. I try to roll onto my stomach. Oh, God! Everything hurts. I see one of my poles and reach for it.

'Argh!' My ribs.

'Chloë!' I hear Theo shout again.

'I'm here!' It hurts even to get that out. But Jed *can't* get ahead. He can't win.

I grab the one pole I can see and use it to get to my feet. I lean down and undo the clips on my skis, slip off the first, then the second, giving another shout of pain. It's my ankle. I've twisted it. I pick up the skis, put them on my shoulder and then, with the one pole, pull myself forward on the snow. Tears are streaming down my cheeks. I can't accept what I know is true. That Jed's beaten me. I've lost!

Theo is running towards me.

'I have to finish!' I put out my hand.

He looks at me in a way no one has ever looked at me before. I've lost my hat, my hair is tangled, and my coat is torn. I'm hobbling on a bad ankle and I've lost a ski pole. But this man is looking at me as if I'm everything.

He gives a little smile, with tears in his eyes. 'It's over, Chloë,' he says, and steps forward. I fall onto his big broad chest and sob. He says nothing more, just lets me cry.

Finally, I take a deep breath. 'I was winning. But the moose came. I turned back to help Jed . . . He scared her and then left me. He wanted the land that badly . . .' I say, shuddering as I sob.

After a bit, he takes the pole and puts my arm around him. I wince in pain. Then Dax, Philippe the mayor, Eli, Nancy, Charlene and Océane are beside me, with their arms around each other and me, walking me to the finish line where Jed is standing, with a wide smile, and Thomas Tremblay. I have a whole range of words that I am putting in order to say to him as we cross the finish line and stop.

I open my mouth to speak, but the only words anyone hears are 'Oh, God, my waters have broken!' We all turn to Bea.

'Looks like we'd better get you to the hospital,' says Theo.

And Jed Anderson is the last thing on our minds.

# 39

'How are you doing?' I ask, pushing open the door to Bea's hospital room.

'They're taking me down to surgery. How about you?'

'Just bruises, and a twisted ankle. Could have been a lot worse.'

'I've known a moose do a *lot* more. Aw!' she says, gasping in pain.

'Okay, let's get you to theatre and deliver these babies.' A doctor has come in.

Bea's eyes are full of tears that spill over and slide onto the pillow. 'I'm scared.'

'You'll be fine.' I hold her hand. 'I'll ring your sister, tell her to come back and be with you,' I say, and make to leave.

'Actually, Chloë,' she stops me as I pull out my phone, 'would you stay with me?'

'Really? You don't want Theo or your sister?'

She shakes her head. 'I'm not sure Theo wants to be in there with me. I know he would if I asked him. But you've been there . . .'

'And not your sister?'

'I don't think any of us need that stress!' She smiles, despite the nerves I can see in her face. 'If you don't mind?'

'Of course I don't. Let me tell Theo what's happening!' I smile. 'It'll be fine.'

'Everything okay?'

Theo is on the bench in the waiting room. He stands up when he sees me, shoving his phone into his jacket pocket. 'Have you been here all this time?' I ask.

He nods. 'How is she?'

I smile. 'They're all fine. Happy and healthy.'

'Two boys?'

'Two healthy boys.'

'Wow!'

'It's all good. But, Theo,' I take a deep breath and say the thing nobody's mentioned until now, 'she still hasn't mentioned the father. She hasn't mentioned Harold.'

'So sad he isn't here to see he has two beautiful boys. He should be part of this.'

'Maybe she should talk about him,' I say.

'He was a good man.' Theo sighs,

The door opens. 'You can come in now,' says a nurse, opening it a little wider, and there is Bea, tired but happy, with a baby tucked into the crook of each arm. She looks up at Theo, beaming.

'Hey, *chérie*!' He kisses her forehead. 'Look at these two beauties! Syrup farmers in the making!'

'I can't wait to get them home, back to the forest.'

'You're going to be taking it easy for a few days,' the nurse instructs her. 'Moving around a little, but we don't want you bursting those stitches.'

'As long as I'm home, I promise to do exactly as I'm told.'

There's a pause.

'Their father would have been so proud of you.' Theo puts his hand to her cheek. 'I'm sorry he's not here to see them.'

'Me too. I wish he was . . .' Her face crumples. 'I'm scared, Theo. What if I can't do this? What if I'm no good at it?'

'You won't be the first new mother to worry about that.' I step forward. 'I was terrified even holding Ruben when they handed him to me. You're doing better than I did already.'

'He might not be here, Bea, but I am,' says Theo. 'I'll be there for you and the boys. I'm not going anywhere.'

'I know. *Merci*,' she says, and puts her lips to the back of his hand.

'Right! Mum needs some rest now,' says the nurse.

'*Merci* again, *mon ami*,' Bea says, resting her cheek to his hand. 'And you, Chloë. Now, Theo, take this woman home and spoil her. A hot bath and a big glass of wine. And some maple cake.'

Theo slides his arm around my shoulders.

'Make the most of each other while you can!' she says, with a crack in her voice as Theo leads me to the door.

'Chloë?' she calls, and I turn back. 'How do you feel about me naming one of the boys Ruben?'

I manage to say yes as tears of happiness spring to my eyes, and suddenly I'm missing Ruben so much it hurts, remembering the rush of love I felt after giving birth to him and taking him home, knowing it was just him and me but we'd do it together. I would make sure he was safe, loved, warm and fed. Just like Bea is probably feeling now. It's a love that takes you completely by surprise, and you'd do anything for them. Just like the moose with her young. It's instinct to look after them.

'Come on! A hot bath, a drink, turkey and maple sandwiches, then the cake. And I'm going to massage your aching muscles.'

And I experience a shiver of excitement.

Back at the diner, everyone is waiting for news.

'Two boys!' Nancy's hands fly to her face. 'A new generation here in Forêt des Esprits!'

'We need to wet the baby's head!' says Philippe, as I limp up the steps to the porch. 'Here, you can have my crutches. Now we've got Theo coaching the girls' team I'm feeling so much better.' He winks at me, but there's sadness behind his eyes, no matter how hard he's trying to ignore what's happening to the town.

Inside, glasses are handed around, corks popped and toasts made. 'To Bea!' they all say. 'To new lives and to lives lived!'

And something scratches at the back of my mind.

Dax is there. 'Jed left. He brought back the key for the *cabane*.'

Theo looks down at it.

'I'm sorry,' I say to him.

'Don't be.' He drops a kiss on my head. 'Like Bea says, let's just enjoy the time we have left.'

With that we pick up our glasses, and I lean into him. I have never felt more wretched or more content, wishing we had more time before all of this changes. And he leads me back to Maple Lodge, where I have a hot bath and he massages every part of my aching and bruised body until it's quivering with delight and we sink between the sheets of the big wooden bed, under the thick quilt . . .

# 40

*27, 28, 29 December*

For the next three days, I spend the mornings baking in the diner and updating the locals on news of Bea and the boys. Océane comes in to help me serve. Philippe has been true to his word about standing down as mayor: he and Dax have put up signs calling for candidates on lampposts and on the porches of the store and diner.

I spend my evenings with Theo at Maple Lodge, cooking, eating in front of the fire and finding out more to love about each other as the snow falls outside. Eventually we head for bed and the joy of the quilt. Grabbing our moment. Living in the now. Not thinking about how it must end.

Until it has to.

# 41

*30 December: 1 day until Ruben comes home*

I push back the covers, stick a leg out and shiver. I don't want to leave this bed. I turn back to look at him sleeping beside me, his head on the pillow, hair this way and that. If I could freeze time, just a little longer . . . But I can't. We have to bring Bea and the babies home today, and then I have a flight to catch.

Ruben is coming home! In time for New Year! We'll watch the fireworks in London on the television and put out all our favourite snacks, just like we always do! I cannot wait to see him again! I don't want to leave what I have now but I must. My time here is done. Everything will change in the New Year and I can't bear to think of it: who will live in Maple Lodge? What will the Forêt des Esprits be like when Tremblay Syrups rolls into town?

I throw myself out of bed and run to the bathroom, hoping the sharp shock of the cold will keep my sadness at bay, giving me something to think about other than the goodbyes I'll have to say later.

When I return, I glance out of the bedroom window. Ike is waiting for me just beyond the porch. I'll go down and stoke the fire, I think, but there's hardly any point: when I close the door on this place today, it'll be for the last time. The house will be sold, along with the land, and the proceeds will go to Jed Anderson. The heir hunters will take their cut.

I pick up the framed photograph I bought at the yard sale, here at Maple Lodge. The man in it is so like Ruben, standing with a First Nations family in their traditional clothing. My great-grandfather, Joseph Jones, and Namid, the love of his life. Never forgotten.

As I'm looking at the photograph, Theo's arms slip around my waist. I feel his body next to mine and lean back into it. I squeeze my eyes shut and try to take in everything about this hug, how it feels, how he smells. I'll remember the taste of his kiss as he turns me around and puts his lips on mine. The picture slips from my hand to the floor.

'Oh, no!'

'Here.' He bends to pick it up. 'Sorry, the frame's come a bit loose.'

'At least the glass isn't broken.' I take it from him, kissing him again, then reluctantly pulling away.

'We'd better get ready to bring Bea home.' I'm trying to stay in the moment, not think about the taxi that is booked to take me to the airport later, then the flight to London. I'll meet Ruben at Heathrow and we'll travel home together. Theo and I clasp each other tightly. I can hear his heartbeat, feel his familiar touch.

My stomach is in knots. I'm beyond excited about seeing Ruben, and I can't stop thinking about the hug I'll share with him, but I'm taking this one with me to remember when I need to.

I'm still holding the picture as I walk towards the wardrobe. I drag out my case and put the picture into it. Theo leaves the window, gets dressed and heads downstairs.

I fold the rest of my clothes and tuck my bottles of maple syrup between them to keep them safe.

It seems mad that the next time I'll be eating this maple syrup I'll be back at the table for two in my little kitchen, in time for Ruben to go back to school.

Outside on the landing Hagrid raises his head as I tug my case behind me and bump it down the stairs. He gets up and follows me.

'I'll take this to the diner,' I say, indicating the case but looking around the living room that has been my home for this part of my trip. And that's how it feels, like home. I have never felt such a sense of belonging

311

in any other house. And this is the hardest I have ever found it to leave somewhere, for all the efforts I've made to stay in the same area, near Ruben's school, making sure things remain the same for him.

'I'll take it to the truck,' says Theo, lifting it.

I close the door behind me and head after him, so many unspoken words hanging in the air.

I hand Theo the key. 'Can I leave this for you to pass on to the new owners? Tell them I hope they'll be as happy here as I was.'

He wraps his fingers tightly around it, as if he's holding on to the last moments of what we had.

'I just need to open up the diner, check everything's okay, and then we'll go and fetch Bea, yes?' I say as cheerily as I can.

He nods, his head low. Then he looks up at me. 'I wish . . .'

'I know. I do too.'

'But we can't.'

The snow falls steadily around us.

'You need to be here for Bea and the boys.' I tell him what we both know.

'And you need to be back in the UK for Ruben.'

We hug, a last one for the memory bank, finding it hard to let go. But Ike is there to keep me on my toes. 'Ow!' He's pecked the backs of my heels.

'He likes you! He'll miss you.' Theo smiles. 'We all

will.' He takes the tips of my fingers in his. The final part of letting go.

'Okay, easy does it.' Theo helps Bea to step down from the truck. The area all around the front of the diner has been cleared of snow and members of the ice-hockey teams, boys and girls, are there with snow shovels and brooms. There's a sign over the door and balloons covering the mayor's posters: *'Bienvenue!* Welcome home, Bea and the boys!'

She takes a deep breath as if the icy air is just the tonic she needs.

*'Merci!* Thank you!' she says, to the ice-hockey teams. 'God, it's good to be home. I hope there's some of Ruben's special left.'

'There is! I made a batch and put some in the freezer for when I'm gone . . .' I tail off. Then I pull myself together. 'Everything's ready for you and the twins. Clean sheets. And I left the jar of Marmite!' I'm trying to jolly things along.

'It's okay.' She holds up a hand. 'I've gone off it now.' She grimaces and I remember how quickly I went off the food I'd craved while I was pregnant with Ruben.

Theo lifts one of the baby seats from the back of the truck.

'Oh, the babies are home!' Nancy comes out of the store, waving a tea-towel like a welcome flag.

313

The diner door opens, and in moments Philippe and others are standing on the porch.

'New members of the community!' He beams. 'Our town carries on. That's something to be thankful for.'

He comes down the steps to meet Bea and offer a hand to help her up them. 'Now, you're not to lift a finger. We've got everything covered,' he instructs.

'*Merci*. Thank you,' she says. 'But who can run the diner?'

Nobody has the answer.

'With everyone else in their jobs and the syrup harvest on its way . . .' Philippe says gently to Bea, and we all know what that means. The doors of the diner must remain closed for the time being. I can see that Bea is winded. But this day was always going to come.

I follow her up the steps to the open door, where my case is waiting. She turns back to me. 'You . . . you're not going already?'

I open my mouth to speak, but can't. The wind is biting, nipping at our noses and ears.

'Taxi's on its way,' Theo tells her, then turns to me. 'I could have taken you to the airport, you know.' Bea looks at us, questioning.

'I told him to stay here with you. You need him more than I do right now.' I'm holding back the tears that are threatening.

Nancy brings in the other baby in his car seat, and I

can see the boys will have plenty of doting adopted grandparents.

'I don't think I can do it.' Bea's face is anguished.

I take her hands. 'You can and you will. I know it seems huge right now but you'll do it. One day at a time. Just live in the moment. Don't worry about what's round the corner. Save that for another day. You need all the energy you can get. And take the help. Remember: one day at a time.'

I look around. 'You have plenty of willing babysitters. Have a bath when you need to. And an early night. Or a lie-in.'

'We're all here for you, Bea. You'll be fine,' says Theo, and my heart swells with love for this giant-hearted bear of a man. I let go of her hands.

Océane is handing around hot chocolate with thick cream and maple drizzles.

'Thank you, for everything,' Bea says.

'No, thank *you*! I'm not sure I'd have got through this month if it wasn't for this place.' I sniff and rub my nose. 'I'm sorry about the land,' I say to her, and then to the group. 'Sorry to all of you.'

'You tried your best,' I hear them reply, and a group hug surrounds me. The tears fall and are lost in a blanket of coats, scarves and gloves. It feels like a very safe place to be.

'But what are the babies' names?' I hear someone say. I think it's Charlene.

We all turn to Bea and the babies.

'This one is Ruben, and this one,' she looks at me, 'is Harold Junior.'

There's a sigh. And suddenly something occurs to me, that I'd not really allowed myself to think about, or even hope for.

'Oh, Bea!' I have to ask the question before I leave. 'Theo told me. They really are Harold's? Does that make me related to the boys?'

She smiles. 'I suppose you are. This one, Harold, is named after their father.' And everyone sighs again.

'But why didn't you want to say anything before?' Suddenly there are so many questions I want to ask, but the taxi is on its way.

'Well, it wasn't how we planned things. In fact, we didn't plan it at all. We just fell in love. But with him being older than me, we thought we'd take our time telling people.'

'But we all knew anyway!' says Nancy, who has been cooing over Harold Junior in his car seat.

'We didn't want anyone to know,' says Bea. 'Not at first.'

'Why?' I'm hungry for more information now.

'It's hard to keep things secret around here. We didn't want anyone to judge us, I suppose. We were happy with it being just us.'

'And we were all happy for you both!' says Nancy again. 'Finding love where you live and being together for the time you had.'

'Hear, hear,' says Philippe. 'Let's raise a glass to Harold, and Ruben and Harold Junior!'

'Harold, Ruben and Harold Junior!' We raise our mugs of hot chocolate.

Just as we do, the white taxi comes into view, drives around the town square and pulls up outside the diner. The driver gets out and runs up the wooden steps. He throws open the door, letting in a cold blast of air. 'Taxi for Chloë?' he calls, gazing at the gathered group.

I clear my throat. 'That's me!' I try for a cheery wave, but I probably look a teary mess.

I reach out for my case, but Theo beats me to it. Our hands clash, sending waves of desire through me that I try to ignore, as the taxi man runs back to his vehicle.

We say nothing. I turn away and hug Bea hard, then Nancy, Eli, who is standing close to her, Philippe, Dax and each member of the ice-hockey team as the driver honks his horn.

'I have to go!' I shout, over the *au revoirs*, and hurry down the steps before I dissolve into a soggy state. My case is in the boot of the cab, with Theo standing there.

'I have to go,' I repeat to Theo.

He nods. 'I know.' His eyes are filled with tears.

'Look after her, and the twins,' I say firmly.

'I will. Take care of yourself and Ruben.'

I daren't look at him.

'I will,' I say, clinging to the taxi door as I open it. I can't resist one last look at him, absorbing everything

317

I have come to love about him. But he can't come with me and I can't stay here with him.

'No promises. No staying in touch,' I say. 'This was just for now, not for ever.'

'I know,' he says, resting his forehead on mine.

'We can't make it harder than it is.'

'No.' He straightens. This man, who'll take on a moose, cut down trees, catch ice-hockey pucks, is standing in front of me, his eyes and nose red with emotion. He brushes at the tears. And I couldn't love him more than I do right now.

With a huge effort, I slide into the back seat of the cab. Theo closes the door and the taxi is away, at speed, leaving the town of Forêt des Esprits behind, and the outline of Theo getting smaller. It's taking all my strength not to shout, 'Stop! Let me out!' and run back. I stare until he's gone. In the past. Now I have to go home to my future.

## 42

*31 December: Ruben comes home today!*

I'm at the airport, watching the Arrivals board.

The Christmas trees and tinsel are still there, a little jaded and tired now. There are no carol singers. But excitement ripples through the air, as people arrive for New Year's Eve. Groups of young men and women, on their way to New Year celebrations. Meanwhile, I know, others are in Departures, leaving the UK with skis and snowboards. Older couples will be wheeling their golf clubs in search of winter sun.

I'm like a cat on a hot tin roof. I can hardly stand still I'm so excited about seeing Ruben. I've been at the airport for a few hours now. I set up camp in a coffee shop, so I'm buzzing with caffeine overload, jet lag and anticipation. I have my phone but I'm trying not to message Theo. I have to let go. But my mind keeps drifting back to the diner. I'm wondering how Bea and the babies are this morning and if anyone's lit the fire. I'm sure they're all fine, I tell myself, one hand touching the little maple leaf around my neck as if it will bring me comfort.

I hold my coffee cup, sad that it tastes so different from what we served in the diner, and focus again on the Arrivals board. Finally, after what seems like the longest wait ever . . . 'Yes!' I shout, with a little fist pump. Heads turn towards me. I hold up a hand in apology for my outburst. 'His flight's landed,' I say, to no one in particular.

I stand, gather my things, including my coat, which seems much too thick for the drizzle outside, and watch the Arrivals doors and each passenger as they come out. Children rush out to meet grandparents, young men run into the arms of partners, and mothers hug their homecoming travellers. I wait for it to be my turn. What if he missed the flight? I know I'm being irrational. Ruben or Lucas would have contacted me.

'Mum!' Suddenly there he is, and my worries evaporate. I'm overwhelmed with relief and love.

'Ruben!'

Neither of us is thinking about whether or not we're being embarrassing. We definitely aren't holding back. My arms are wide open, as are his. He's wearing a new baseball cap and there's a new rucksack on his back. It's like my little Ruben left and a bigger one has replaced him. But as he throws himself into my arms and wraps his around me, I close my eyes tightly, breathe him in and he's my Ruben again. His cap tips back on his head and I rest my face on his hair. I wonder how much longer it will be before he's taller than me and is hugging his ageing mum. Suddenly time is whizzing away, galloping along, like the electricity meter when the tumble dryer's running.

Eventually I pull back. 'Look at you! You've grown!' I say, gazing at him from arms' length. He's definitely grown. And I missed it! But it's so good to have him back with me.

Lucas is behind me.

'Hi, Chloë.' He leans forward to kiss my cheek. Unexpectedly, I wonder what it's been like for him all these years, seeing Ruben so rarely, missing out on the little steps. The growing. The passing time. It must have been hard.

'It looks like you two had a great time.' I try to take Ruben's rucksack from him, but he gently pulls it further onto his shoulder.

He looks around at Lucas. 'We did! Didn't we, Dad? And I got you a present,' he says, keen to make sure I'm not left out.

'Your advent calendar was present enough!'

'Darn it!' he says, surprising me with a new word

he's picked up on his trip. 'Knew I shouldn't have bothered!'

'It's just something from all of us,' Lucas says.

'Thank you, Lucas,' I say softly. 'For everything.' And I want to say, 'Because if it wasn't for you I wouldn't have Ruben,' but I think he knows what I mean.

'He's a wonderful boy!' and Lucas's eyes sparkle with a few tears that I know will fall when he's on his own. 'Now, give me a hug,' he says to Ruben.

Ruben does, and my heart fills with joy. Even though Lucas and I weren't meant to be together, I'm so pleased Ruben has Lucas in his life. You can never have too many people to love you, and my mind leaps to Bea and the twins, the town that will look after them as if they were their own.

'Let's get home,' I say. 'You're staying for a night or two?' I ask Lucas.

'Thought I'd tie in bringing Ruben back with a couple of meetings while I'm here, and catching up with some old friends for New Year.'

'You'll miss Lizzie and Jodie,' I say.

'Lizzie and Jodie will be fast asleep way before midnight. Lizzie wanted me to make sure this one got home safe and sound. And it's a good chance to catch up with the old gang. She insisted.'

'Well, happy New Year. Message us when you get home,' I say, then lean in to hug him. 'Thank you for bringing him back.'

'Maybe you should come too next time,' says Lucas.

'Maybe I should! Meet the rest of the family!' I say, and that's how it feels, not them and me, but a family brought together by Ruben. We're Ruben's family.

With that, we begin to walk away. Ruben turns and waves to his dad, as I do. I can't imagine how Ruben must be feeling right now, or Lucas. I have no idea how to make this better. Ruben's dad lives in New York and we live here. This is always going to hurt. I try to focus and walk steadily, one foot in front of the other, keeping a rhythm, just as I have done for all these years of Ruben's growing up, trying not to rock the boat. But maybe it's time to find a way to rock the boat, to make this better for all of us.

At home, I push open the door. Despite the heating being on, the house is cold and lifeless. I shiver, sensing Ruben's anticlimax at being away from the excitement of New York, his dad and the flight home.

'I'll turn up the heating,' I say quickly, but the idea doesn't fill me with the same satisfaction as lighting the wood-burning stove in Maple Lodge. 'And then I want to hear all about your trip. See the photos.'

'You've seen them,' he says, sliding his baseball cap off his head. I can tell he's missing where he's just come from. This must be so strange for him, being back here, just the two of us, away from the hustle and bustle of family life.

'How about a Chinese takeaway?' Everything seems flat. It isn't the New Year's Eve we used to know. 'And we'll watch the fireworks.'

But Ruben is already watching the feed from Times Square on his phone. The countdown to the ball dropping is not for five hours after we see in the New Year here, but there's ice skating, performers, and crowds. He peels off his jacket and dumps it on the floor behind him, glued to the screen.

Outside, it's dark and raining.

It's barely evening. The Chinese takeaway has hardly been touched. Ruben has fallen asleep on the couch and I've put a blanket over him, just wanting to be near him for a while longer before I chivvy him up to bed. I look at the present he brought me from New York, a calendar of all the pictures I sent him from Forêt des Esprits, one for each month, right up to December next year, and I can't help but wonder where we'll be by then. Will we have gone back to doing what we always did, the same traditions, or will everything have changed? I look at the pictures of me skiing, the mountaintop picnic, the tree-lighting ceremony, the line dancing and the lantern walk. I think about the skiing and how I would have loved Ruben to be there, to meet Hagrid and the horses – and Ike, of course.

I pull out my phone. No messages. I hold it to my lips. This is what we agreed, I tell myself again, and wonder if he's thinking about me like I'm thinking about him. I imagine what they'll be doing for New Year in the square tonight, and wonder how they're coping without Bea to organize something. Maybe they're all pitching in to make it a special evening in honour of the new arrivals. Is Ruben disappointed to be home? Does he wish he was still there, seeing his dad and sister, being in New York for New Year? I know he'd never say so – he wouldn't want to hurt me – but I also know he's missing them. I wish I could make it better, but I can't. Lucas and I are never going to be together and I know that's what Ruben would like, for us all to be living together, one big happy family.

I yawn. I may not even make the New Year fireworks myself.

I look around at the bare room. No decorations. I can't help wishing that Ruben and I were at the diner this evening, celebrating with the town.

I look at my still packed case on the floor and open it. I take out the maple syrup and put it in the kitchen. Four little bottles, one of each grade: golden, amber, dark and very dark. I unscrew the lid of the amber bottle, trace my finger around the top and put it into my mouth. The deep, rich, sweet flavour transports me to the diner, to Maple Lodge, to Theo. I screw the lid back on the bottle. I have to try to forget about Forêt des Esprits. There's nothing there for me any more. I lost the land. It will be sold and the whole town will remember that while it takes many generations to build a community and a business like theirs, it takes just one, mine, to destroy it.

I feel wretched. I go back to my case and pull out the picture of my great-grandfather with Namid, now loose in its frame from when I dropped it in Maple Lodge. A bit like the land, it survived for generations, then one silly mistake and it's all fallen apart. I'm so cross with myself. If I hadn't agreed to the sap race, if I hadn't stopped to help Jed, if I hadn't gone out to Canada in the first place, all this might have been different.

Ruben is sitting up, his hair on end, rubbing his eyes.

I pick up my coat from the chair where I left it and go to hang it by the door. A scrap of paper flutters from the pocket as I pull out my thick gloves. I have no idea when I'm going to need gloves like this again. Probably never! I bend to pick up the piece of paper. I unfold it. I know what it is straight away. It's from the advent calendar.

'What's that?' says Ruben.

'It's one of the messages you sent me in the advent calendar.' I hand it to him. ' "Say yes." ' I smile. 'But in Forêt des Esprits we say, "Oui!" '

I think about the skating lessons, gliding across the frozen lake with Theo, the downhill skiing, Ike, the moose, falling in love. And stop myself. It all scared the life out of me. But I loved it.

Change is scary. Saying yes is scary. I look around the familiar blank walls that I can't even hang a picture on because the place is rented. All these years I've lived here because I was too scared to make a change, to say yes. I stayed in my job at the campsite café because I wanted everything to remain as it was.

'What's this?' Ruben reaches for the picture.

'That's your great-great-grandfather . . . I think!' I say, trying to work out the relationship. 'But it doesn't matter how many greats there are, or how many times removed you are. He was your ancestor, Joseph Jones. A brave man who went to make a life for himself and the generations to come in Canada. Him and his brother.'

'Wow! And who's that?' He points to the man in traditional costume, with a feathered and beaded headdress.

'He was the father of the woman Joseph fell in love with. She's sitting there, beside him. Namid.'

'Namid?' Ruben says. 'That's your middle name.'

I nod. 'It means "star dancing",' and the words catch in my throat as I remember the stars back at the *cabane*. 'They were going to be married.'

'And what happened?'

'Joseph was called home to Britain, to help out with the family business, the corner shop. His father was ill.'

Ruben frowns. 'Why didn't his brother go?'

I shrug. 'I don't know. Joseph was clearly a kind man.'

'And what happened? Did Joseph and Namid get married in the end?' His eyes widen. 'Am I part First Nations?'

I shake my head. 'His father died and Joseph stayed to help at the shop. He sent for his bride-to-be to join him, but his brother wrote back to say she'd died.'

'Oh, that's sad.'

'The piece of land, the forest, the maple trees, they were all part of the wedding gift for the couple due to be married, from her family. It was given to him.'

'So then what happened?'

'He never returned. His brother took over the land and the maple-syrup business and handed them down to *his* family.'

'And?'

'Joseph eventually married someone here in the UK. But . . .'

'Yes?' Ruben's eyes are agog.

'His brother never told him . . . so he never knew,' I'm feeling quite emotional all of a sudden, 'that there was a baby. Namid died in childbirth, but their baby survived.'

'So I have relatives in Canada?'

'I suppose so, yes. The baby was brought up by her family. Grew up and had a family of its own.'

'Tell me all about them! Have I got relatives there now?'

'The baby would have been my grandfather's half-sibling I suppose. They're distant relatives but the same roots, yes.'

And I tell him about Dax, and Océane, and the night she sang. All the time he's holding the picture close to his chest.

'Still, I wish I could meet them.'

'I know,' I say. 'But there's someone else I wish you could have met. Twin boys, who I think you would have loved.'

He pulls the picture away from his chest and stares at it. 'We should hang it up.'

'We can't. The landlord won't let us put any nails in the walls,' I remind him. I miss Maple Lodge and that feeling of home all over again.

'I hate being here! Why can't we just go and live in New York?' Ruben blurts out, in a sudden fit of fury. I've hardly ever seen him like this. 'Why can't we just be normal?'

He slams down the picture, which slides from the sofa and hits the floor.

'Ruben!' I call, as he crashes out of the living room and storms up the stairs.

I seem to be spectacularly good at getting things wrong, I think. I regard the cold Chinese takeaway and the picture, its frame now broken, lying on the floor.

Why can't we be 'normal'? Not that I know what

'normal' is. Is it Bea and the boys in the diner, without a father, but happy in their home? Nancy and Eli tentatively rekindling a teenage romance in their later years? Océane living with her grandparents? None of it is 'normal' but they're happy. Are we happy here? Just to keep everything as it was? Or should we be looking for something else? Something to say yes to.

I pick up the picture. The back of the frame falls off, making me want to cry. I don't think I've ever cried more than I have in this last month. Usually I hold it all together, for Ruben's sake, so as not to embarrass him. At that point I dissolve into floods of tears.

I don't hear Ruben until he's beside me. 'Sorry, Mum. I know you're doing your best.'

'No, I'm sorry, Ruben. I wish I could have done things differently. Not worried so much.'

We hug each other.

'I promise I'll try to say yes more often.'

'*Oui!*' He smiles. 'Be brave! Like our relatives, setting out on an adventure, a new life. Maybe we could think about going away next Christmas.'

'Somewhere different,' I say. 'Have a change. Now,' I look down at the picture between us, 'let me sort this out, get a new frame. One we can put on the table. So they'll always be with us.'

I pull the photograph out of the broken picture frame, and as I do, some folded, faded pages fall from the back, right into Ruben's lap.

# 43

I stand to shut the curtains and see a car parked out-side. I go to the front door and open it.

Nigel, from Berry and Brandy, the heir hunters, gets out of his car.

'I'm sorry it's late, Mr Berry, and New Year's Eve,' I say. 'I didn't expect you to come straight away. I just wanted to leave a message. I wasn't sure who else to call.'

'It's no problem. And call me Nigel. I've only got two weeks left at Berry and Brandy. Like I say, I'm retiring. So I'm keen to get this sorted before I leave for good.'

'Oh, really? What are you doing for your retire-ment?' I feel compelled to ask. Ruben is sitting next to me nervously.

'Something I wish I'd done years ago. Selling up and moving to Spain!'

'Wow!' says Ruben.

'Are you scared?' I ask.

'Yes!' he answers directly. 'But that's a good thing. At least, it makes me feel alive!' He puts on his reading glasses. 'So! Let me see what you have here.'

I hand him the folded papers, smelling of woodsmoke, with shaking hands.

# 44

'Thank you, Nigel,' I say into the telephone. 'And a happy New Year to you! Enjoy Spain!'

'Good luck to you, dear, in whatever you decide to do next. I'm sorry that this inheritance didn't come to anything, for you financially, I mean. But I've spent years watching people fight over money from people they've never met. It's been such a blessing to meet someone it meant more to than money.'

'It does, Nigel. The town will be delighted that the will is legitimate.'

'It is. All checked and verified. The will states that the land cannot be sold to anyone outside the town. And if no one is in a position to buy it, it stays within

333

the cooperative and the profits from the syrup are to be shared between them.'

I'm choked up all over again.

'I'll let the mayor know as soon as we've finished.'

'*Merci*,' I say automatically. 'I mean, thank you.'

'Sounds like part of that place has stayed with you,' he says.

'I think it has,' I say.

'And, of course, as I said about the house . . .'

'Maple Lodge.'

'Yes. It isn't mentioned in the will, so that does come to the heirs. Maybe there will be a little money in that for you when it's sold.'

'And . . .'

'Yes?'

I'm wondering whether to say anything. Is this like letting the genie out of the bottle, telling him what I'm thinking? What if I'm mad?

'Mum?' Ruben's listening to everything on speaker phone.

'What if it doesn't sell?' I ask.

'Well,' Nigel says evenly and clearly, 'I'm assuming that if one heir wanted to live in the property, both parties would have to agree to its sale, or buy the other out eventually. It could be a matter for the courts. You would need to come to an agreement.'

'Okay, thank you, Nigel. For everything. Happy New Year again.'

'And to you, dear. And don't leave it as late as I have to live out your dreams. It might scare you, but it may just be the best thing you've ever done.' With that he says goodbye and hangs up.

Ruben is looking at me. The word 'yes' is whizzing round my brain.

'What if . . .' I say slowly '. . . I could find a way of you seeing your dad more often?'

'YES!' Ruben shouts.

'It would mean leaving school, moving, changing everything about our lives as they are now.'

'YES!' he yells. 'Term's only just starting!'

'Even if it meant moving abroad? I'm not sure where our long-term home would be, but I do have somewhere we could stay for now.'

'YES!' And then he pauses. 'You want this too, right?'

A wide smile spreads across my face.

'YES!' I cry.

'Then what are we waiting for?' He jumps down from the settee and runs to grab his case, still packed from his month in New York.

# 45

*10 January*

'Hello? *Bonjour?*' I call, as I open the door on an extraordinarily tidy general store. Everything has been sorted, folded and stacked. I half wonder if I'm in the right place. But Hagrid, lifting his head from the floor, still looking like a moving rug, lets me know that I am.

'Whoa!' says Ruben. 'Can I?' He bends to pat the dog's big head.

'*J'arrive!*'

I hear his voice, and my heart flips and spins, like a skater on the ice. Ruben is entranced, looking at the neat rows of shovels and snow shoes.

Theo appears from the top of the stairs and stops. He's holding a baby, rocking him, a cloth over one shoulder, a bottle in the other hand.

336

'It's you!' he says, amazed.

'Hi.' I'm suddenly panicky. Should I have called him? Let him know my plans? Find out if he'd be pleased to see me?

'But I thought you said . . .'

'I said we shouldn't call each other again.' I smile.

He looks at my son. 'You must be Ruben!'

'I am!' Ruben grins. 'How do you know?'

'Oh, you're pretty well known around here,' Theo says, coming down the stairs. He puts the bottle under his arm and a hand out to shake Ruben's.

'I've heard all about this place. Except Mum said it was pretty untidy.'

I blush.

'I decided to turn over a new leaf. All thanks to your mum's visit! And your advent calendar. Bea told me I should tidy the place up and I said—'

'*Oui!*' we chorus, and the baby stirs.

I bend over to look at the bundle in his arms. 'Sorry!' I whisper. 'Which one is this?'

'This little fella, well, you'd better get properly intro-duced. He's also Ruben,' says Theo to my Ruben.

'After me?'

Theo nods.

'Mum told me that, but I wasn't sure I believed her.'

'You'd better. You and your mum made quite an impression around here.'

'How's Bea?' I ask.

'Getting some rest but doing fine,' he says, staring at me, as if he still can't believe I'm here. I can't quite believe it either.

'I saw the diner was closed,' I say, remembering the '*fermé*' sign on the door.

'She can't run it and look after the babies. Would you like to hold him?' Theo asks Ruben. 'And with the harvest coming soon, everyone is tied up in the forest and at the sugar shack.'

Ruben nods and Theo gently puts baby Ruben into his arms.

'I'm good with babies. My dad says so. I have a new sister.' Ruben gazes at the baby, then up at Theo.

'So I hear.'

I can tell Ruben's wondering how Theo knows quite so much about him. 'Theo and I are . . . good friends,' I say, by way of explanation.

'Really? That's brilliant! Wait till I tell Dad you've got a boyfriend! He'll be made up!'

'Well, erm . . .' I stumble, feeling giddy with excitement.

'What about you, Ruben? Would you be okay with it?' Theo asks.

'It'd be great!'

'Really?' I say quietly to him.

'Yes! You should have a boyfriend. Dad's got Lizzie. It's normal.'

'So, you wouldn't mind?'

'No. Especially not if he's as cool as this.' Ruben has noticed the newspaper cuttings and medals in frames on the wall, and the cups that are now in a trophy cabinet.

'How long are you here for?' Theo asks.

'Well, I wanted to deliver this news in person. You heard about the will?'

'Yes. It was the best news! The land is to stay in the community. And Philippe is so happy he's called off his resignation as mayor.'

'Great! No one is better suited to being mayor of this town,' I say. 'So the land was in the will. But the cabin . . .' I shake my head '. . . wasn't.'

He's studying my face as if he's trying to read what I'm saying.

'It's not in the will. So . . . Maple Lodge will be divided between the heirs.'

He frowns.

'But we both have to agree to sell. Nigel, the heir hunter who tracked me down in the first place, contacted Jed. The cabin's not worth much in the condition it's in. We're waiting to hear what he says. All I know is I own half a house right now. I've offered to do it up. Maybe we'll find somewhere to rent once it's sold. I just know I needed to make the leap, or nothing will change. So you may have something that belongs to me.'

'What? Really?'

I nod and smile, even though I'm exhausted from the journey back. 'I'm here for the key to Maple Lodge.'

The bell rings over the door.

'Hey, look who's back? Or did you even go?' It's Dax, a smile on his face.

'And this is Ruben!' says Theo, pointing out Ruben, who is rocking the baby.

'*The* Ruben?'

'The very same!'

Ruben smiles.

'We have new residents in Forêt des Esprits!' Theo throws open his arms.

'Wait!' Dax opens the door of the store and shouts to Philippe, 'Chloë's back and she's moving into . . . Where are you moving into?'

'Maple Lodge,' I tell him. 'For now.'

'Maple Lodge,' he shouts, and Ruben is beaming.

'Nancy!' calls the mayor across to the grocery store. 'Have you heard the news?'

'Wow! News travels fast around here,' says Ruben.

'What are you going to do first?' asks Theo.

'Well, I want to spend some time with Ruben, show him around, if that's okay?'

'By all means. Meet back at the diner later? I'll light the fires. I'm sure we can rustle up something to eat.'

Ruben hands back the baby, fast asleep, and everyone falls into whispering.

'Help yourself to skis, whatever you need!' Theo says, beaming, and my heart squeezes.

# 46

'So, that's the town, and the lake, and all of this land was where your ancestors harvested the sap to make maple syrup every year. They looked after the trees and the trees looked after them,' I tell Ruben, as we stand on the mountaintop, reminding me of the picnic I had that day with Theo.

'Wow! And that's where the ice-hockey teams train? On the ice?'

I nod.

'I saw a game with Dad. It's awesome.'

I smile at his Americanisms. 'This land is special. It was always at the heart of the community.'

'It's amazing.' He stares out in wonder as I did the first time I saw it.

'So, how would you feel about liv—'

'Yes!' He cuts me off, making me laugh.

'The cabin, Maple Lodge, it's not much to look at the moment. It needs some work. Which is why the other heir, our very distant cousin Jed, isn't interested in it. It'll probably cost more to do it up than he'd get for it. We can live there, make it our home. Then we can sell it and either try to buy something else or rent. It doesn't matter as long as we're here.'

'And I could go to school here and play ice hockey?'

'You could. And it's only about six hours' drive from your dad, so you could spend weekends and holidays with him.'

'And they could come here!' He's about to explode.

'They could.'

'Let's do it!'

'But it's a lot of change, Ruben. New schools, new country and a new language. You'd have to learn French.'

He shrugs. '*Oui!* It'll be fine, Mum. Just fine.'

The snow is falling, the bald eagle circling, and in the distance, I swear I see the moose among the trees. And in that moment I know he's right.

Back at the diner, everyone is there. The fire is roaring and the candles are lit on the tables.

'Did you have a good time? Everyone, this is Ruben!' says Dax.

Ruben gives a little wave and they all gather around to say hello.

'What's happening?' says Nancy.

'Well, as you probably know, we found the will in the back of the old picture of Joseph and Namid.'

There's chatter.

'Why did he keep it there?' asks Charlene. 'Seems a daft place if you want people to find it after you're dead.'

'He always used to say he'd written a will and it was in a safe place. It never occurred to anyone to ask where that was,' says Nancy.

'We knew it was in the cabin, just not where. And when nothing came to light when we were preparing for the barn sale,' Philippe shrugs, 'we assumed it was lost for ever.'

'He wasn't that old. No one expected him to die so suddenly,' says Nancy.

Bea raises her head. 'That's why we have to seize the moment and live every day as if it's our last,' she says.

'And you're joining the community?' asks the mayor.

I look at Ruben, who nods and grins.

'Well, as mayor, I'd officially like to give you a warm welcome to our town.' He shakes Ruben's hand.

'Finding the will means that the land stays in the community. The syrup, too,' I continue.

There's a mutual sigh of relief.

'Everything will stay as it was, just like the generation that's been and the one to come.' I look at Rubén, who is beaming. 'We're moving into Maple Lodge, to make it our home for now . . .'

And everyone cheers.

'Unless Jed decides to sell.'

Suddenly all the joy is sucked out of the room.

# 47

*Later the same day. The first day of the rest of our lives*

'Take it! We all agree! We discussed it while you and Ruben were out seeing the area.'

'I can't!' I exclaim. 'That money is for the new sugar-shack equipment.'

'It'll pay off Jed Anderson and the commission to the heir hunters. It's a loan. If we all pull together, we'll find a way to raise the cash for more equipment. Now just phone and offer the money,' says Philippe. 'It's what we do around here. Look after our own. And as the mayor, I'm insisting on it.'

'The land is in the right hands,' says Bea. 'As long as it stays in the community, that's what counts. It's for all our boys' future, so that they can call this place home. And you and your boy need someone you

can call your own. This is us, looking after our family.'
I hug her.

Then I dial the number.

'Sorry to disturb you, Nigel. I'm in Forêt des Esprits right now. Actually, the thing is, you were right. I've decided not to sell the cabin. I want to keep it, move out here. I'm going to learn to tap trees for a living.'

'I'm delighted, my dear.'

'I can afford to buy Jed Anderson out of Maple Lodge. Could you make the offer to him and get it finalized?'

'I'll go to the office to sort out the paperwork. A few emails and it'll all be taken care of.'

He makes me smile.

'And could you tell me how much the commission will be? I'll make sure the loan covers that too.'

'I could. But I'm not going to. This is my leaving present to you. I'm going to waive the fee. As I said before, I've spent so many years watching people fight over legacies and rip each other apart to get their hands on the money. You're a breath of fresh air. I wish you and your son a very happy new life. Just send me a bottle of maple syrup every year. That'll be plenty in the way of repayment for me.'

I hang up. 'There's no commission to pay. Just a bottle of maple syrup,' I say. 'Every year.'

'So that's it? With what's left over, we get to buy some new equipment?'

I nod.

'And you get a brand new life, you and Ruben, here in Forêt des Esprits.'

'I have to phone Dad!' Ruben starts to FaceTime him. 'Dad! Guess what?'

I can see Lucas smiling.

'It's great news. Mum texted me to ask what I thought.' He nods towards me, standing behind Ruben.

And I love that word. Whatever happens, wherever life goes, whatever changes take place, that's the one thing that will always stay the same: I'll always be Mum and I'm so grateful for that. But Mum can change too!

'Hello, Lucas.' I smile.

'We're moving here, Dad!' Ruben shouts, as if all his Christmases have come at once.

Theo comes to stand with me, as drinks are being handed out. I turn to him, leaving Ruben to chat with his dad about their plans for more ice-hockey games and weekends in New York.

'So that's it. You're here for good.' The smile I've missed is pulling at the corners of his mouth.

'Yes,' I say, still letting the information sink in.

'And you're going to tap trees with us.'

I laugh. 'I am. But I'll need to learn the ropes, so to speak.'

'I know someone who'll help with that.' He chuckles.

'Good!'

'What made you change your mind?'

'I think I'd forgotten that children are really good at change. It's adults who aren't. It was Ruben who taught me to just do it. The advent-calendar message to say yes. Even if you're scared. To be brave, like my great-grandfather. So I am!'

'And how are you feeling now?' He slides his arm around me.

'Terrified!' I laugh. 'And alive!' And very, very happy.

Bea walks towards me. 'How do you feel about partnership in the diner?' she asks. 'What with me having my hands full.'

I look around at the candles on the tables, the red and white checked tablecloths, the counter and the kitchen where I've spent the last month cooking, and realize how much I've missed it. 'I'd love it!'

'And having her hands full means Bea can't make lists. That's why she was given twins!' says Theo.

'Fancy being deputy coach for the ice-hockey team?' shouts Charlene, across the diner.

'You're on!' I call back, and the girls do high-fives.

As we leave the diner, after a dinner of marinated maple-glazed ribs and cheese burgers, crunchy sweet-corn dripping with melted butter, a big bowl of colourful coleslaw and Ruben's special for afters, the three of us, Theo, Ruben and I, walk hand in hand towards Maple Lodge. I'm finally home. As darkness starts to fall, the stars come out as if to welcome us. This is where I plan to put down roots, for me and the generations to come, grateful to the past for what I can pass on to the future. A family, a community, a place of belonging, and a new life in Maple Lodge.

# ACKNOWLEDGEMENTS

This book began in my head many years ago when I went to Canada on my honeymoon. I loved it. The trees, the wildlife, the way of life. I just fell in love with it all! I even bought my husband a checked red jacket and hat to match, which he's still got!

I got thinking about this book again a few years back when we had members of a rugby team from Vancouver stay with us. They brought us maple syrup in leaf-shaped bottles and told me about the maple production there on the island. Once again, I knew I had to write about this ingredient.

So, thank you for leading me down the research rabbit hole that is maple syrup and Canada. Once you start googling these wonderful farms, you won't come out for a very long time. Thank you to the farmers who do such a brilliant job of documenting their working lives online and letting us see a slice of maple syrup country life. And to the brilliant Sam and Shauna, the Welsh BBQ stars and authors of *Hang Fire Cookbook*, for inspiring me as official ambassadors for Canadian Maple Syrup and showing me how maple syrup can sprinkle a little something special into my cooking.

# Acknowledgements

If you're looking to buy Canadian Maple Syrup I got mine from https://www.puremaple.co.uk and it's delicious. I love to use it in roasting, over a glazed ham or parsnips.

Thank you to my team at Transworld, my editor Francesca Best, my marketing team Julia Teece and Sophie MacVeigh, Becky Hunter for her brilliant publicity work and the rest of the gang there. And to Larry Finlay, Managing Director at Transworld, for letting me move in and make Transworld my home. I wish you all the best on the next chapter in your own story. And finally, thank you to my agent David Headley for loving the idea for this book and all his support.

Thank you to my lovely writing friends in the SBC! You are all so great and supportive. Thank you for being there Katie Fforde, Judy Astley, Bernadine Kennedy, Jill Mansell, Milly Johnson, AJ Pearce, Janie Millman, Catherine Jones and as always Jane Wenham-Jones for always being with us.

I hope you love this trip to Canada, to Maple Syrup country, as much as I did writing it!

With Love
Jo
x

*Read on for some delicious
recipes and more information
about Jo's uplifting and
heart-warming books . . .*

## Pancakes and Maple Syrup

This delicious breakfast pairing is a staple in the diner for a reason – everyone loves pancakes and maple syrup. You can serve these in a few ways, but my favourite is with bacon as I love the sweet and salty combination. But you can also serve them with any fruit of your choice and some whipped double cream. Here's my go-to recipe.

**Ingredients:**

240g/1 cup plain flour
2 tbsp sugar
2 tsp baking powder
½ tsp salt
240ml/1 cup milk
1 egg
2 tbsp melted butter
Maple syrup for serving

**Method:**

1. In a large mixing bowl, whisk together the flour, sugar, baking powder, and salt.
2. In a separate bowl, beat the egg and then add the milk and melted butter, stirring until well combined.
3. Add the wet ingredients to the dry ingredients and stir until just combined. Be careful not to overmix; there should still be some small lumps.
4. Heat a non-stick pan over medium heat. Once hot, spoon 4 tbsp (¼ cup) of batter onto the pan for each pancake. Cook until the surface is bubbly, then flip and cook until golden brown.
5. Repeat with the remaining batter until all the pancakes are cooked.
6. Serve the pancakes hot, topped with maple syrup.

# Bread-and-Butter Pudding

And now for Ruben's special, the bread-and-butter pudding. This is the perfect dessert to serve if you have family and friends visiting for Christmas. The caramelized crust and soft, pillowy centre make this dish a real crowd pleaser – and not just in the book.

**Ingredients:**

8 slices of white bread, crusts removed
4 tbsp softened butter
470ml/2 cups milk
120ml/½ cup double cream
120g/½ cup granulated sugar
3 large eggs
3 tbsp maple syrup
1 tsp vanilla extract
½ tsp ground cinnamon
¼ tsp ground nutmeg
½ cup raisins (optional)

**Method:**

1. Preheat your oven to 180°C/160 fan/gas mark 4.
2. Butter each slice of bread with the softened butter and cut them into quarters.
3. Arrange the bread quarters in a 20x20cm (8x8") baking dish.
4. In a medium saucepan, combine the milk, cream, sugar, eggs, maple syrup, vanilla extract, cinnamon and nutmeg. Cook over medium heat, whisking constantly, until the mixture is heated through and the sugar has dissolved.
5. Pour the milk mixture over the bread in the baking dish. If using raisins, sprinkle them evenly over the top.
6. Allow the bread to soak up the liquid for 10–15 minutes.
7. Place the baking dish in the preheated oven and bake for 35–40 minutes, or until the top is golden brown and the custard is set.
8. Serve warm. I would recommend adding a dollop of whipped cream or a drizzle of custard sauce.

## Maple Glazed Ribs

But maple syrup isn't just reserved for sweet dishes, as these glazed ribs prove. These are so juicy, sticky and spicy – the perfect combination!

### Ingredients:

2 racks of baby back ribs (about 2kg total)
1 tbsp smoked paprika
1 tbsp garlic powder
1 tbsp onion powder
1 tbsp chilli powder
2 tsp cumin
1 tsp salt
½ tsp black pepper
120ml/½ cup maple syrup
60ml/¼ cup apple cider vinegar
60ml/¼ cup ketchup
2 tbsp Dijon mustard
2 tbsp Worcestershire sauce
1 tbsp soy sauce
3 tbsp olive oil

### Method:

1. Preheat your oven to 145°C/120 fan/gas mark 1.
2. In a small bowl, mix the smoked paprika, garlic powder, onion powder, chilli powder, cumin, salt and black pepper.
3. Rub the spice mixture all over the ribs, making sure to coat them evenly.
4. Place the ribs on a lined baking sheet and cover tightly with foil.
5. Bake the ribs for 3 hours, or until they are tender and the meat easily pulls away from the bone.
6. While the ribs are cooking, prepare the maple glaze. In a medium saucepan, combine the maple syrup, apple cider vinegar, ketchup, Dijon mustard, Worcestershire sauce, soy sauce and olive oil. Bring the mixture to a

simmer over medium heat, stirring occasionally, and let it cook for 10–15 minutes, or until it has thickened slightly.

7. After the ribs have cooked for 3 hours, remove them from the oven and increase the temperature to 220°C/200 fan/gas mark 6.

8. Brush the ribs with the maple glaze until they are evenly coated.

9. Return the ribs to the oven and bake for an additional 10–15 minutes, or until the glaze is sticky and caramelized.

10. Let the ribs rest for 5–10 minutes before serving. Chunky wedges and a simple salad are the perfect accompaniments to this dish.

11. Enjoy!

# Maple Taffy

This is a classic Canadian sweet treat that is really fun and easy to make. Traditionally, maple taffy is made on fresh snow but if you don't have access to that, finely crushed ice works too. These delicious lollipops are the perfect treat to enjoy in the run-up to Christmas.

## Ingredients:

240ml/1 cup maple syrup
10g/2tsp butter
Finely crushed ice
10 wooden sticks

## Method:

1. Pack finely crushed ice into a large bowl or baking dish. Smooth the top and place in the freezer.
2. Pour maple syrup into a medium-sized saucepan.
3. Grease the top 1cm of the saucepan. This will stop the syrup from bubbling over.
4. Bring the syrup to a boil.
5. The mixture is ready when a sugar thermometer reads between 112°C and 118°C. If you don't have a sugar thermometer, drop a small amount of syrup into cold water and if it forms a ball, it's ready.
6. Remove the ice from the freezer and set on the counter. Pour about 2 tbsp syrup per piece over ice in thin lines about 13cm (5") long.
7. Let syrup strips cool for 3–5 seconds until they have firmed up slightly.
8. Pull the taffy strips out of snow, then wind into a lollipop around the end of a wooden stick.
9. Eat while still a little warm.

*Jo's next summer novel will whisk you away to Provence . . .*

*Coming summer 2024 and available to pre-order now.*

**One Icelandic Christmas holiday. One snowstorm. An adventure they'll never forget!**

Twenty-five years ago, Freya and her three best friends created a bucket list. The future seemed bright and full of hope . . . But now they are travelling to Iceland in memory of the friend they've lost, determined to fulfil her dream of seeing the Northern Lights at Christmas.

They didn't count on an avalanche leaving them stranded! Handsome local, Pétur, comes to the rescue, showing them how the community survives the hard winter. With Christmas approaching, Freya and her friends throw themselves into the festivities, decorating and cooking for the villagers using delicious local ingredients.

**But will they manage to see the Northern Lights? And can Freya's own dreams come true, this Christmas?**